Voices From the Dust

A Song of Beginnings

Voices From the Dust

A Song of Beginnings

A NOVEL BY

Susan Evans McCloud

Bookcraft

SALT LAKE CITY, UTAH

Library of Congress Catalog Card Number: 95-83704
ISBN 1-57008-226-X

First Printing, 1996

Printed in the United States of America

For Connie Drummond, whose friendship,
insight, and faith have been absolute.

Apart from historical figures with
whom the author has taken the literary license
customary in a work of fiction,
all characters in this book are fictitious, and any
resemblance to actual persons,
living or dead, is purely coincidental.

Preface

The major thrust of the Book of Mormon—the very reason for which it was brought forth and translated by Joseph Smith—is stated on its title page: "To show unto the remnant of the House of Israel what great things the Lord hath done for their fathers; and that they may know the covenants of the Lord, that they are not cast off forever—And also to the convincing of the Jew and Gentile that Jesus is the Christ, the Eternal God, manifesting himself unto all nations."

In no place and at no time did Joseph state the exact geographical location of Lehi and his people; where they landed on the American continent and where they built the first city of Nephi and their subsequent flourishing civilization has never been precisely and unequivocally proven. President Joseph F. Smith, "when asked to approve a map 'showing the exact landing place of Lehi and his company,' declined, saying that the 'Lord had not yet revealed it'" (John L. Sorenson, *An Ancient American Setting for the Book of Mormon* [Salt Lake City: Deseret Book Co., and Provo, Utah: Foundation for Ancient Research and Mormon Studies, 1985], p. 4).

In any case, I have drawn upon detailed research by scholars and archaeologists concerning the mountains, rivers, flora, fauna, wildlife, temples and other structures, highway systems, calendar, food, crops, clothing, medicines, warfare and weapons, and other features of ancient civilizations in Mexico and Peru. I have also drawn upon research and records of life and customs in Israel and the psychology of the Bedouin or desert dweller at this time.

In contemplating the Book of Mormon from a scriptural standpoint, we ofttimes fail to take into account the idea that there may have been other peoples in the area besides Lehi's group. The fact that Nephites had to contend with large numbers of Lamanites during the early years suggests that perhaps other peoples united under the banner or generalized designation of "Lamanite" in opposition to Nephi's small band.

The knowledge we possess of Book of Mormon peoples and their times is sufficient for us to reconstruct possible scenarios of the things they might have been doing, the issues which would have concerned them, the conflicts between Nephite and Lamanite cultures and creeds. The rich, full details are missing, and I believe we must be careful in drawing them in. Human nature, consistent through all times, can in some cases help us. But nationalities possess characteristics unique to themselves which must be taken into consideration, as well as times and circumstances which we have never and can never experience. Respect and care are essential, and an unflagging awareness of our limitations and of our purposes. In the case of this novel, the purpose is to depict believable people with believable struggles in the context of Book of Mormon times, which might help to illuminate and define our struggles as followers of Christ in these last, perilous days. The record was preserved and brought forth for our benefit, so that we might learn from the mistakes and challenges of a time very much like our own. If this book assists us in coming to understand our own mortal natures more clearly and in appreciating the purposes of America as the promised land, if it increases our testimony of the mission of the Savior and strengthens us in the fulfillment of our individual missions, then I shall be well content.

Susan Evans McCloud
Provo, Utah
October 1995

Nefer

CHAPTER ONE

He is dead. Our great prophet-leader. The dreamer of dreams. He who followed Jehovah and was brought from the land of our fathers to this vast, distant place. We are here by his hand. Here, on the edge of the ocean, on the edge of the world. And now Father Lehi is dead.

I hear murmurings; there have always been murmurings. Anger and confusion as well as sorrow seethe in some hearts. Thus it has been among us from the very beginning, though I was not there. I am one of the children of promise born in the wilderness—the lonely, brooding deserts beyond the Red Sea. That I remember. I am Neferure, daughter of Zoram, servant of the great Laban. My mother is Hannah, daughter of Ishmael. We are of the people of Lehi, who left the land of Jerusalem at Jehovah's command, traveling for many days south-southeast down the great trade road that coils like a snake across the ageless expanse of white sands. For many days, for many years, were our people nomads and travelers and dwellers in tents. We have a story, a story most strange and marvelous. I am Neferure. I am not a prophetess or a dreamer of dreams, but I am a weaver of words. And I tell our story. I tell what I saw with my own eyes, and I write what the Spirit whispered to my listening heart.

My sister, Bentresh, and my best friend, Esther, entered the room where I sat weaving and thinking. They had been crying. I placed my hands in my lap and allowed the loom to go silent.

"Come, Esther," I said, holding my arms out to her. She is a daughter of Sam, one of the sons of Lehi and Sariah. She had a right to her tears. Her soft hair, the color of sun-warmed figs, fell over a cheek as smooth as white honey. I gathered her into my arms and let her weep against my shoulder.

"I remember his kindness on the journey," she sighed, "his patience with us when many of the other adults were cross and out of temper."

"Remember too the long, happy days in Arabia when we camped by the cool blue-green sea, and he would join in our games—running along the damp sand as though he were no older than Himni, his gentle eyes spilling over with pleasure."

She smiled through her tears. She was fourteen years old to my sixteen. But she was only three when we left the land of Bountiful in Nephi's new ship. There were six of us, and we were like so many steps carved into the cliff side: Rensi and Shemnon were the oldest, being seasoned men of six years; I was five; my sister, Bentresh, four; Esther, three; and my younger brother, Amon, but two. The group stuck together, we older ones watching out for the younger.

Oh, what a place Bountiful was! Lush grasses and meadows spread up the steep, sea-facing mountains to tall stands of sycamore, tamarind, and boscia trees. Date palms, figs, and vegetables grew in uncultivated abundance around us, as well as other full, exotic fruits. Friendly swarms of bees produced sweet, wild honey. White-fleshed fish and lobsters teemed in the frothy waters, and the men caught them bare-handed while standing on the rocks by the sea. A large freshwater lagoon provided water for our drinking—all this after the travail of the parched and colorless desert. It was a little paradise God had prepared for his weary travelers. We lived in a spirit of gratitude and rejoicing, or at least the grown-up people did. We children, born of the desert's travail, had never before set our eyes on such wonders. Our unhampered spirits opened like flowers, drinking in the beauties of creation as thirsty petals drink in the dews. We were content. Our limbs and hearts knew a freedom that seemed as pristine and unspoiled as this gentle, hallowed place.

I remember all this. And though the memories must be only vague impressions for Esther, I wished to turn her heart to the good.

"He is with us still," Bentresh murmured, remembering the strength of Lehi's spirit and the benediction of his last blessings.

"But his death marks an end," Esther cried out. "And I am afraid."

She feared what we all feared, but were loathe to put words to.

"Amon comes!" Bentresh called, hearing steps in the outer chamber.

"I will go to him." A soft light touched Esther's brown eyes.

"Yes, by all means. He will comfort you." I gave her a gentle push with the tips of my fingers as she slid from my grasp. My brother was a year younger than Esther, but she had loved him since they had toddled along the cool sands together, mere babies, her chubby little hand closed round his as she tugged him along.

He is used to her leading, I thought to myself. *It will probably always be so with them. But she leads him well.*

I thought of Leah, my aunt, married to Simon, a son of Ishmael. She had led him, too. When he would of his own will have given heed to the entreaties of Nephi, she sowed new seeds of discord and fanned the pride and greed of his nature until he was won entirely to Laman and Lemuel's manner of thinking, until sloth and envy consumed all his finer virtues. A shudder ran through my frame. Shemnon, son of Simon and Leah—the fairest, the finest of all of us—enmeshed in his parents' darkness, endangered by other men's sins?

I arose. I could not bear to think such thoughts. I could not bear to think of Shemnon at all, he who was spirit of my spirit, who shared every thought of my heart. Shemnon—a partaker of darkness, as my parents believed he must be? Sooner could the sun reflect shadow than his soul reflect evil!

I paced in agitation the length of the narrow room. How the hours dragged by! The evil day clung with the tenacity of tragedy, so that even the smothering blackness of night seemed a relief when it came. Lehi dead. The patriarch gone, and our small, fragile tribe split in two! Nephi was strong. Not one among us doubted it. His spirit was pure. But purity cannot cajole evil. Benevolence cannot bring avarice and cunning to shame. Had we not all witnessed it dozens of times—hundreds of times—throughout the years of our wandering and during these years we had already spent in the promised land? Even angels—messengers from God's throne sent to chastise them—had not softened Laman and Lemuel's hearts. How could their brethren, whom they hated and despised, hope to bring them to reason?

After the evening meal was eaten and the remnants of food taken away, my father cleared his throat and began to speak solemnly of memories that stirred his heart.

"Oh, that night," he began, "when I walked through the darkness with him who I supposed was my master, only to discover that I had been discussing secret affairs of state with an imposter! I could feel death sitting astride my shoulders as he held me in an iron grip and demanded that I swear a solemn oath to him."

Oaths are sacred among our desert people. Even when a man's life is threatened, he will not break his oath. To swear by one's own life is most solemn, but Nephi pronounced the highest oath of all to my father: "As the Lord liveth, and as I live, no harm will befall you," he said.

"I went down into the wilderness with them—a free man," my father continued. "For so Nephi had promised me. I saw Lehi's great joy at the safe return of his sons. I watched the yearling camel brought to his tent and prepared; I watched the sacrifice and burnt offerings ascend to the God of Israel for the successful completion of his sons' most dangerous task. I knelt by the altar of stones and pledged my solemn word that I would tarry with these people from that time forth."

My mother sighed. Right now this story was not pleasant to her. My father turned his eyes toward her.

"Mine was a good strong arm, and they were glad to have it. But when Nephi again went forth and returned with the fair daughters of Ishmael—"

Hannah waved her hand at him, a sharp gesture meaning "I am not in the mood for this." But he would not be waylaid.

"I had moved among the great and powerful," he said, "and my eyes had looked upon many fair and noble women. But when I saw you . . ." His voice was becoming a caress, low and gentle. He reached out for her hand. "How can I describe the delicate force of your beauty—your sweet, modest ways?"

"To what end?" she answered. "That I might be withered like an overripe tamarind by the cruel desert years—all my soft beauty dried out and bleached by the desert sun?"

In truth, she was not in a mood for fond speaking and kind remembering. I attempted a different vein.

"Tell me of Bountiful, Mother," I asked. "Was it truly as beautiful as my child's memory paints it?"

"Indeed, and more," my father said, speaking before she could, which was his way.

"Rather ask me what it was like on the plain of Wadi Jawf when my father died." Her voice rose and became shrill with emotion. "To bury him at Nahom, his bones mingling with the bones of strangers! How his daughters did mourn at such a cruel fate—how bitterly did we lament him!"

I placed my hand on her arm. It was only natural that Lehi's death should bring back memories of her own father's passing.

"None of us wanted to go!" she continued. "My father had a lovely home in the land of Jerusalem—outside the city; filled with fine, costly wares; surrounded by vineyards and ripe fields and orchards. To leave all that we loved, to become outcasts and wanderers!"

"Not so, Hannah!" my father retorted. "You are too distraught to think clearly. There were other prophets besides Lehi, and all preached the same warning: to be led away as slaves to the Babylonians, to taste their cruel oppression—"

"You do not know this is so!" she interrupted, a tremor in her voice.

"I know! For so the prophets have told us."

My mother covered her face with her hands. She would talk no further this night, and my father and I both knew it. I stood to leave them. My mother had her concerns, but I had my own, which weighed with an awful heaviness on my mind.

ᴄ·ᴐ

He came to me, though he knew the possible danger in doing so. The hour was late. I heard him at my window and slipped out of the house to meet him. The moist night clung to us, heavy and still. Confusion would break out, no doubt, after we buried the patriarch. But now a gloom sat upon all.

I took his hand. It felt cool to my touch, and his lean fingers wove quickly, comfortably around my own. By silent consent we turned our steps toward the sea. As we reached the rough, pebbly shoreline, he placed his other hand at my waist to steady me. The touch of him was familiar and comforting. The sound of the unseen surf had a soothing effect. Had we not cut our teeth, in a manner of speaking, on that fair distant curve of shore where warm blue water shimmered toward us in long graceful lines, constantly moving, constantly murmuring, misty and mysterious, and endlessly delightful to gaze upon?

"There will be a storm," Shemnon said. "That cannot be avoided. But we have weathered such storms before. This one will make no difference to us."

I wanted to believe what he said. My whole being yearned to let his words flow through me with the assurance I craved. I parted my lips to protest, to disagree with him. But I closed them again, letting no more escape than a sigh. I had not the heart to stir even the slightest discord between us, to tatter the delicate fabric of hope he had woven out of our shaken dreams.

He pulled me close to him, and my lips met his eagerly as shivers of delight traced my flesh. Our breaths mingled; then he murmured my name with his lips to my cheek.

"From before we could speak, from before we could understand, we knew we belonged to each other!" His terse words revealed the agony he was trying so hard to hide.

I reached up and pressed my lips to his forehead.
"We will see what we will see, my dear one," I murmured. "Until then, we must try to have faith."

"When you speak such words a warmth surges
through me," he replied. "But when I am separate from
you, when I hear the bitter arguments of my father, of
Lemuel, I am no longer so sure."

"So sure of what?"

"So sure of all the things you are sure of." He
laughed. I loved the sound of his laughter.

"Surely you do not doubt that it is the hand of God
that has led us?"

"Not now. Not when you speak the words to me."

"Well, you cannot doubt one thing."

"And what is that?" he asked, pressing his lips
lightly to my hair.

"You cannot doubt the native goodness and gentleness of your own nature, Shemnon. You are not like
them."

"I do not feel that I am. I do not like the darkness I
sense in them. I do not want the things they want. Their
words stir my own thoughts into an unhappy confusion."

"And in this manner God warns you of the evil of
what they are doing."

"It is true," he said thoughtfully. "When Nephi
speaks, when he explains to us the ways of God, when
he draws our future with his bright words of promise,
everything within me responds. I feel strong, I long to
serve, to endure, to be part of those things which he
speaks of."

*My poor Shemnon. It was not right that he should suffer,
that he should be torn by the errors and willful blindness of
his parents.*

"So let it be," I said. "You will become what you
desire. If you and I desire righteousness, God will show
us the way."

In time, we drew apart with reluctance. Together we were whole; none of the dangers of the world could touch us. Separated, we became little more than two young and vulnerable creatures, afloat on the strong currents that surrounded us and swept up all in their powerful course.

Great were the weepings and wailings, the moanings and lamentations, when we laid our beloved leader to rest. His final blessings had reached to every one of us, and we felt his absence, each in his own way. Mourning always has a draining effect upon both body and spirit. For the first while following Lehi's burial, people seemed to walk about as though dazed, unable—or unwilling—to accept what had happened and the changes it would bring. At once there was a vying for leadership and power, though, to a degree, each family dwelt within its own circle of authority: the sons of Laman, the sons of Sam, the sons of Ishmael the younger, and so on. Even those most greedy for dominance were reluctant to openly declare themselves, to force some kind of a schism—not yet. But the rumblings, the veiled threats, the alarming rumors shuddered through us like shock waves and left not one among us in peace.

Thus we stumbled on, until the weeks counted themselves into months. What occurred behind closed doors I could not say. Nephi and his brethren still taught those of us who would listen. We harvested our grains and prepared for the coming winter—drying and storing food, slaughtering animals, gathering and preserving fruit. The men went about their trades, the women went about their weaving and sewing, and all seemed as usual—but only on the surface. We lived from day to day, not knowing what tomorrow would bring. And such a life does not foster unity or comfort or content.

Shemnon was forbidden to associate with me, and I with him. My people did not trust the sons of Ishmael, and the sons of Ishmael despised my people. In the beginning it had not been so bad. In the beginning, when we were yet children and the promise of a new land hovered beyond the horizon, boundaries were not so harshly set. Surely, we thought, boredom and rebellion and jealousy would all be sorted out once we left the irritations of the desert and the uncertainties of our nomadic existence. Surely the land of promise would engender peace and unity in every heart.

So now, as things settled more and more into their harsh, unrelenting pattern, Shemnon and I felt the strain. Of the six of us who had grown up inseparable, Shemnon was the only one who came from the camp of the dissenters—Laman, Lemuel, and their followers. He and I had always believed—we had always *known*—we would spend our whole lives together. But as we grew older and our own feelings grew stronger, we experienced tighter and tighter constraints.

And then there was Himni. Himni could very nearly be said to be one of us, though when we had played on the seashore he was much older than we. He was the only son of Levi, a trusted servant of Ishmael, and his mother had died long before they followed Lehi into the wilderness. My mother was one of several who took him under her wing, but he was a lonely and cautious young boy. Boy he was, while we were only children: thirteen years old when Rensi and Shemnon, the oldest among us, were six. Often he did little more than watch us at our antics, appearing with amazing speed and efficiency as soon as someone was injured, frightened, or in any way in need of his help. At last he won his own awkward place in our circle, awkward because he acted more as teacher and mentor than as comrade and friend. He taught the boys skills with bows and slings, even the baiting of fish, until he became a hero of sorts in their eyes. We girls he kept at a distance with a mixture of shyness and respect that pleased our exacting feminine natures. And he concealed very well the adoration he felt for me. I had no idea of his feelings, no idea at all until two months after Lehi's funeral when he presented himself at my door.

Perhaps I had been blind by choice, by dint of my preoccupation with my own affairs of mind and of heart. I saw that now, as I noted the way his eyes looked at me, his nervous and obsequious manner, the way he hung on my every word.

He is twenty-four years old, I thought, *a man full grown, eight years older than I am. He would have my youth and spirit, he would have my heart, which is not mine to give.*

My mother was nearly as deferential to Himni as he was to me. I watched as she drew him into conversation, praising his opinions, his cleverness, even his habits. He was not an unpleasing man to look upon, though he was a bit short of build. He had a beautiful head of black hair, but his eyes were too small, and so dark that they seemed to obscure the expressions of his soul, which might otherwise mottle and shade them. Both his chin and his nose were sharp angled, giving him the appearance of one who is crafty and not to be altogether trusted. But I knew he was not like that. His mouth at least was generous. When he smiled it warmed all his features and softened the angled lines.

So unlike Shemnon, I thought. *His hair has the shades of fire and the uncooled ashes running through it, the burnish of glowing metal new from the forge. His eyes are as a child's eyes, round and guileless, stained with the cool greens of the sea. His manner is open and mild, he moves with unpracticed grace and ease.*

It was unfair to judge between them, to draw comparisons. I could not view Shemnon in an impartial light. He was too familiar, too close in thought and sympathy to hold at arm's length and examine.

I walked with Himni where the lush jungle growth
skirted the shore. Brightly colored birds screamed from
the broad leaves above us and darted in flashes of yellow and crimson from tree to tree. Dozens of birds and
small creatures, before unknown to our people, had
emerged in all their curious splendor to be examined
and given proper names. Had Father Lehi felt like
Adam, set down in an unspoiled, uninhabited Eden,
given the enviable task of selecting the names which
plants and trees and creatures would be known by from
this time forth? Or had there been people living in this
silent, vast land before we came who spoke a tongue of
their own, preserved now only in the sighs of the wind
and the rustle of the slick, rain-washed leaves? If we
could understand the call of the shy, graceful birds,
would they tell us that they already had names of their
own—more ancient, more pure than our designations?
It was a curious thought.

"You are quiet, Neferure. What does your fancy
muse upon?"

Himni's voice stung me back to awareness with the
unpleasantness of a gnat. But I could not brush him
aside.

"This place," I answered honestly. "And how
strange it is that we dwell here, much like the first
people of creation—with a clean, empty parchment to
write upon, never yet touched with the pen of man's
experience."

"Every person's future is an empty, unwritten page,
Nefer."

"Ours more than others," I persisted, resenting a
little his use of my familiar pet name, as though intimat-
ing some intimacy that did not exist between us.

"Yes, and we may be even more so. For the plots
against Nephi thicken."

"Meaning?"

"Meaning that plans are underway. It is only a matter of time—the Lord has already spoken to Nephi."

"And who told you so?"

He smiled with an indulgence that maddened me. "Ask your father. He too knows of what has been happening."

"I have not exactly been playing with dolls," I countered.

"No," he replied slowly, his narrow gaze appraising me. "But you have been closing your eyes."

"Such a criticism from you is unwarranted—and what I do is no concern of yours."

"Oh, but it is."

His words fell like hard stones into the pit of my stomach. "I say it is not."

He smiled again. "I have spoken with your father, Neferure." He reached for my hand, but I slid it behind a fold of the cotton skirt I wore, at the same time lowering my eyes.

"The time is soon coming," he said more gently, "when we must stand and be counted—counted as those who follow the prophets and the word of the Lord."

I knew what he was referring to, precisely, and he knew that I knew. The sun felt suddenly hot, spattering through the variegated covering of trees.

"And in your superior wisdom you have already predetermined the stands that others will take? Pray, enlighten me."

"You are hard on me, Nefer. Some things are plainly stated."

"And you would condemn a man for the sins of his parents?"

"Not I. But those parents would."

"Let time decide it," I snapped, moving yet further away from him.

He sighed in frustration, but I did not relent. All my sympathies rested with myself and Shemnon, not with this man who had wheedled into my father's good graces and then taken it upon himself to plot against my happiness—to presume a hand in my future!

"As you will. But time is a commodity we have very little of."

I could not read his thoughts from the careful tone of his words. But I could feel his frustration, more palpable than the heat thrown up from the jungle floor over which we walked.

"You were once his friend." My words were an accusation I did not attempt to soften.

"I still am!" Himni insisted. "But I am not blind, as you are. What you want cannot come to pass!"

I hated him for the truth of the words he was speaking, for the fact that he chose to speak them and strike this blow to my heart.

"Better myself than another," he said, as though reading my thoughts. "For I love you, too." I glanced at him involuntarily. "Is that so difficult to believe?"

"You were always much older than I—we were only children—"

"But I loved you even back then," he broke in. "Even as a child you had a grace the others were lacking—a gentleness, despite your wild ways. You were—"

"No more!" I held my hand up as if to stop him. "I do not wish to hear!"

"You may, in time."

In time—in time! His cruel warnings mocked the pain that threatened to spill over and betray me.

"Leave me, Himni," I demanded. "You have given me too much to think about. I wish to be alone with my thoughts."

"It is not my intention—it is not my desire to hurt you."

His dark eyes were misted over. I looked away from his pain. *Pain?* The word had no meaning for him to whom I was still largely a stranger, a sought-for prize. To me Shemnon was the other half of my being, the only other person who could make my life whole.

I walked the curve of beach concealed by scrub growth and thick foliage. I walked until the departing sun bleached the sea and the sky, a sky as colorless and bereft of lustre as my own cheerless heart.

Nefer

CHAPTER TWO

My mother watched me, like one of the long-tailed hawks that hover over our skies. I gave her no sign of my feelings and refused to discuss Himni with her until, in her frustration, she took to muttering old Hebrew curses upon my head. I felt she had betrayed me, and would betray me further. Caution became my watchword. Shemnon and I still met, though our meetings were fewer and always clouded with the doubts and fears that clung to us like a shroud.

"It will not come to what you think," he tried to assure me. "My people bluster much, they like to preen and pride themselves, but when it comes down to action . . ."

My people. He had taken to calling them that. So few of us, and all from the same source—how could we be such strangers, in both matters of heart and of head? Shemnon showed great skill in the use of weapons, and his father trained him with pride. Indeed, he was already a hunter of repute who brought in choice meats for the pleasure of his father's table. There is wild game in plenty here, from the boar and the deer to the rabbit and duck, and other strange fowl. There are signs—many signs—that others before us have been brought to this land. For are we not promised that only those led by God will inhabit it? Yet, for what purpose? Certainly all who have been or remain here do not serve Jehovah as we do. In this, too, there are signs.

"You brood too much," Shemnon teased me. "Let me cheer you as I used to."

Then he would catch up my hands and run with me along the warm sand. The sea birds would cry out our pleasure as the white foam curled round our ankles and the blown spray wet our faces.

But such moments do not last forever. Only in the memory do they take root and live. The reality was that my parents called me to them one day to inform me that Rensi had requested Bentresh's hand in marriage, and they had given consent.

"These are unsettled times," my father stated bluntly. "Best to take care of such matters while we have the luxury to do so."

Bentresh is younger than I; it is not seemly for a younger sister to be married before an elder, so I knew well what would come next.

"It could easily be a double wedding, an occasion for much rejoicing," my mother suggested. Though her tone was cautious, there was little warmth in it. She was trying to tell me, without stating it bluntly, that she expected compliance from me.

"I think it a good idea," I replied evenly. "I too would wed the beloved of my childhood, as Bentresh will do."

My mother glanced at my father; he shook his head slightly, and the black of his brow furrowed into one long, worried line.

It was he who sought me later, away from the others. I sat in the cool dimness of my chamber, which meant he had to come in to me, which made him feel ill at ease. Nevertheless, he was yet lord and master, as every man is of his household, and he could take comfort in that.

"You prove difficult on purpose, daughter," he

began, mincing no words, making no light, insincere ovations, as my mother might do. "You must come round to our way of thinking, and well you know it."

"You wish me to marry Himni."

"He is a man of honor, a skilled workman who will provide well for a wife and a family."

"And?"

"Yes, since you deem it important, he loves you, Nefer."

"Or so he says."

"What more can the man do than state his affection with his intentions? You give him no other choice."

He was a man, and he envisioned himself allied with Himni, who was also a man. Shemnon was an unseasoned boy yet, to be taken with a measure of salt, especially in light of his other unstable conditions.

"I love another," I said. "I have always loved Shemnon; you have always known of my love for him, and his love for me."

"Circumstances alter, Neferure. You are wise for your age, and you know this; indeed, you see it as many do not. It is only in this one thing that you choose willful blindness."

"Perhaps you choose unwise caution—"

He laughed lightly, glad for an excuse to slacken the tension. "Can caution be unwise when it is applied to a daughter's happiness?"

"Yes!" I urged, reaching for his hand, weaving my slender fingers around his thick, solid ones. "You would abandon Shemnon because of the sins of his parents— and this when you know his heart, when you can see the promise he carries."

He was listening; I could see in his eyes how he considered my words.

"We are his hope, Father! With our strength to back him, he could break away from them and make a life of his own." I tugged impatiently at the hand I

held. "He *is* my happiness, Father! If you truly consider this of importance, then do not separate him
from me."

He sat silent. Sorrow filled his eyes. I could see both
sorrow and defeat there. He tightened the grip of his
fingers on mine.

"'Tis sad, indeed, and it may seem unjust as well.
But the lad is under his father's direction—and is not
Shemnon his father's pride?"

I could not belie this; I held my breath as he continued.

"His father will never let go of him. And, if I were to
give you to him, I would see the day when I would lose
you, daughter."

I suddenly gasped for breath. "What do you mean?"

"There will be a split, an alignment along two
sides—I know whereof I speak," he stressed, answering
the protest in my eyes. "And, when that occurs, the sons
of Ishmael will be on one side—and ourselves on the
other."

I said nothing; I could not at that moment find
words to speak.

"A wife, by law and custom, goes with her husband's people. You would be lost to us, Nefer, and lost
to the Lord."

This last he spoke softly, with the tenderness one
would expect of a woman. And still he held tight to my
hand.

"Might you be wrong? Might Shemnon defy his
father?"

"Such a thing could happen," he conceded. "But,
what think you of the odds? Or of the tragic mess which
must ensue?"

I shuddered at his words, and he fell silent as the
weight of them sat heavy on his heart.

"I cannot . . . marry Himni . . ." My words were no
more than a whisper.

"I will make it right with your mother," he promised. "We will wait yet a season."

I rested my head in his lap. *Wait yet a season*. "While we wait, will you pray with me, Father?"

"Think you not that I already do so?"

His words were a reproach of sorts, which I deserved. I buried my face against the soft cotton of his tunic, and he remained motionless, patient as a great rock of the desert, until my tears were all through and I could dry my eyes and lift my face, which he cradled between his big hands and kissed—the only way he could think of to comfort me. Then he strode from the room.

Egyptian legend tells of two sisters, princesses of Bakhtan, who were both wise and lovely. The eldest, given by her father to Rameses II, won the Pharaoh's heart. He gave her the Egyptian name of Neferure and made her his chief wife. Though she missed her home, she lived in Egypt with her husband in great joy, until one day messengers arrived from her father saying that her beloved sister, Bentresh, lay at the point of death and could not be healed. In honor of the love he felt for his queen, Rameses did all he could to assist the dying girl, at last sending the god Khons to drive the fever demon from the princess's body. In this way Bentresh was saved, and her sister rejoiced.

When a daughter was born to my parents, they named her after the Egyptian princess; a year later, when another girl came, they gave her the name of the little sister. Both Bentresh and I were well named, for surely she looked to me for strength and assistance in all things, not only because I was the eldest but also because of her cautious and delicate nature.

"Neferure was born at an oasis," my father liked to tell us. "A garden spot on the desert where clear springs bubbled forth. She sings like the bright springs, with the same energy and passion. But you, little one"—and he would tweak my sister's cheek as her solemn eyes watched him—"you were born at a desert spot, dried up and hard bitten, where the sands always shifted and the winds always moaned through the dim desert air."

So he believed we had taken on ourselves the characteristics of our birth places, and perhaps he was right. Bentresh certainly was fearful, uncertain, and easily frightened. But then, she had me to lean upon, me to stand out before her. And, true to the legend, we adored one another. Yet when Amon was born (named as well for an Egyptian god), we took him into the mysterious alliance of childhood, and we three reflected one another as the waters of the still lake reflect the morning and noontime and evening sky. Omni was born as we journeyed toward the Promised Land, and the little jewel Isabel was born in this place. My mother had never been well since Omni's birth, and Isabel's told hard on her. But, to do her justice, she never complained. If I did not please her, if we did not understand one another, it was no more her fault than mine. She moved slowly; her life on the desert had aged her. Perhaps her own youth had dried up within her, so that she had no sympathy for the passions of mine.

Bentresh understood, but only to a degree. She had always been docile and compliant. Besides, the will of others had seldom clashed with her own. Certainly now as she prepared for her marriage to Rensi, her very happiness stood as a barrier between us.

"Surely Jehovah will not abandon you to an unhappy fate," she would cry. But the words were as much a question as a comfort, and I knew well that God's ways are not man's ways. Nephi had preached much about the agency each man has to choose truth and happiness, or wickedness and misery. But it was not even as simple as that. No man's agency operates in isolation, and lives are altered by the choices of those around them, sometimes as much or more than by what they themselves do. God would not interfere with what was happening down here. He had given us all he could give us—the remainder was in our hands. Either to salvation or destruction—and we took others with us. And the only comfort God gave us is that we grow from those things which we suffer, and, if we are faithful, all things will work for our good. Vague words, speaking of a time beyond this time, a world beyond this. I found it very difficult to live for such things. In the here and now the boy I loved walked this fair world like a young stripling god, and I wanted him—I wanted to walk through life with him! The ease of Bentresh's happiness smote at my heart. Not that I envied her, that I desired less for her—I loved her too much for that. But the contrast was a constant cruel reminder of my own wretched state. And to feel her happiness, like a sweet perfumed essence enwrapping her, then to live with the acrid taste of my own bile and bitterness, was nearly more than I could bear.

One week before the date of the wedding I chanced upon Rensi in the street; he pulled me into his shop and entreated me to stop and break bread with him and grant him a bit of my company. What reason had I to refuse?

Rensi was a quiet young man with features nearly as finely drawn as a woman's, and soft, doe-like eyes. He smiled much; though his smile was slow, it came easily, and there was something in his manner which put those around him at ease.

"You look as fresh and beautiful as this rain-washed morning," he said, spreading his arms out in a gesture of welcome and appreciation.

I smiled in return. "Little good it will do me. No one is fitting *my* wedding gown. What beauty I possess will never glow for the delight of my loved one."

He pushed a low chair toward me and helped me sit down.

"I fear you are right," he said, meeting my angry gaze levelly. "I have prayed these past weeks—you and Shemnon have been constantly in my thoughts and prayers, Nefer."

"Well, if your prayers have been to no avail . . ." I spoke the words sincerely. Rensi had always been the most righteous among us, the most in touch with the Spirit. Most young men preparing for their nuptial delights do not concern themselves with the disappointments of others, but Rensi was not any young man.

"You are already like a brother to me," I said. "To know that my lovely Bentresh will be in your care forever brings great joy to my heart."

"I know this and shall strive to justify your faith in me."

"Oh, Rensi," I cried. "How can I bear this anguish?"

He knelt beside me and drew my head to his shoulder. "Only with God's help," he said. "He will help you, Neferure; he will not leave you comfortless."

I managed a weak smile through my tears. "Have you spoken with Shemnon?"

"No, he sulks. I believe he avoids me. He does not possess your generous heart." He wiped the tears from my cheek with the end of his slender, tanned finger.

I spoke quickly. "He possesses many fine qualities which should not be wasted, nay, twisted, by those who—"

Rensi pressed his finger against my lips. "You torment yourself, Nefer. And to so little avail."

There were tears in his voice and tears in his eyes when I left him. I turned away from home and toward the outskirts of our settlement, to where a low hill rises, a gentle, tree-covered slope. Here I could lose myself and cry out my entreaties to heaven. Would Jehovah listen to one such as me? Surely so, for I knew he was mindful of us, knowing exactly our whereabouts, knowing his own reasons for bringing us here.

I prayed for a long time, with the hot sun beating down on me and the noisy winged insects making their claim on my silence. I received no sense of peace, no feeling that what I desired would be granted me. In some way I could not see, was this cruel denial part of God's plan for us? I dared not believe it was so. At last I walked home, exhausted by my efforts and by the moist heat which drains the energies and muffles the head.

Shemnon was sulking. He blustered and protested, he boasted and threatened—and the words he spoke were his father's, even the tone of his voice when he spoke them.

"You are a man," I said to him finally, "and I understand that a man responds to pain and disappointment in his own way. But all this bitter ranting and raving?"

He dropped down on the sand where I sat and placed his head in my lap.

"It is my helplessness that drives me mad, Nefer!" he moaned. "That, and your pain. I could bear mine with more grace—but to watch you suffer, to be powerless to deliver you!" His fierce hunter eyes melted with tenderness. I stroked his thick, sweet-smelling hair. But my fingers ached at the touch of him, at the terrible love that coursed through me and must yet be contained.

"Will you come to the wedding?"

"No. Bentresh will understand."

"It will look ill if you do not."

"It will be cruel if I do!" He reached up and placed his warm hand on my face. "You may just be able to bear it if I am not there. I will not add to your torment— I will not push your soul into madness!"

I kissed the rough fingers that caressed my skin. I knew Shemnon was right. I realized for the first time that he was suffering much more than I had imagined before.

Among our people we make much of weddings. We prepare special wines and meats and sweetbreads, and there is dancing with the feasting—oh, how the men of Israel can dance! And with what harmony and delight do we lift our voices in song. All that is holy, all that is beautiful within us overflows like sweet honey, and our very joy is a sacrament unto our God.

Bentresh wore the dress our mother brought with her, across desert and ocean, the dress she, herself, had been married in. It was fashioned of the finest soft linen and embroidered with subtle and intricate patterns by the hand of my mother's mother, she who buried her husband on the desert and now sits among us an old woman, gentled and wrinkled and seasoned by age. Bentresh was a fair, modest bride; blushing every time her eyes met Rensi's; dancing with demure, graceful measures the ancient, honored rites. Beneath the stretched canopy the marriage couple received their blessings and mingled their voices in prayer. From the sacred writings the sacred words were spoken over them, and the two were made one by God's hand, as it has been with our people since the beginning of time.

I cried for Bentresh's beauty, as tender and wistful as her spirit, and I cried for her joy. A sense of solemnity settled over my spirit, and I felt the presence of our ancestors near us, those whose bones rested beneath the rock and soil of Jerusalem. Could it be so? The sensation came strongly. To me our people had seemed out of place here in this lush, sea-bordered land. But perhaps in time we could make it our own. If our ancestors' spirits could whisper over this green place and bless it, then perhaps God had been right in sending us halfway around the world to inhabit it.

I was tugged away from my reverie by those who

would have me join in the celebrations. I allowed myself to be led, talked to, danced with, toasted as part of the bride's family—until I found myself face to face with Himni. For an awkward moment we both stood there, gaping stupidly. Then he reached for my hand.

"You are a fine, brave woman, Neferure," he said, "and I salute you."

He lifted my hand to his lips. His rich voice rolled over me like pleasant shock waves. I had not expected this from him. Releasing my hand, he turned to leave me, adding, almost timidly, "And you are also, in truth, the most beautiful woman who graces this wedding today."

I stood stunned by his graciousness. I believed it was true understanding I had read in his eyes.

I was the last to kiss the bride. "Go, and be happy," I murmured.

"I have never lived without you, Nefer!" she whispered, clinging suddenly to my hand.

"I shall be near," I assured her. "We shall never be separated, Bentresh, you and I." I kissed her high white brow. "You are simply adding the care and devotion of one more, my darling, to bless your days."

Rensi heard this last, as he came up upon us. He too pressed his lips to her brow.

She will be well-cared for, I thought. *Yet, she needs me. She always will.*

Somehow the realization comforted me. Should it not be so between sisters—sisters of flesh and spirit, threads of the same fabric, woven by life to strengthen, enhance, and beautify one another as long as the cloth shall endure?

Nefer

CHAPTER THREE

Like a cruel jagged rift in a mighty mountain were the sons of Lehi torn one from the other. The hearts of the tender lamented, and the heavens themselves gathered in black turbulence above us and mingled their tears with our own.

The Lord commanded, and Nephi obeyed the Lord's counsel. We who supported the prophet made preparations to leave. We packed up our tents and all our implements of housekeeping. We brought out the black goat's-hair sacks and packed supplies of wheat and seeds in them, each holding from 150 to 180 pounds. The men had animals and tools to sort out and manage, and yet, by and large, we would travel lightly, as the people of the desert are accustomed to do.

At times it seemed like nonsense to me, like the quarrels of naughty children who needed a good hard scolding to set their tempers aright. Preposterous this, that we must skulk away from our brethren who would rather see us dead—or never set eyes upon us again in this lifetime—than to bridle their passions and jealous desires.

Nephi's life was in constant danger, even now that he had given in to his brothers' pleasure and no longer sought influence over them and their families. The people of Nephi did not speak to the people of Laman if

they could avoid having to do so. No help was
extended toward us as we made our methodic, sorrow-
ful preparations. I watched the faces of the older
women, who had gone through this process before. In
quiet submission they placed their lives in God's keeping, and I marveled at their strength and the dignity of
their obedience.

There was not much here I would miss, save the sea.
If we might but dwell within sight and sound of the
ocean, I could leave this dense jungle behind me with
ease. But, of course, that was not all I would be leaving
behind me.

The last time I met Shemnon we walked the night
shore, silvered by the light of a full moon and brushed
by the tide whose rising and receding murmurs seemed
to echo the anguish that surged in my own heart.

"Your god has not answered your prayers," he said.
"Perhaps we should take matters into our own hands."

I laughed bitterly. "By all means! This is not the land
of Jerusalem. There are no other cities or settlements we
can run away to, no other people we can hide among—"

"Why can we not live by ourselves? I am a good
hunter. I can provide for our needs."

I was shaking my head as he spoke. "You cannot—
not all of them. Even your skills do not extend that far."
I placed my hand over his fist where it sat clenched on
his knee. "But that is not the issue. We would not be
allowed to find out, Shemnon. Both sides would hunt
us down, as an example, as a detested type to be
avoided."

He ground his teeth in frustration and the angular
lines of his face hardened. He wore only a cloth about
his loins and his bronzed skin gleamed in the moonlight.
I closed my eyes, concentrating on his image, wishing to
imprint it forever upon the screen of my mind.

"You could run away with us."

"I would like that," he mused. "I have felt the spirit

of this God who led us into the wilderness. I have felt it
when Nephi speaks; I feel it when you speak, Neferure.
It is a feeling I shall cherish after—" He could not go on.

"You must come with us! I cannot leave you in the
hands of these people!" *What will become of you, my
heart cried, when the light is taken out of your life?*

"That too would be impossible," he said. "My father
would come after me, and many lives would be sacrificed for the sake of my recovery."

I knew he was right. We talked daydreams and
impossibilities, as if we were children, pathetic in our
hopelessness.

"It is worse than death and yet, in the end, just the
same. When I walk away from this place it shall be as if
you have died, and I have left you in a living grave
here." I choked upon my own words. He drew me into
his arms and cradled me like a child.

"Nefer," he breathed. "You must do something for
me. Promise you will."

"Anything," I replied, sick with misery. "Ask me
whatever you will!"

"You must marry Himni."

I drew away in horror and stood facing him. I was
trembling all over.

"Do not ask that of me!" I cried. But his eyes, green
and blinding as the sea, gazed back at me. "I am yours. I
could never belong to another! For the mercy of heaven,
Shemnon!" I swayed on my feet. He reached out to
steady me. I could feel in his touch the pulsing strength
of his love, of the sacrifice he had already made in his
heart.

"If I *were* to die, which I could do in the forest any
day when I venture out with my bow, then you would
enshrine me, a fallen love, in your heart. It must be so
now. You spoke truly a moment ago. *Think of me as dead,
Nefer*, and I shall always live on in the very soul of
you—untouched, undiminished."

I was weeping now. He stood and moved close beside me, and drew me again into his arms.

"How do I keep living when I have no desire to go on, when every breath I draw is unbearable torment?"

I could feel the trembling of his body. How like a woman for me to turn to him for strength. He had nothing with which to comfort me. That should be my task, not his. I was the one who knew the truth, who had been given the answers.

"All I know is that you must go on! You have too much life in you to die with my death. Live for me, Neferure! Live a strong, noble life for the both of us, and our sacrifice will be requited."

I held him close to me, praying for Jehovah's mercy upon his gentle and noble soul. *Temper the spirit of this land for his sake,* I prayed. *And temper the pain which he has taken into himself that I might not perish from mine.*

In good time our people—the people of Nephi, as we called ourselves—were ready for the journey ahead of us, and there was no reason to stay. Nephi had his brass ball and the promise of direction from the Lord, and we felt peace among us for we kept the statutes and commandments we had been given.

The people of Laman hated us; there was not one among them to wish us Godspeed. Rather they cried curses and vile words upon our heads. Thus we turned our footsteps away from the place of our landing, heading northward and upward, always upward. Our people had crossed the Arabian desert with the aid of camels, which can carry loads of a thousand pounds and go two to three weeks without water, surviving at the same time temperatures that seem to boil the blood of a human. Here we had teeming jungles and deep roaring rivers, great fissures in the rock and mountain gorges, steep and treacherous, yawning beneath us like giant chasms of the underworld.

We were a small group, consisting of less than sixty people. Yet since our coming to the New World, we had grown indeed. God sees to that through the miracle of children, and we had our share. My own youngest sister was only four years old, and my middle brother, Omni, but nine. He was a gentle lad, who looked after Isabel with untiring patience and affection, sparing my mother what little extra strength she had.

Bentresh was happy. She still held the honored position of the newest bride among us, and she still basked in her husband's adoration and that glow of well-being which new wives often wear.

The day of our departure my father had given me a blessing. He knew not how sorely I needed it, but his heart went out to me, as far as it was able. Encouraged by this, I told him somewhat of my conversation with Shemnon. Because his feelings were already tender, my words brought tears to his eyes.

Fighting the terrible ache in my soul, I told him what Shemnon had asked me. His eyes grew wide with astonishment.

"There is more to the lad than I believed, and I'll gladly admit it."

My father was like that, generous and effusive.

"Lass, you will do well to heed him." He spoke the words in a low tone, respectful of my emotions. His softness brought tears to my eyes.

"Not quite yet. Will the journey be long? Perhaps some place on the journey."

And so it came to pass that we arrived at a small river valley with a stream running through it where Nephi decreed we would stop, replenish our food supply, rest the animals and give respite to the women. This was the logical time—and a lovely setting for such a solemn thing as a marriage.

Up to this moment I had allowed myself the weakness of thinking of Shemnon almost constantly:

wondering what he would feel about this thing or that; describing beautiful scenes and interesting oddities to him in my mind; pretending conversations; imagining his responses, the expression in his eyes, the touch of his warm, calloused hand upon mine. It was innocent, but it was foolish, and I realized that now I must stop it, now I must put him behind me indeed.

Let him die, as you both decided! I would tell myself fiercely. *Imagine a scene, if you must. Bury him and mourn him. Otherwise there will be nothing left to give to the husband who awaits you.*

It was not an easy task, made harder yet because I did not wish to perform it. I could not yet live without him; I could not imagine doing so. In the end it was Rensi who helped.

He came to me our first night in the valley. "The moon is lovely," he said, gazing at the low yellow orb which sat above the purple-blue mountains that terraced their way into the heavens.

"Will we cross those mountains?" I asked.

"I do not think so, though we may go some distance into them. But where we go does not matter."

"Indeed? It matters to me."

He was getting at something. I glanced at him sharply and drew one of his slow, thoughtful smiles.

"Are you preparing to preach to me?"

"Yes." I had drawn his eyes to me, and now they lingered, discomfiting my usual sense of ease with him.

"You do not know your own powers, Neferure. If you did you would relax a little; you might even rejoice."

"This is enigmatic talk," I countered.

"Yes, because I am nervous." He smiled again and rubbed his hands together—slender, well-shaped hands, only a little bit larger than mine. "Even when we played on the shores of Bountiful as children I saw the strength in you—true strength because it was tempered with kindness and untouched by pride. I loved you then as I do now, not as a man loves a woman, but . . ." He paused, seeking a suiting expression. "I loved you as the tree loves the soil and the bird loves the sky."

"You are being enigmatic again."

He shrugged his shoulders. "You are a giver, a nurturer, Nefer."

"I do not take great pleasure in it. Sometimes I nurture, as you put it, despite myself."

"You are young. It will get better and better, I promise you."

"Oh! Well, I shall look forward to that."

He did not laugh. He leaned closer, his face intent. "I want you to be happy. You, above all of us, deserve it."

"Your wish is too late," I replied.

"Let go," he said, ignoring my self-pity.

"I shall never let go of Shemnon!" I snarled.

"I did not mean that." His patience was as gentle as the peaceful night which enfolded us.

"Let go of your desire to control what cannot be controlled. Let go of the pain—and the terrible loneliness."

I caught my breath; he knew I had taken his meaning.

"Can I?"

"It is the only way, especially for someone like you."

He spoke no more; nothing more needed saying between us, except perhaps my gratitude, which I expressed with a hug. After he left me I walked alone along the flat valley floor, skirting the tents and the enclosures of sleeping animals. There were a few fires yet burning, and I avoided those too. I moved toward the low spot where the stream dug its channel and a small copse of bending willows formed a natural enclosure.

Here I sank to the ground, alone save for the melody

of the moving water. I stayed on my knees a long time, longer than ever before in my memory. I could not speak the words — I could not utter the plea without meaning it. *Thy will be done, Father. Thy will. And give me the faith to endure it, to place my days in thy keeping* . . .

After many long moments I became aware of a peace settling over me, a peace so strong that it carried a sense of light with it, and I opened my eyes, expecting to see a flood of glory surrounding me; but the water and grass remained dark. Yet the silence was sweet, the light still encompassed my being, and I knew whence it had come. It was enough. I arose, walked stiffly into the darkness, and worked my way back to our tent.

Could the Spirit extend beyond myself? Himni tempered his own enthusiasm with an obvious respect for what I was suffering when he might have done differently, for does not the male creature love to exalt in his conquests? His consideration spoke more clearly than anything the truth of his avowals and convinced me that, indeed, he did love me. *Many marriages,* I told myself, *must begin with less love than this one will.*

Bentresh too was sensitive, but she could not hide her pleasure, a somewhat selfish sensation, for she wished me to share with her in that mystical realm of wifehood where she had been dwelling alone. We had shared all things since her life had begun, and she was not comfortable going before me.

My mother did not even attempt to temper her ecstatic sense of triumph that I had submitted at last. All was as it should be, all was well as far as she could judge. She would not admit to my pain. This present was reality; anything beyond reality was a waste of her time. I was lucky to have such a man as Himni to love me. I should be grateful and happy; I would be wicked to behave in any other manner. So it was with her, and I had to accept her for what she was. Wishing for something more would have been futile. Anyway, I had Bentresh to stand in the stead of a mother.

This was a strange sort of marriage. I did not look upon it as mine, not in the sense of something I had dreamed of and looked forward to since I had become old enough to realize that I was a girl. It was something I must do—and I was willing to do it. I could even admit to the good that lay in it. But it did not belong to me. There existed no deep desires or hoped for fulfillment on my part. If my heart still whispered that there was only tragedy when the dreams of a young girl are denied her, I stopped my ears to its temptings. My course had been set, and I must go forward in honor, trusting in Him who had heard my entreaties and bestowed His blessings on me.

The wedding was lovely, set in the cool green of the little valley, with fresh flowers to wreathe my forehead and grace the long tables of food spread out for us. I moved as if in a sweet dream, basking in Himni's joy, which was a rich and palpable thing. Only for one moment, as I spoke the vows, weighty and eternal, did my resolve waver and fear strike my heart. Otherwise, beauty wrapped its arms around me, the peace I had desired was granted, and the day passed as it should. I could see my father heave a visible sigh of relief once or twice as he watched me. Poor man. He had concerns enough of his own, yet he had been worried about me, frustrated that his accustomed power could not extend far enough to ensure the happiness of his daughter. I returned his gaze and smiled, wishing I could tell him how tenderly I loved him at that moment.

A small tent had been lavishly appointed for us, with silk hangings above our heads and Turkish rugs at our feet. A miniature lamp sat on a low table, releasing clouds of pungent incense. A deep bowl of perfumed water stood beside it, with two linen towels draped

over the wide lip. I had removed my shoes to enter, and
I stood now perplexed, my mother's soft dress seeming
to whisper around my stiff legs. This was part of the
strange drama I was enacting, to come here with Himni.
A sense of panic rose within me. *Home.* It was preposterous to believe that I could leave my loved ones—the
dear, familiar pattern and people I was accustomed to—
and dwell here with a stranger, no matter how ardent
his feelings.

"It will not be as devastating as it seems. You may
arrange all to your liking. I will alter my tastes and patterns to fit yours."

He had come up behind me. Now he placed both his
hands on my shoulders. I felt myself stiffen. There had
been as yet no physical contact between us, no outward
expression of affection. He stood still. I knew he was
trying to make all of this easy for me.

Suddenly I felt like a baby. I did not desire my marriage to begin in this way. I did not desire Himni to look
upon me as someone who was weak, who needed coax-
ing and pampering! Far better to embrace my new life,
to take part in it, rather than simply let it happen to me.

I turned slowly to face him. His hands still rested on
my shoulders. He brought one up to touch the curve of
my neck, my cheek, my hair. I made myself relax
toward him, and when his lips covered mine I
trembled—but there was some of pleasure in the sensation, as well as reluctance and fear. I closed my mind;
thought does not belong to such moments. I gave in to
Himni's tentative caresses—and to his desire, which
reached out with an almost melancholy yearning, loos-
ening the painful constrictions that had imprisoned my
heart.

Nefer

CHAPTER FOUR

We stayed nearly a week in the quiet, enchanted valley. The herds grazed and the men hunted. The women washed and mended and cooked food for the next stage of our journey. And I began to learn somewhat of the gentle secrets that pass between a husband and wife, the delicate, incredible entanglements in attempting to weave two separate, dissimilar lives into one. If at times I lamented the fact that I was not sharing these wonders with him whom I loved, there were yet other times when I rejoiced in simply being alive. The days were long and mild, and I sensed a harmony in my being I had never felt there before. Bentresh said I glowed, and that did not altogether displease me.

When at last we struck the tents and packed again for our journey, I felt a real sadness at the prospect of leaving this hallowed place. Here my spirit had encountered Deity and been strengthened and comforted. Here I had passed from maidenhood to womanhood and, with the sanction of heaven, bound my soul with a covenant that would affect me throughout the eternities. These were great, solemn things which made my thoughts pensive as I rode out beside Himni. He sensed my mood and did not distress me with importunings toward more mundane things. He merely gazed on my face, transfixed with that awe, that affection which

made the other men laugh at him and mildly tease him
for his daft devotion to a woman. He took it all in good
humor because, in truth, he did not mind their gibes.

"I have obtained what I never dared to hope would
be mine," he had whispered to me one night. And on
yet another he said, "I knew you could make me happy,
Neferure. But I knew not the meaning of the word itself
until these last days."

It was not always easy. Sometimes his devotion
stifled me. Sometimes I wanted to shout, "Why should
you experience this passion of joy and fulfillment, while
Shemnon and I are bereft and cheated—when I am
merely his sacrifice to you?" But none of these things
were Himni's fault. In my cooler moments I acknowl-
edged that, and felt wicked in being able to resent the
adoration and devotion of a man, something many
women longed for, wept for, and were denied.

We traveled slowly, our progress laborious, sometimes almost painful. But we moved through a world
wild with beauty—expansive splendor generously,
abundantly, almost carelessly, tossed by the gods. Every
spot the eye rested upon would arouse some sensation
of wonder, astonishment, or pure simple pleasure. And
we nudged ever upward, water in sight on either side of
us, forests and cliffs and massive cloud banks tumbling
over our heads.

We were so few that each person was precious, more
than commonly so. We exercised caution beyond the
customary, for danger stood undisguised all around us:
long dropoffs from jagged cliffsides; narrow, unstable
paths; poisonous snakes and insects; bold, yellow-eyed
predators, both in river and jungle. Yet who can prepare
for all eventualities?

We experienced much rain as we went: at times fine
mists which seemed to merely moisten the air and stick
like gossamer webs to our hair and our clothing; at
other times dense, drenching water pouring from the

heavens, a deluge unleashed by the furies, creating a dim, twilight atmosphere through which we passed hushed and expectant.

On one such day we had labored for hours beneath an obscuring veil of rain, cold and drenching. Moisture here renders the foliage and rock and mud beneath one's feet slick and treacherous. For miles we plodded close beside a swollen torrent, which at length we were required to cross. Grown men paled at the sight, but postponement was futile.

We raised temporary shelters and huddled beneath them while the men, lugging large, fallen trees and worm-eaten logs from the forest's edge, attempted to construct some sort of causeway for us to pass over. We were miserable and wet, with no prospect of comfort for hours to come. Some of the women took up singing in hushed tones to their fretful little ones. Pressed in close, denied freedom and action, many of the children were behaving poorly, even the older ones. The truth is, there was much to distract us, so when Isabel, my four-year-old sister, darted out of the rough enclosure and started down the bank to the river, precious moments passed before anyone noticed at all.

Omni was the first to catch sight of her—a small streak of color dashing dangerously close to the water. With a cry he leapt after her in his long, boyish strides, but her baby eyes had spotted her father among the working men. Stretching her arms out she scrambled toward him, slid on the steep bank of mud, and disappeared into the flood.

Omni paused but a moment. I, who was close behind him, saw that brief hesitation. Then he plunged into the swirling water, and both disappeared from my sight.

The torrent was so swift! Eddies swirled and collided with one another, and debris nearly as treacherous as the pounding water drove and leaped through the shivering mass. I saw Isabel's head surface, and I cried out to her, stricken by the frozen terror on her face. Then Omni was there, lifting her somehow high above him, out of the water's reach. He was straining for the shore, but the powerful currents dragged against him, and the frightened child's strugglings tired him. He could not hold on for long. Some of the men had waded nearly waist deep into the stream, extending their long arms toward him, encouraging him on.

Exerting all his fine young strength, Omni thrust within feet of the shore and literally tossed the child to the straining men who waited. Relief flooded through me. "Save yourself now!" I whispered. But then it happened. If I had glanced away, I would have missed it. I wish that I had. A large log, torn from the forest and trailing long roots and clumps of soil, burst through the torrent and struck Omni full on the back of his neck and head. For one moment his white, tired features bore a startled expression. Then his eyes clouded, dull and sightless, and he slipped beneath the churning water, never to surface again. Shuddering uncontrollably, I turned away.

With a roar of rage Amon attempted to dive in after him, but the other men held him back. The current would be death to any who attempted it; they were firm about that. A few claimed to have seen his legs, tossed like those of a child's doll, flash above the deadly froth twenty feet downstream. Amon's sacrifice would be to no purpose now.

Limp and listless, we retraced our steps up the slope toward where the others waited. It may sound strange, but the grief I felt seemed to blind me. I groped my way and saw only dimly that Rensi held Isabel's shaking body in his strong grasp and was drying her off. Then suddenly, like an arrow of flame, Bentresh shot into my arms. She was sobbing uncontrollably, and she felt rigid and cold as I pulled her against me. The other women formed a tight circle of protection with their bodies to shield our grief. I sank exhausted onto the ground and rocked Bentresh in my arms, like a baby. Our mother was nowhere in sight. I closed my eyes and tried to pray, but all I could think of was Omni's stark face. Then, with a cruel flash, the features of Shemnon arranged themselves out of the black mists in my brain.

You would have saved him, I thought. *You were the strongest, the boldest of all. You would not have let Omni die.*

It was a foolish thought, but it had come unbidden. Now it only increased my misery. I huddled beside Bentresh, arching my body above hers, until Himni and Rensi came to gently disengage us and lead us away.

We did not cross the river that day. Instead, we marched inland from the scene of the tragedy and set up a wet camp. The misery was something palpable that sagged the men's shoulders and twisted the women's faces into lines of vulnerability, awful to see. *Who next?* was the question on every grim face. We knelt in prayer—that was one of the first things we did, and again when night came—around a hot yellow blaze whose roaring tongues leapt up to meet the pale, half-obscured moon that dimly lit the moist sky. Prayer is our way; we turn to our Maker in all things, both happy and sad. He is always there: how many times has he proven this? But we are not always able or willing to draw his comfort into us. It was so with me now. The hard pain inside would neither dissolve nor soften. I did not remember what Rensi had told me. I did not remember the night in the valley I spent on my knees. Is that not the way of mortals, that we hunger and thirst, that we stumble and suffer, because we forget?

My mother did not return that night. She had run into the forest to try to escape her own grief. My father followed after, calling her name out softly: "Hannah!

Hannah!" The frightened syllables sounded hollow and eerie as they rose from the cold, mist-choked glade.

He did not find her, which meant she had secreted herself from him, and I know that wounded his heart. "She needs me, but she will not give in to even that need," he told me. And I looked down discreetly to avoid the pain in his eyes.

I roused myself a little upon his return. Is that not the way of women? Here were two men who had need of me; I postponed my own grieving to succor theirs. My father was as still as a stone and as watchful as a hawk, but my brother, Amon, was wild, bearing a burden that was not his own, torn apart inside by what might have been. That was foolish, as foolish as it was tragic.

"You did not kill Omni," I said at last. "Nor could you have saved him."

My words were as poison to him. He had no wish to be comforted; his pain was too great, and rage was his only defense.

So the evening wore away and the fire burned low, and people finally sought the warmth of their tents. Amon had paced the stretch of shadow just outside the reach of the firelight like a mad, hunted thing. Just as I was thinking how reluctant I was to leave him there, I heard a sound at my elbow. Believing it might be my mother I turned, startling Esther, who had crept up behind me.

"May I go to him?" she whispered.

I clasped her little cold hand in mine. "You are heaven sent," I breathed. "Please, Esther, do."

She smiled weakly. She was older than Amon by one full year, a small, birdlike woman who would appear frail if one did not know her. She and Amon were two sides of the same coin, and if she was the front, or the head, so much the better. Hers was a wise, gentle lead which my brother had been following since they were children.

I watched her move into the shadows to stand beside her beloved, and a sharp pain caught at my heart. I ignored it, turning my back on their tenderness. Himni waited inside my father's tent with Rensi, who had soothed Bentresh into an uneasy slumber. If only I could go in to him with that love in my heart which I knew Bentresh felt for her husband.

"Hannah will return," my father said from his place by the fire. "But she will not recover from this."

His words sent a tremor of anguish along my skin. "Do you feel so—or fear so?" I asked.

He moved and looked up at me. "I know so, daughter."

I went to stand by his side. It was then that we heard it, like the cry of a wild animal, piercing and stark. I shuddered and leaned against my father's broad back for comfort. The high keening repeated itself, shuddering through the black forest.

"She mourns all things from the beginning," my father said, his eyes reflecting her crazed pain. "The coming away from Jerusalem, our travails in the desert, the death of her father—and now the death of this child—all as strands of one single fabric."

And so they are, I thought. *The fabric of her life.*

"Is not that a woman's way?"

He reached for my hand, and his was cold and clammy. The anguished cry echoed from the cavern of the forest and tore through us again.

"Would you go find her?" I urged, unable to help myself.

"I will wait here by the fire. In good time she will come—and I will be here."

Tears stung my eyes. I could not face the company of the tent yet and stumbled off on my own, more unnerved by my mother's abandon than I would admit. Loneliness settled like a mantle over me. *Strange,* I realized, *Omni was born on the ocean — and now the water has claimed him—given him life, and taken it.* Isabel had been born in the new land—a child of promise, a child of our inheritance. But Omni, if one wished to maintain it, had never possessed a home. The land of one's birth: our people use that phrase strongly. Had Omni been borne on the surface of life, as on the surface of the water, for his brief sojourn on earth—a wayfarer, a bright soul lent briefly to us? My spirit wondered, darkly, uncertainly, but could come to no rest.

I shivered as the sound of my mother's lamenting carried to me again. Suddenly the closeness and light of the tent was just what I craved. I ducked in through the flap, blinking at the sudden brightness, though only one small lamp was lit. Himni sat in a corner, bent over a pile of parchments. When he lifted his face and saw me, such pleasure came into his eyes that I could feel it reach out and caress me. I opened my tired arms wide, wooed by my need and the willingness of his love. As he gathered me into his arms I clung to him fiercely, wanting for the moment nothing more than his tenderness and his strength.

We spoke the same words over Omni as if his body had been there to represent him. I could not bear to think of him dying in the cold, drowning terror of the water. To straighten his poor limbs and cleanse his fair skin would have proven a comfort. But this was denied. Instead we sat and imagined him in our minds as he used to be, as he had been when he died: a lithe, beautiful boy, scarcely more than a child himself, with dark, playful eyes and a mouth nearly as sensitive as a woman's.

My mother had returned sometime during the night, but she and my father did not come into the tent. I never knew where he took her, but he protected her from all pitying eyes, even ours. When the words of death and dedication were spoken over her son's spirit, she sat pressed against my father with a dark veil drawn over her face. I knew she wanted to melt into him, to run away from the cruelty of this intended kindness.

She was closed to all of us, save my father. Even Isabel who had been finding comfort in the arms of Bentresh and Rensi was consigned to remain there. Mother had no strength, no tenderness; she had nothing to give.

We packed our tents and belongings and prepared to move on. I had been anxious to leave, to never set eyes on this landscape of horror again. But when I walked away I realized that the last of Omni was left here in this strange country that had no name, no history to whisper over it, nothing to hallow the spot. In great heaviness of heart I walked, Himni beside me, bending to study my face now and then with a grave and cautious attention. All our people observed a respectful silence until we had crossed the cursed stream and left all traces behind us of our great sorrow and pain. Mother kept apart, riding on one of the animals, and all respected her silence. And the misshapen day wore on, and all to me seemed lamentable here in this wild foreign place. I longed to be where the blood of my ancestors called me, to the hot plains of Jerusalem where grew the vine and the olive and the sweet brown fig. What were we doing here, walking into isolation and possible destruction? It seemed like a form of madness to me.

I expressed as much to Bentresh and the men by the fire that evening.

"It is your weariness and your sorrow that give birth to such thoughts," Himni said gently.

But Rensi, the theologian and philosopher, replied softly, "We have no enemies save those we carry with us, tucked within our own bosoms." He tapped his chest to emphasize his meaning.

"What of our brethren who are now called the

Lamanites?" I pressed. "They hate us. They would delight to bring suffering, even destruction upon us."

"They will never find us again." Bentresh spoke the
words more as a plea than as a statement of fact she
believed in.

"Oh, yes they will." Himni leaned forward. "God
would not make it that easy."

We all laughed uncomfortably.

"Nephi teaches us through the words of Isaiah that
this exile, this scattering of Israel, is part of God's plan.
We are meant to form a nation that can have a claim on
his covenants and his blessings." Rensi spoke kindly; he
always did. He was never one to exhort or coerce. But
tonight his words were just that; merely words. Melancholy sat too heavy upon my spirit to admit any light. I
sought my bed early and slept as though drugged,
blessing that slumber which brought blank incompre-
hension and release from pain.

We traveled and we traveled. Our route passed
through rugged mountains of fantastic shapes, so high
that I could believe with no doubt that we stood on the
very top of the world, gulping into our lungs the pure,
thin air of heaven where no man yet had stood. Sometimes we found tunnels that had been hewn by water
and wind out of solid rock, and we passed through their
dank, dim expanses with a hushed expectancy,
entombed as we were in the heart of the earth. We
crossed swamps, forests, and places like my gentle valley. And always the sea was on the left of us, the great
sea we had crossed, with the waters of an unknown
continent stretching away to our right.

We were well organized: there was no laziness, no
contention among us. I believe each of us remembered
well enough where that led. The ruling elders blessed
and encouraged us, and the spirit of Lehi went with us,
embodied as it was in his prophet-son. But that is nei-

ther quite fair nor quite accurate. Nephi was a great leader himself, filled with vitality and confidence, yet touched by humility and honest concern for our welfare. He was a true man of God—what more can I say? We knew he led us not as he would, but as God would, as he was instructed to do.

We moved methodically and we moved with purpose and thought for the future, building bridges and steps of stones in the sheer cliffsides, clearing and leveling stretches of road which would remain for our finding if we wished to pass this way again. Thus I knew that Himni's terse words were true: the people of Laman would find us. In this great, seemingly endless wilderness, there would be no place to hide.

We moved on and on. And we of the house of Zoram laid not down our burden of sorrow. It grew so heavy and loathsome that our hearts bowed beneath the load. At last my father stepped forward to exercise his rights as patriarch. He gathered us all in his tent and spoke of that which our mother had forbidden.

"You owe your mother all respect and obedience," he began, "whatever she may ask of you. This is as it should be. But sorrow is not meant to oppress and hinder man, nor yet to hamper the progress of him who has gone."

My mother glared at her husband, but she did not move a hair, and she spoke not one word.

"We will lay Omni to rest once and for all and free his noble spirit, for that, too, is as it should be."

We knelt and he offered a prayer. Deep and sonorous was his voice; when my father speaks to his God, there is such warmth of entreaty, such depth of devotion, such delight, such yearning—one cannot listen and ever again doubt the existence of that Being whom Zoram addresses. When he was finished and done, he came to each of us in turn, placed his hands on our heads, and gave us a father's blessing. But Mother warned him away with her eyes. He spoke no word of censure; indeed, he was so gentle with her that it brought tears to blind my gaze and sting my throat. Then my mother did a strange thing.

She rose from her seat—graceful, I remember, the way she must have been as a girl. She raised Isabel from the low bed of skins where she rested and lifted her high into the air. Mother's body trembled, her face contorted, and she appeared to be trying to speak. *What in heaven's name is she doing?* I remember thinking. "Hannah! Hannah!" I heard my father mutter under his breath.

Rensi rose in his slow, matter-of-fact way and moved to stand by her side. She whirled to face him— her eyes frenzied with emotions I had no names for. Rensi solemnly lifted his arms and extended them toward her. "We will take her," he said.

I drew my breath in so hard that the sound was audible. What in the world did he mean?

"We will take the child to be our own daughter, Bentresh and I."

I could see tears in his eyes, and my mother was crying now, great wrenching sobs.

"We love her," he said, "but no less than we love you." He reached out a hand to steady her, and she clung to it with a tight, clawlike grip. Then almost with a shove she placed Isabel into his grasp and turned away herself, the skin on his arm showing white from where her fingers had pressed.

Thus it happened that Rensi had seen what Hannah's own children were blind to, and he had answered her need. She relinquished all, and was left with only the burden of living life out day by day.

We moved forward. We traveled far from the site of our landing. With prayers and patience we made our way, and thus progressed toward the place the Lord would choose for us, which was to become our new home.

Nefer

CHAPTER FIVE

I t came to pass that we followed a great noisy river that provided a pass between two ranges of mountains, one on the north and one on the east, and reached a valley set high above the level of the blue ocean and the coastal plain where the people of Laman yet lived. This river, which we came to call the "Great Speaker," forms our western boundary, and a knudo, or mountain knot, bounds us on the south. The climate here is temperate and gentle, with very few cold rains or violent squalls.

And so we laid down our packs and our burdens and gave thanks unto God. Jacob, brother of Nephi, sensing our mood and our need, exhorted us thus:

"My beloved brethren, let us not hang down our heads, for we are not cast off; nevertheless, we have been driven out of the land of our inheritance; but we have been led to a better land, for the Lord has made the sea our path, and we are upon an isle of the sea. But great are the promises of the Lord unto them who are upon the isles of the sea. For behold, the Lord God has led away from time to time from the house of Israel, according to his will and pleasure. And now behold, the Lord remembereth all them who have been broken off, wherefore he remembereth us also. Therefore, cheer up your hearts, and remember that ye are free to act for yourselves."

Jacob's benediction sufficed, at least for my sake. I felt blessed of the Lord—to be remembered of God, what a glorious thing! And this was a fair place, "a better land," as Jacob had said it. My heart was moved to rejoice, for, in truth, I fell in love with this valley when first I drank it into my sight. In the dappled light of morning its green depths, pristine with promise, deep with the silence of the ages, delighted my heart. Untouched by man, this spot which God had preserved for us. Under the careful hand of Nephi it would blossom and grow as it should.

How do I tell of those early days and months which blended into one another—and yet unfolded, one following another, in natural splendor like the petals of a rose?

We had flocks to care for, crops to plant, and the intermittent harvesting of those natural fruits and foodstuffs which already grew in this land—these were our first concerns. Those already skilled in such matters took over the organization and execution of the work.

There was the building of homes to see to, the establishment of a community. Nephi laid out the city which would be named after him in ample squares or blocks, intersected by straight, well-paved streets. Large public plazas and baths were built into the pattern, places reserved for houses of higher learning, lots for buildings of government and industry, where our women would spin and weave cloth or our goldsmiths hammer out delicate trinkets and jewelry. All was thought of; all was provided for. Nephi taught well, omitting and uprooting, through the guidance of the Spirit, those practices of the Jews which he considered weak or wicked. I believe we all were aware of the sacred trust, the exciting opportunity to form all things from a point of beginning. Every pattern we set, every decision we executed would influence countless lives, countless generations beyond our own.

Nephi and his brethren were well educated and possessed many skills which they taught with care to the people. We built substantial homes of dressed stone fitted together without the aid of mortar so perfectly that the thin blade of a knife could not be inserted between them, so great was the proficiency of our stonecutters. The land about us was exceedingly rich in gold and silver and precious things. These we mined and refined for the edification of our people. But there were also needs more practical. We constructed a system of irrigation for the fields and drinking water for the city, as well as a system to carry off the sewage and refuse. Nephi directed the building of a wind-furnace, fashioned after the manner of Solomon's smelter which had required no hand bellows to fan the flames. Constructed circular in shape, with the mouth facing windward, the strong currents which exist here produced the draft necessary to sustain high temperatures and melt the precious abundance of gold and the steel needed to fashion swords after the fashion of the sword of Laban. This too was a necessity.

We were an industrious people, and the Lord blessed our industry and began to prosper our hands.

Adjoining one of the public squares, Nephi directed the construction of a lookout tower, sixty feet high, topped by a spire. From here we could watch for our enemies. Did Nephi see, through the eyes of the Spirit, events yet hidden from us? So we built and we prospered. And in all things we remembered our God. South of the tower, Nephi designated the spot where a temple to Jehovah, worthy of the temple of Solomon, would be built.

How can I tell of the doings of those days? We labored, but we made time to rejoice with our families, time to teach our children the scriptures and raise them up unto the Lord. I say time, and yet time, as we commonly think of it, had no meaning for us. The seasons for planting and growing and reaping were long and sweet. We had nowhere to go, no one to deal with but ourselves. We carded wool and spun thread, our men killed game and cured meat, we domesticated the wild deer, we increased our flocks and our herds—indeed, in all things we prospered.

Yet, I go ahead of myself, for even as these things happened, life happened too, the inner struggle of each soul as he walked along his own path.

Omni was not the only one of our number to be lost on the journey. We guarded our young people jealously, those who were our future, who must learn skills and carry on traditions. Each loss affected the community, the whole, as well as the particular family who would, of course, mourn its loss. Some lost more than others; some accepted loss better than others. Since that day in the tent, my mother had begun to fail fast. She took no interest in what went on around her. By some eerie choice of her own, life was no longer happening to her; she had taken a step back, a purposeful step. Now she merely existed until she would be allowed to let go.

Despite my enthusiasm for our new destination, I found myself dragging, tired long before the day was, irritable, with a vague sensation of illness which I could not explain. Then one morning my stomach was unable to hold down the food I had eaten. When the same thing happened at noon I knew suddenly, with that instinctive assurance, what was the matter with me.

It seemed impossible, yet it was true. How could I be with child? I was not ready to be a mother; in fact, I was afraid of the role. I was not ready to let go of the freedom of girlhood. Then I realized with a jolt that I had already done that. But Himni had made it so easy for me that I had failed to fully realize the realities of my existence.

Again I painfully evaluated my life, from the inside out, and I did not like much of what I saw. I was yet selfish, tuned to my own needs and desires. I could be strong, I could do the noble thing, I could trust to the wisdom of heaven, but only now and again. I was not consistent; I was not deeply committed. Now, too, I must face the fact that the child I carried was not Shemnon's, but Himni's. It would be both foolish and wicked to wish it were otherwise. Thus I stood, trembling and uncertain, and feeling wholly unworthy.

Then one thing happened that made all the difference. Rensi and Bentresh announced proudly that they were expecting a child. I laughed out loud, in relief and pleasure, and Bentresh laughed back, knowing instinctively what my reaction meant. So it came to pass that we walked hand in hand through this experience as we had everything else in our lives.

Of course there was Isabel, who was nearly five now, old enough to be told. I marveled at how easily she had accepted Bentresh and her young husband as her parents. Once that strange scene had taken place, she never returned again to the tent of my father. My mother never approached her, contriving somehow to ignore her altogether, which seemed a cruel thing indeed. Did the child in her innocence sense the reasons for this rejection and find ways of her own to compensate? I cannot say. It was my father who, to all appearances, suffered the most.

He was a strong man, the patriarch of his family in every sense. Why had he submitted to this? I asked myself that question hundreds of times as I watched him with his youngest daughter. He still poured his love out upon her and exercised a gentle guidance, but he could not impose parental authority and undermine

Isabel's own welfare. He was too wise for that, too well disciplined. But the bearing of it was hard for him. I could see it in the sagging lines of his face, in the way he ground his back teeth together in an effort to contain himself. But what of the years to come? And how would it go with Isabel, pretty and pampered though she was, when she grew older and we all tried to explain?

I was always one to court trouble by trying to out-guess the future. But in the case of Isabel I did not even try. Bentresh and I simply loved her and made her a part of our new adventure, and the busy months passed.

She could not, or would not, stay long enough. And for a long time I resented that most of all about my mother.

Two months before I gave birth to my first child, my mother died. Even in this, she had her way. No one was there when it happened. As though she sensed its coming, she put her whole house in order; this much was easy to see. Her cooking pots were scrubbed clean, the work on her loom completed and neatly folded, her linens freshly washed and scented by sweet herbs tucked in with the folding. Her floors were scrubbed, her rugs beat free of dust; she must have worked like a veritable demon to have achieved so much in one day! Most unexpectedly, in an earthenware jar on her table was gathered a profusion of wildflowers. She who sneezed at the slightest whiff of their pollen. Why did she place them there?

Father was the one to find her, as I am sure she had hoped he would be, lying placidly on her own bed, dressed in the gown she had made for her burial while she was yet a young wife. At her neck rested the golden pendant he had given her on their wedding day, and her thick auburn hair, with no silver in it, was coiled in a braid round her head, an intricate braid as lovely as lacework.

We gazed upon her in astonishment. This did not seem possible. She had not been ill; indeed, there had been no signs beforehand, save her increasing weakness and withdrawal. Yet there she lay, and I thought, *She is at peace at last.* But it is strange how my father put it. He said, "She is at peace once more."

I grieved more in my heart than I let anyone see, even Bentresh. I grieved for the hollow tragedy of her life more than for her death. I grieved for what had never been between us, things I was only beginning to understand now that I was a wife.

But Isabel grieved as though her heart were broken, amazing us all. No one could comfort her, not even Rensi. It was not until my father drew her into his arms that she began to quiet, that her terrible sobs became even and controllable. He rocked her in his arms, crooning something over her which the rest of us could not hear. When she slipped at last into an exhausted slumber, he refused to move or to release her.

"I will sit where I am," he insisted. "In good time she will wake, and I will be here when she does."

His words haunted me until I remembered that other night, dim and gray in my memory, when my father had sat by the fire waiting for a wailing mad woman to come in from the dark.

"I will wait here by the fire," he had said. "In good time she will come, and I will be here."

Only then did I give in to a weeping that was bitter indeed, mourning all things, as had my mother, as have all women since the beginning of time.

Bentresh feared that her time would come before mine, and she did not want it so.

"It is right that you should go first," she would say. "I do not enjoy it the other way round."

I was working that morning in my garden, terraced down from the low hills backing my house. Father says the people in Palestine would weep to see a garden like mine. I have beds of fragrant roses, brilliant gold and crimson poppies, gaudy hibiscus flaunting above sweet pearly violets and cool lacy ferns. I can even boast a few elegant orchids to set off some of the more common flowers. But I love every one. I was humming as I worked when suddenly a tight pain caught at me, and I dropped the bone-handled spade I was using and sat back on my heels, a bit dazed. I knew, as women know, what was happening. I left my tools where they were and moved slowly back into the house. Through my open door I can see into Bentresh's kitchen, and if I call loudly enough she can hear me. I called out to her between the binding pains, and soon I saw her arms waving madly back.

"Stay where you are, Neferure. Lie down and be still. I will bring help."

I smiled at her frantic concern. Since I had guessed what was coming, a strange calm had rested over me. *I am in God's hands,* I thought, *as my kind has been since Eve brought forth the firstborn of all our race.*

Our midwives are skilled in the use of medicinal herbs and ointments, and I was made quite comfortable. But childbirth is still childbirth—a demanding, all-consuming procedure. I had not realized there would be so much hard work involved. But after the pain and labor came such a sense of well-being—and then I heard my child cry, and lifted my head, and realized that I had brought forth a son. Joy flooded every pore of my being and I thought in my heart: *Not only is God with me, but I am with God, working a miracle that no man who has lived or will live can understand.*

I kept in my heart the sanctification of what I had experienced, while Bentresh, slipping into the room as soon as she was allowed to, placed her hand on my head.

"Me next! I can hardly wait my turn, Nefer. You look—radiant! Was it so wonderful, then?"

I shook my head weakly. "I cannot tell you, but you will soon learn for yourself."

Himni was stunned by this abundance which heaven had given him. He was exultant, too, carrying his son up and down the streets for people to praise and admire. We named the boy Seth—an Egyptian name of great power. I thought in my heart: *For these few precious moments our joy is full. Even mine. I wish nothing more, nothing different. I shall savor this, remember it, put it away in my heart against the times when I may have need of it.*

The child grew well and was of a calm, pleasant nature—curious and alert, but never fussy or hard to please. Precisely two weeks following Seth's birth, Bentresh's time came. She had not as easy a time as I, and the midwife allowed me to come into the room and help. I was not yet considered recovered from my own confinement; among our people we have very set rules and customs regarding the times and conditions under which a new mother may resume normal life. Nevertheless, I stood beside Bentresh and allowed her to cling to me when the bearing down came; I sponged her hot brow and soothed her with words of comfort and encouragement.

When she too was delivered safely of a son, oh, what rejoicing there was among our family. Rensi was quiet, almost solemn; the more quiet he grows, I have come to learn, the more moved is his heart. They named the boy Jarom.

"The two will grow like brothers," my father pronounced, holding one grandson in each of his massive arms. "Noble children come of noble parents," and there were tears in his eyes.

c⋅ɔ

Thus came into our home a joy we had never imagined. Who can explain the spirit of peace and love—whispers of a world beyond this—which a new infant brings? Seth united me to Himni in a way I had not thought possible. He was flesh of our flesh, but more; he was spirit of both our spirits. We had something in common which had not existed before. As we marveled over him together, as we shared our delights and our concerns for him, our own hearts were woven together with strands both bright and tenacious, and the weaving was good.

So the gentle and busy days crowded against one another, pushing relentlessly forward, and for us the living was good. The hum of our people's industry was like a tune in the air, and the music grew sweeter each day as we surveyed the many fruits of our labors. Progress marked our diligence and our faith. Bentresh and I often worked side by side, with our babies bound in their cradles and cooing to one another, Isabel watching over them, delighting in their antics, loving them as only a young girl-child can do.

Thus the pleasant days passed. And thus we established ourselves in the new world as Jehovah had commanded, directed by a wise and fearless prophet, who led us well.

Nefer

CHAPTER SIX

We had not been settled long in our new home when signs of a disturbing nature began to appear. There were, as we had suspected, peoples here other than ourselves. We had seen what we believed were indications of them back on the coastal plain, where the thick jungles revealed only slight evidences here and there: human tracks along what were obviously well-used trails, signs of burned out fires and temporary campsites, and at times an animal carcass with an arrow point rusting inside its ribs. Not arrows shot from fine steel bows such as our men carry, but cruder weapons less skilled than our own.

And then there were the animals, many so similar to the ones we know and have uses for that we could not help but wonder by what power and for what purposes they were brought here.

All men know the power and influence of the Phoenicians; even Ezekiel in his writings praised the extraordinary skills of these seafarers and the quality of the fine fir, cedar, and oak they used for their ships, which also boasted benches of ivory and sails of the finest Egyptian linen. Surely it was possible that they, as well as others, had touched on our shores. The Lord told us that he had led away others besides ourselves.

But to think of them here—to wonder at their origins, their state of civilization, their language, the actual look of them—seemed an eerie, almost unnatural thing.

These strangers, these other remnants or branches, began to come forward and make themselves known. We communicated only in a tentative fashion and agreed to some cautious trading—their knowledge in growing certain foodstuffs, such as corn or maize, for the products of our artisans.

"They are a fearsome lot," Himni reported after meeting a few who had come into our settlement to meet with the elders.

As I said, our people moved cautiously in our dealings with them. In the meantime, we continued work on the temple, constructing it with the fine cedar, rosewood, and mahoganies that grow in this region, as well as the hard white stones and the precious jewels, gold, silver, and other metals which we have found here. After the manner of Solomon, we built the temple on a platform, with each room inside having a distinct and different sacred function. Outside the temple was a courtyard protected by a wall. Here were constructed terraced altars, representing the layered universe as we understand it. The building was so situated that on the solstice day the earliest rays of the rising sun would slant in through the opened door to shine directly upon the holy of holies—"the glory of the Lord" lighting up his earthly temple.

Amon, my brother, is greatly skilled in the use of his hands, most especially in the carving of wood. He can feel the spirit of the wood and, with his care and patience, release it, reshape it, enhancing the beauty which was already there. Thus he became one of those privileged to labor on the house of the Lord, and that pleased all of us well. It also provided him with a means of supporting himself and establishing the independence he believed he needed in order to make

Esther his wife. She waited patiently, longer than I would have, so that he could have things in order just the way he thought they should be. While they were waiting, our infant sons grew, our crops grew, our city grew. And from time to time Nephi called us together to give us certain counsel and instructions.

On one such occasion he reminded us of the sad state of our brethren, the Lamanites, who had rejected the Lord and now sought dissension with us. For this purpose he had instructed our men in the making of many fine swords after the fashion of the sword of Laban so we might be prepared should the Lamanites come up to battle against us.

"Come up against us. . ." The people of the glades and forests had found us, appearing from nowhere and melting away just as swiftly and suddenly. Would the Lamanites use our own roads, the great highway Nephi had caused to be built along the route we had taken? Of course, it was not completed as yet. But, as in all things, we were building with care, terracing along the incline of mountains, forming retaining walls along river banks, and constructing steps and resting spots in the high, wind-swept heights. Along this entire length the road would be cleared and leveled before laying down a hard surface which would make it superior to the roads any of us had yet traveled. *Come up against us . . . the Lamanites . . . Shemnon, a great hunter and warrior . . .*

Nephi was yet speaking. I pushed my thoughts aside to make room for his words. He was saying that our brethren, the Lamanites, because of their disobedience had been cut off from the presence of the Lord. Then he added, in a voice that pierced through me, "And he has caused a cursing to come upon them, yea, even a sore cursing, because of their iniquity. For behold, they have hardened their hearts against him, that they have become like unto a flint; wherefore, as they were white and exceedingly fair and delightsome . . ."

An image of Shemnon rose at its own bidding inside my head. *Fair and delightsome . . . yes, I remembered . . .* "That they might not be enticing unto us, the Lord God has caused a skin of blackness to come upon them. And thus saith the Lord God: I will cause that they shall be loathsome unto thy people, save they shall repent of their iniquities."

I returned to my home in a sort of stupor. Nephi's words yet ran in my head. I had done as Shemnon had bid me—as both duty and wisdom had bid me—and considered him dead. *Yet, he is not dead!* He was living in darkness. Darkness and misery. And though he was still dead to me—with Nephi's words, more than ever—I could not bear to think on his state!

The mood hung over me for days, inducing a gloom that was uncommon to me. Himni noticed, of course, but he was reluctant to intrude, to ask questions. Irrationally, his reluctance irritated me as though he were subtly stating his lack of confidence, admitting that he had no real claim on me or my affections. I wanted him to fight for me, to stand up to the ghosts and shadows, indeed, to expel their heavy weight from my heart. I wanted his comfort and his assurance, but he could not give them to me. And I began to see with clarity that I shunned the weakness of his love. Yes, he adored me, worshiped the ground I walked on, and was quick to serve me and please me in little things. But his love for *me* was a tonic for *himself*. It served his pride and his confidence; he cherished it as he would cherish a fine and costly possession. His love existed there, within himself, not as something extended to me, not in those ways which would require studied thought and painful effort. His devotion was too sweet to himself to be drawn down to such a pedestrian, work-a-day level.

I suffered terrible nightmares. In the deep silences of night, tossing fitfully, I would see Shemnon's face before

me, lit as if by a soft inner light—so fair, so finely
molded, with his green eyes glowing like bits of jade.
Then the darkness would begin to alter his features:
first a dull, mottled brown that deepened to black, a
blackness so dense that the green lights blinked out
and became empty gray sockets. Then the black face
crumpled into a pile of ashes and I would wake up with
a scream.

The dreams exhausted me—the dreams, and the
constant worry, and the sense of aloneness I felt. Bentresh noticed at once, but she knew she was helpless to
aid me so instead increased her kindness and attentions
to me, doing her best to ignore the problem. One
evening my father brought over a toy for Seth, a small
horse set on wheels that he had carved, mounted and
painted himself. The child was delighted, and while he
played on the floor my father revealed the real intent of
his visit.

"It is not mine to meddle in your life any longer,
daughter," he began.

"It is always your place to advise and counsel me," I
returned with a smile. For truly, I hoped for some help
from him.

"You are a good, obedient daughter, Nefer," he
replied, "and I mourn to see you suffer as you do."

I held my breath, waiting for him to continue.

"You have a husband now to whom you owe alle-
giance. Turn to God for strength and comfort, child.
That is all you can do."

It is not myself I am worried about! I wanted to cry. But
I kept my words to myself. For I could see from my
father's expression that all his concerns were directed to
me. Shemnon existed no longer, except as a possible
threat to his family, in which case no mercy would be
shown him.

I kissed my father good-bye when he left, feeling his
loneliness as his strong arms closed round me. *He should*

have a wife by his side, I thought. But, of course, what should be is seldom what is. I watched him walk away, tall, dark, and sure of stride. But also alone, so alone, carrying burdens that no one could see.

The day for the marriage was set, and still my great sorrow brooded over me. *I must not darken the union of Amon and Esther,* I worried, but that only worsened the matter. *Shemnon is all alone,* I kept thinking. *Nephi said that God has removed his presence from the Lamanites. He is doomed to misery and destruction.* The realization made me feel unworthy, guilty for enjoying the abundance of happiness and light that was mine. We began those most pleasant tasks that precede a wedding, Bentresh and Esther and I. Rensi, coming often upon us—in search of his son or his supper or his unwashed linen, neglected for other fine, pressing duties—became aware of my pain. And, being Rensi, he confronted me in his gentle but most forthright manner.

"I will walk our sister home this night," he announced to Bentresh one evening when I was preparing to leave.

She raised an appraising eyebrow, but made no reply. The sky was light yet, and I lived but a few steps away. But Rensi could be trusted and was therefore not to be gainsaid.

"Nefer, Nefer," he began in a gentle scold, as soon as we were out of earshot of his house. "You torment yourself, and the very torment is your enemy."

"What do you mean?" I answered with a surly growl, thinking he deserved no better.

"Your unhappiness blinds you to the very thing you are seeking."

"Stop talking in riddles!" I said.

He laughed softly, and his laugh was like a kind word from others. "God has not forsaken Shemnon as you fear that he has."

I whirled on him. "Nephi told us—"

"What did he tell us?" I knew he wanted to make me think.

"That God has removed his presence from our brethren, the Lamanites."

"Exactly."

He was exasperating me, and he knew it. Yet his own spirit remained patient and calm.

"His presence, Neferure. What does that mean?"

I remained silent; I did not wish to attempt to answer his questions, as though he were a schoolmaster set over me, and I a dull, unruly child.

"His presence, I believe, means his priesthood—his keys and authority—and the nearly as important direction that can come to each man through the promptings of the Spirit, that inspiration which can speak only to a worthy and interested heart."

Of course! His words were so simple, yet so illuminating.

"And," he continued, "by removing his presence he is not forsaking them. It is they who have forsaken him, who have themselves made it impossible for his presence to dwell with them."

"So, what of Shemnon and others like him?"

"Well, what do you think?" That gentle remonstrance again. Rensi will make a good father.

"Perhaps he will not forsake them altogether. Nephi did say 'if they repent . . .'"

"Yes, and if there are good desires in any of them already—light within their own spirits—he will try to speak to that light."

I nodded, no longer able to trust my voice to answer him.

"Pray for Shemnon, by all means, Neferure. He is God's child as much as you are; He will not fault you for the concern you yet feel for him in your heart."

My eyes swam with tears, and I wished the dark

cloak of night had already fallen to cover me. But Rensi smiled.

"Submit Shemnon to God's care, and then trust him, Nefer! You have such trouble with that."

He spoke the words with such concern that they warmed me, urging me to the faith I was lacking.

"I shall try harder," I promised. "You make me wish to be good and wise; yes, and even obedient! God bless you, Rensi." I leaned over and gave his cheek a quick peck, then hurried into my house, lighter of step and lighter of heart than I had been for weeks.

For Amon and Esther the wedding ceremony seemed but a formality; it certainly was not needed to unite them in purpose or harmony or solemnity of commitment. High and noble purposes already moved in their hearts, and their hearts were already as one.

Yet how wondrous a wedding time is! It seems that God himself bent down and whispered to each of us, stirred our hearts to remembrance and our spirits to joy. Ourselves and all we love seemed newly baptized and newly blessed.

Thus it came to pass that in the twenty-fourth year after Lehi and his family left Jerusalem, my brother, Amon, was married; my firstborn son had his second birthday; and all things were well with us.

All things prospered with the people of Nephi. We lived richly in the hollow of our luscious, gentle valley which the River Sidon runs through and the ocean winds blow across with mild and beneficent caresses. The harsh weather seldom reaches us; we know only the bracing effect of our clean air, winter or summer, with skies scrubbed a cheerful, often dazzling blue. We eat well. Even I remember the raw meat and jamid of the desert—that rock-hard mixture of herbs, grasses, and camel's cheese which our women placed in a skin bag, kneaded, then dried on the tent roofs beneath the hot sun. Here we have fresh game and fish in abundance and vegetable crops that range from maize, beans, and pumpkins to potatoes, sweet potatoes, peanuts and yucca, to mention only a few. And fruits such as must have been found in the Garden of Eden—guanabana, papaya, pineapple, pacai, yacon, oca, lupin, and the incredible cocoa bean, which possesses a sweetness and flavor that no fruit has.

Nephi had brought us here; Nephi had made all these things possible; and many among us wished to make him our king. But Nephi was wise, wiser than us all, and he would have none of that foolishness. Instead, he used our vain desires to instruct us again, reminding us of the fate of our brethren in Jerusalem who had become proud and idolatrous. Even the homage paid a king is a form of idolatry. Corrupted by riches, undermined by greed and dishonesty, the people forgot the precarious position they occupied, poised as they were on the path between two rival powers, Babylonia and Egypt. They ceased to care. They desired ease and continued prosperity, despite the cruel and uncomfortable warnings of prophets like Jeremiah and Ezekiel, Nahum and Zechariah and Lehi. They ignored these speakers of doom, then they mocked them, then they imprisoned and killed those who would have been their help and salvation.

"A wicked and blind generation," Himni observed as we four sat together one cool, still night. "I do not understand how they could be so self-willed, so proud."

"Let us see that we never do understand our fallen brethren," Rensi replied. "For I fear Nephi speaks of their ignorance and misery as a warning to us."

"To us?" Himni was almost offended.

"We too are wealthy and independent, and we too

are human. I believe he wants us to see well to ourselves."

Himni brushed Rensi's words aside, but I remembered them then—and long afterward.

Nefer

CHAPTER SEVEN

In the twenty-fifth year, measuring the time of our exile from the land of our fathers, Esther gave birth to her first daughter. They called her name Hannah, and all was well. Two years later a second daughter was born to Amon and Esther, and her name was called Miriam. In that same year Bentresh gave birth to a second son, whom his father named Ethem. The Zoramites grew and prospered, but I remained strangely barren. At first it puzzled me, then it grew into a great source of sorrow. I had once given birth with no sign of distress or problem—less than Bentresh experienced, or other women I knew. My body had proven that it understood the patterns and was able to function as God had designed it to. What could the problem be then?

I prayed. I spent days in fasting; I received blessings from the hand of my father, and the hand of my husband; still I failed to conceive. Failed—I was made to feel like a failure, though I had produced one healthy, very charming, very intelligent male child. Seth was now five years old and could carry on an intelligent conversation with the various adults he lived among. He was sober and watchful, as though he believed his small mind had to figure the meanings of all that happened around him. Thus, he constantly asked questions

of anyone who would answer him. My father began to
teach him somewhat of the writings of our people.
Young Seth loved words the way I do, and he had a
quick memory.

"He is too old for his age," my father would tell me.
"Give the boy child's toys to play with."

"He will have none of them, Father. Think you I
have not tried? He is with Bentresh's Jarom every day,
but before long he often wanders off to clamber his way
to the high shelf where Rensi keeps his prized scrolls.
He pulls down the heavy, unwieldy writings merely to
look through them."

I smiled at the memory of the last time we had
caught him thus. I was mixing tonic as my father and I
talked, one of our favorite beverages, made by boiling
the powder from the bean of the cacao bush with honey,
vanilla, and pepper. The sweet fragrance brought the
occurrence back to my mind.

"When I began to scold him, he placed his little
hand on my arm and spoke so beguilingly. 'Mother, I
will not hurt them,' he said. 'I like the way they feel
when my fingers touch them. I like the way that they
smell.'"

My father shook his head and gave up; in truth, he
was proud of his first grandson, and everyone knew it.
Then he spoiled it all by saying, "We need more like
him, Nefer."

I swallowed my ire but replied with an edge of
sharpness still, "There could not be another like him,
Father, if I bore a dozen children."

If the truth would be known, I was growing weary
of the male expectation that surrounded me. Himni, his
father, my father, even Amon demanded on a regular
basis to know just when I intended to produce another
child for my husband. Never for me or for us. In
heaven's name, what had I to do with the matter, more

than I was already doing? Their attitude caused a rest-less resentment to grow in my heart. *Am I good for noth-ing else then?* I wondered. The women of my acquain-tance never plagued me about my inability to bear more children; rather, they showed sympathy for my situation and spent their time with me talking of pleas-ant and useful subjects. In their company, I too felt use-ful.

In my frustration I took to writing down my feel-ings, ofttimes in song or verse, which has long been cus-tomary among our people, many of whom are born with a strain of poetry already woven in with the other, more mundane threads. Paper, or papyrus, as the Egyp-tians call it, we consider the handmaiden of the Spirit, and we hold in great respect among us the written word. Paper we can make according to our needs from slices of reeds, as the Egyptians do, laying the thin strips of the inner pith in layers at right angles to one another, then compressing these until they adhere and mat into a porous but very white paper. Ink we procure from the juices of wild nuts and berries. Nonetheless, we choose carefully what we write. Scribes record things of importance in matters of business and keep histories of our doings. The sacred record which Nephi is preparing is, of course, quite a different thing. His words must endure past more time than we can imag-ine and must be carved into metal plates which are diffi-cult to write upon and bulky to store. And what he records must be of spiritual value to those who come after us, as God himself has directed.

Thus, even I move with respectful caution before I put pen to parchment. Yet it is only natural that I claim for myself the role of our family scribe, for someone must record the births and deaths and happenings of our tribe. No other among us is skilled in this manner, nor shows the interest which at times burns through my

veins with passion, and I know I have the poetry within
me, weaving its golden thread in and out of the dull,
darkly shaded ones.

Among our people is a beauty beyond describing. It
is the beauty of truth. It seems to bless the very water
we drink and the air we breathe. Day and night, waking
and sleeping, God watches over us, he who is God of us
all, Father to his children, he who will send his Only
Begotten Son to redeem the whole earth.

During these early years Nephi unfolded the writings of Isaiah to us, for his spirit glories in plainness,
and he wished us to know what would befall our
people, the Jews, from their captivity in Babylon up to
the crucifixion of Jesus, the Savior. Therefore, Nephi
made it known to us that the Messiah will come to the
earth in six hundred years from the time our people left
Jerusalem. The name of this Messiah shall be Jesus
Christ, and he shall in truth be the Son of God. The
prophets have spoken it, and an angel of the Lord has
spoken it unto Nephi himself.

This is sacred knowledge. Can we comprehend its
great import? Can we treasure it in our hearts?

"Will our descendants be in this valley still?" I asked
Himni.

"Not unless we are blessed with more children," he
quipped. Then he saw the hurt in my eyes and
shrugged his shoulders. "It is too hard to tell. Six hundred years."

"But Nephi did say that the Savior would visit our
people."

"Yes, he did, didn't he?"

I did not pursue it, but I thought to myself, *I want to
know these people, these sons and daughters of Zoram and
Hannah who will live in the time when eyes of flesh shall
behold the Savior and hear his voice.* I wrote of it; I wrote a

song of praise that my own heart would sing if I were to stand there among them and see his face. I wrote in small letters, with words close together. But the writing felt good, and the song of praise echoed in the silence of my own heart for many long days.

Savior
Thou Lord of Love whom prophets praise,
Who shall redeem the future and the past.
All flesh is naught without Thee.
Thou who wilt come . . .
And Oh, that blessed day!
To gaze upon thy face,
To hear thy voice
Speaking the strains of salvation!
Would I could stay!
Linger to sing thy praises
With those few
Who will in time come forth
To live their span,
To welcome Thee,
Their Redeemer, and their God.
That day is not even a whisper on the breath
Of the high mountain winds,
Only a promise in hearts
That choose to believe.
Messiah
Born of a virgin,
My mother-heart
Longs for the time of thy coming.
Would I could praise
Thy majesty and grace
Upon that day!

We are to go to battle against the Lamanites. And this is not the first time. They have come by the highway we built with our own hands, and they harry us here. They are wild men. They have taken to wearing nothing but skins and loincloths, and some shave their heads. Their skin is darkened, as Nephi foretold, and their eyes are dull. They are an idle people, we have learned, and they do not live in permanent homes but dwell still in tents and wander about in the wilderness. Yet they have cunning enough! And they all want the same thing: spoils and bloodshed and suffering.

"We brought the seeds of our own destruction with us," Rensi says whenever Bentresh and I express our fears to him. "What other way could it be?"

"Lehi could have left Laman and Lemuel in the desert to perish," I snap back, but he only smiles.

"To understand happiness, we must taste sorrow; it is the way of mortality. We only learn by opposites."

"I do not like that way," Bentresh pouted.

"I think you do, my sweet," he answered, kissing her forehead. "More than you know."

My husband, Himni, was a goldsmith, a worker in fine metals. He crafted jewelry and costly ornaments, and he had prospered from the very beginning because of the skill he possessed and the many hours of careful work he was willing to spend. But he had partaken of the spirit of keen competition, the pressure to do better and earn more than the next man, and there was often a tenseness about him that reflected this inner driving and ambition to please and excel. Rensi was a husbandman of the soil and a keeper of flocks and herds. His spirit reflected the peace of the open fields and the sky, and the solemn miracle of the cycles of life and of growing things. Rensi was fortunate; his way of life had protected him. Or perhaps he chose well, and chose purposefully. Himni stood often in harm's way, exposed to the baser aspirations and appetites that dull a man's spirit even as they sharpen his wits. I feared for him, and I grieved for him, though that may sound a strange thing. For he did not see, did not even feel the slow robbing of his integrity from him.

Yet he still loved me, in that simple, effusive way of his that was both curse and blessing, as far as I was concerned. If I had allowed my feelings to show, if I had acted anything less than the dutiful wife, my father would have scolded me, and Rensi would have shaken his head, and both would have reminded me of how ungrateful I was. Many women live and die never knowing what I seemed to take lightly. Perhaps they are right. My son tipped the scales. Next to the light of heaven he was the brightest orb in my sky. He colored everything with a tinge of hope, and gladness and gratitude, like a sweet wind, blew through my soul.

In the twenty-ninth year after Lehi left Jerusalem, my sister-in-law, Esther, gave birth to her third daughter and called her name Sariah. And we, the people of Nephi, began to figure our time from the prophecy spoken that in six hundred years from the time of our going out into the wilderness, the Savior would be born. Thus, it was the year 571, and our people continued to prosper, and my husband's house continued to prosper, and all was well, save for the coming of the Lamanites to war against us from time to time. We fashioned many fine swords and taught our young men the art of warfare. I asked Himni one day, "Will it be thus always, that we must defend ourselves against our brethren, the Lamanites?"

"I fear it may well be so. As we grow stronger and more prosperous, they will despise us more and more, and delight in our destruction."

"So do we raise up our sons only to perish on the point of a Lamanite spear?" I asked, and even speaking the words aloud made me tremble inside.

Himni glanced over at our son where he sat bent over blocks of wood and sticks and a pile of small, rounded stones, which he was using to build a fine miniature palace of his own imagining, and he answered, "God willing, it will not be so, my love."

Himni no longer deprecated me for my failure to bear him another son, and we had taken to not speaking to one another of our disappointment. Seven years had passed since Seth's birth; very soon he would be no longer a child. We took great joy in him, as parents do with their firstborn, and tried to be grateful to God despite our terrible longings.

Then, in the year 570 before Christ, thirty years since our leaving Jerusalem, I conceived. And Bentresh also. Again we were to bear our children together, and my heart, sore and shrunken so long with bitterness, was glad.

In the full bloom of the year, when the golden-throated birds sang above my lilies and poppies, when the maize and cotton were growing high in Rensi's fields, I gave birth to a daughter. Himni felt a keen disappointment, which was only natural—because of his growing business, if for no other reason, he needed another son. Maybe next time; surely there would be another next time now. I felt a grave sense of satisfaction which I did not try to hide.

"God is mindful of you," Rensi told me. "He has blessed you with your heart's desire to demonstrate the love he feels for you."

He spoke the words as naturally as if he had said, "Your father loves you," or "Bentresh loves you." Could it truly be so?

"Yes, it is so," he assured me, his quiet eyes laughing at my unspoken question. "Your poet's heart will not trust him, Nefer."

"A poet above all should trust the God of truth and beauty."

"A poet above all cares deeply and can be destroyed by disappointment and hurt."

But now there was no hurt; now there was only joy. We named our new daughter Awhere, a good Egyptian name, as was her brother's, as was mine. My father, frail now with age, gave her his blessing, and said that this small one had the eyes of her grandmother. I agreed it was so.

Six weeks after Awhere's birth, Bentresh brought forth her third son, and they named him Helam. If Himni was envious of the bounty of sons God had blessed his friend with, he lived to repent of his pettiness. The child was listless and frail and did not breathe as he should; his color was pale as the moon or one of the sweet, green-veined roses that drooped in the hot sun of my garden. Before the harvest was brought in, ripe and full from his father's fields, Helam faded away, gently, as did the last of my roses, their petals blown and scattered by the faintest breath of a wind.

Bentresh grieved, but Rensi grieved more, though it was hard to see it. His calm grew more deep and impenetrable, but the sparkle was gone from his eyes.

"I am a fine one to preach the ways of patience and goodness to others," he confessed to me as we stood over the grave of his child. "Now God requires that I seal my words with my actions."

"You have always done so." I closed my hand over his, uncommonly slight and uncalloused for one who works in the soil. "How else do you think that your words have had power with others? God is simply purifying you further—because you are worth the refining."

My words brought him some little comfort, and I was pleased to be able to help him who had so often helped me. Bentresh was another case altogether.

"All for nothing," she mourned. "The pain and suffering, then the unbearable hope! Why did God take him? I see no reason, no possible reason!"

No explanation satisfied her; she refused to be comforted.

"You have so much," I kept telling her. "And this one precious child is at peace. You need not fear that he will give way to the sins Nephi warns us of, nor will a Lamanite spear find him and cut down the promise of his youth."

It would take time with Bentresh, for time alone could wean her heart away from fascination with its own loss. Discouraged, I found myself stealing off to the child's grave on many a cool, dusky evening when the autumn sky was loud with the rook's calls and the hollow, trumpeting cry of the winter-shy geese. I wished to write something to comfort or cheer my sister, but no words would come, and I would walk home while the cold shadows closed round me and the black birds wheeled overhead.

Then in mid-autumn a small, marauding band of Lamanites, moving along the great highway which we had constructed, came upon a group of our people going down for the purpose of trading with the peoples of the sea plains. The robbers fell upon them and murdered every last one, even the half-grown boys who had gone along to learn the ways of their fathers. When our people discovered what had happened, we sent out for the bodies and brought them back for a proper burial. They were not the first ones to be killed. But the senselessness of it, the cold thoughtlessness, came home to my heart. Sons not much older than my Seth were buried beside their fathers, leaving sorrowing mothers bereft both of present and future.

Then the singing words came, as I thought: *We are making this land our own because we are sowing it rich with* our blood—the blood of our dead, and the blood of our slain. And their bones shall lie here, in remembrance, for generation following generation. And their bones shall go into the soil which nourishes their children's children. And thus the spirit of the land shall mingle with the spirits of the living, and the two become one . . .

> Thy sons and daughters whom thou didst lead forth
> In pettiness defile the promised land
> With bitter strife and dark, unworthy deeds,
> Even unto the shedding of men's blood.
> And the silence of night is rent with the widows' wail,
> And the moaning of the fatherless.
> Beneath thy arm
> Where we, thy people, have sheltered,
> The shadow of sin
> Trembles more black than the storm clouds
> That seethe in the sky.
> We bury our dead, our beloved, in this new soil,
> Hallowed now by our sufferings.
> We are sojourners here,
> But already our spirits mingle with sun and loam
> As we sow and reap new harvests,
> As we plant our dead in this earth,
> And watch season following season pass over us,
> Thus our memories are born,
> Yesterday blending with tomorrow
> One day at a time,
> And the land becomes ours,
> And we become part of the land.

My little Awhere thrived, and we all doted upon her. Amon and Esther had daughters in plenty, but we had just this one. She became the spoiled plaything of Bentresh and me, and of Isabel too, who was now a young girl of thirteen, with at least one foot poised on the threshold of womanhood and feeling the stirrings of hunger for babies of her own, as only a woman can feel. My father too spent many long hours just bouncing her on his large, bony knees, crooning my mother's old songs over her, and sometimes nearly breaking my heart as I thought of how much my mother was missing.

The following year a fourth daughter was born to Amon and Esther, and they gave her the name of Rebekah. Hannah, named after my mother, had been the first. Then Miriam, named after Esther's mother, then Sariah. Beautiful girls, blending their father's fire with the gentle, sure strength of their mother.

Each one a family line, I thought, *to branch out on her own when the time is right, to bear daughters and sons who will in turn bear sons and daughters. How many fair branching tendrils will there be by the time that our Savior is born?*

So I wondered. And, as I wondered, time slipped away from me, and life took its course. And all things changed, for is anything living ever ordained to hold still? And we, the people of Nephi, continued to prosper in the land.

Women are preoccupied with the affairs of their own hearts and their own busy hands. I failed to see the power and influence which my husband was gathering to himself outside our home. An abundance of the goods of this world and the ability to amass them—both are looked upon as admirable things. In this way did Himni rise in the estimation of his fellows, until he was appointed to a government office wherein he ruled over his brethren. He was considered clever, his opinion nearly as much sought for as were his gold-leafed figurines and his delicately formed anklets and bracelets. All this felt right to Himni as he basked in what he considered were his just, rightful dues.

One evening he brought home an amulet for Seth, a heavy gilded disk which the boy clasped to the shoulder of his tunic with pride.

"There!" Himni pronounced, gazing at his son. "Just look at you already. One day you will grow up to be a great man, like your father!"

Seth strutted beneath the praise.

"That is no way to talk," I said after the boy had left us to go in search of his cousin.

"Well, I am a great man, Nefer. How could I be otherwise married to you?" He came up beside me and kissed the soft hollow of my throat. "And I have for you here, my sweetest, a gift which will put Seth's bauble to shame."

What was I to do? I could not scold the poor man then. But I accepted his extravagant gift with some misgivings. Nephi warned against pride and the wearing of costly apparel and jewels. Himni liked to flaunt his finely made jewelry as much to show off his workmanship as to boast of his wealth. No woman among us was more cunningly adorned than was I. It sat uneasily with me, though Himni claimed that my long white neck and my slender arms and wrists enhanced the beauty of his creations and made other women imagine that they would look as dazzling and inviting as I did if they wore ornaments of Himni's making. So it went, season upon season, year following year, as his prophecies proved accurate and the women of our people purchased their adornments from him.

One evening, several days following the incident with the presents, I took occasion to remind Himni of his humble beginnings.

"It is marvelous indeed," I began, "that you and I, both being the offspring of servants, could live as we do."

"What do you mean?" His head snapped up sharply

and his eyes narrowed to regard me with sudden caution.

"Is it not true?" I continued in a mild vein. "Zoram was servant to Laban, though he married Ishmael's daughter. And both Levi and Miriam, your parents, were servants."

Himni knit his dark brow, and his chin and nose appeared even sharper than usual. "There are servants, and then there are servants," he muttered.

I laughed at him gently. "Nevertheless, we are fortunate. What might our fate have been otherwise?"

He did not like this vein of talk. "Otherwise?"

"If our people had stayed in Jerusalem, if we had been taken along with the others. If this bountiful land had not been prepared for us?"

He shrugged his shoulders; pointless questions, his eyes said. "We are here, and we have proven our worth, and God has been good to us."

"Yes," I agreed softly. "He has." I remembered the words Nephi had spoken to us—words of truth, but also words of poetry, as many of his sayings were:

"Behold, the Lord hath created the earth that it should be inhabited; and he hath created his children that they should possess it. And he raiseth up a righteous nation, and destroyeth the nations of the wicked. And he leadeth away the righteous into precious lands, and the wicked he destroyeth, and curseth the land unto them for their sakes. He ruleth high in the heavens, for it is his throne, and this earth is his footstool. And he loveth those who will have him to be their God."

I looked at Himni, smug and unbending. *Is he Himni's God?* I wondered. Then, rather than censuring my husband for his weaknesses, I found my thoughts turning inward upon myself. *Is he mine? How many idols do I hold above thee, Father?* I prayed in my heart. *How many things of this world do I take delight in, which are not of thee? How often do I forget thee?*

I walked quietly into the room where my two children lay sleeping and dropped down onto my knees, desiring suddenly to have God's blessing upon me and to feel his presence near.

Nefer

CHAPTER EIGHT

Marriage is a sacred sacrament between three parties: a man, a woman, and God. I could not see our little Isabel, though she was now eighteen years old, participating in such a solemn ritual.

"She has never grown up in your eyes," Himni tried to explain to me. "I think both you and Bentresh will always see her as she was when Omni died and your mother . . . well . . ."

"Yes," I agreed quickly. "I suppose you are right." We had not spoken of those painful events for years; we had not allowed them to surface, and yet, they were there.

"It is all right," Himni encouraged, crossing the room and planting a kiss on my cheek. "All will be well. Is our beautiful Isabel not marrying the man of her dreams?"

It was true. Onihah was nearly as beautiful as Isabel, though in a different way. Isabel had hair as black as the wing of a raven, with the same shifting, shining glisten of purple and blue when the sun lifted and lit her tresses. Her skin was as white as the sand on the beaches of Bountiful, her eyes a mixture of hazel and green, so that she looked nearly as exotic a creature as the turquoise Xiuh-totl or the flaming Tlah-Quechol which grace our blue skies with their irridescent plumage. Onihah, on the other hand, was the golden boy: hair like burnished copper, with strands from the summer sun and the autumn corn in it. Even his smooth skin seemed stained the color of gold dust. At times he looked like a young lion with his great mane of hair and his warm brown eyes, which were flecked with gold, like all else about him. He even walked with the ease and surety of that noble creature of the wilds who is confident of his own powers and the pride of his place.

Well matched? Most would say so, but I harbored a few secret doubts, and I knew that Rensi did too. Onihah had ambitions, but they were all of a worldly nature, and he was, well, how can I say it, too taken with himself. There was among our people no maiden more pure and guileless than Isabel. Could she influence him in the direction of virtue and wisdom? Perhaps. For the present she was glowing with happiness, and that would have to suffice.

Scant months before her sister's wedding, Bentresh gave birth to another boy. His name was called Melek, and he made up the fourth son born to my sister, counting Helam, who had died. I thought it good that she had a son to dispel the pain of the lost one, but she did not see it that way.

"Melek cannot replace my little Helam," she kept saying, and she held herself aloof from the child a bit, as though she shied from really loving him for fear of what might happen then. Besides, although she teased, she was half in earnest when she complained that Esther had all girls, I had a girl of my own, but she had none. And, indeed, Esther had given birth to her fifth daughter, Anna, the year before, and a sixth, whom they called Ruth, had been born only weeks before Bentresh's son.

"All boys for me," she would moan, "and I could

have been happy dressing and playing with a dozen Isabels."

It was true. Her gentle, timid nature did not take well to the loud ways of young men, nor to their outgoing, blunt, plainly stated needs. The quiet subtleties of the female mind were the only safe ground for her. Rensi, not really meaning to, had nurtured her weaknesses, and now she found it difficult to adjust to the demands made upon her by her own growing boys. Ah, life is not plain and simple, not for the least of us. That is how God means to stretch us, to reshape us in his image. It is all part of his plan.

But these, our last days with Isabel, were laced through with magic so potent, so tender, that I found myself catching my breath and holding quite still, as if I might capture them and carve their impression deep and true into my heart.

Bentresh and I had discussed it and decided that we must broach the subject of our mother with her. It would be unfair to send her off into life with unanswered questions, unresolved fears, and uncertainties. We had shrunk from the task for so long, postponing it each time Isabel reached an age or a stage of development when we thought that, perhaps, she ought to be told. Now we must do justice by this sweet girl who was in some ways sister, in some ways daughter, to both Bentresh and myself.

We selected an evening several days before the planned ceremony and invited her out to walk with us along one of our favorite paths that wound up a gentle green hill which stood only half a mile from our houses. Secreted in its dense green foliage was a miniature pond whose waters were as blue and unruffled as a young peacock's breast. We sat there, the three of us, our skirts spread among the ferns and flowers that scattered their beauty through the tall grasses and cattails which the wind stirred into melody as it shivered over the land.

Are we the first, I wondered. *The first of Eve's daughters to fill this sweet air with our voices, to pour out our dreams and longings into this pristine glade?*

Bentresh leaned close and spoke to her sister-child. "Isabel, my dearest, though it may cause you pain, Nefer and I want to speak with you of our mother."

Isabel's lips parted in an expression of pleasure which startled both of us. I reached for her hand. "Bentresh and I have many memories of Mother, but you were young when she died. Perhaps no one has fully explained what happened when you came to live with Rensi and Bentresh, when—"

She wound her slender fingers through mine and tenderly interrupted, "She explained."

I blinked, and my sister smiled back at me. "Mother explained it to me many times during the nights we spent together."

"Isabel, what in the world do you mean?" Bentresh had gone white and had clasped her hands, almost in supplication.

Isabel sat back and gazed, first upon me, then upon Bentresh. "You do not know of those times? When I was small, after I first came to stay with you?" The pleasure she felt made the lines of her face more beautiful than I had ever seen them before.

"Then, I shall tell you!" she cried, rejoicing as a child would at the thought of sharing a secret of great worth with a friend whom she loved. "Mother came every night to sing me to sleep. But first she would hold me in her arms, and we would talk about things."

Bentresh was shaking her head. "I would have known, I would have heard her, at least some times—"

"You are a deep sleeper, Bentresh. And do you not remember, Rensi placed my bed in the small alcove on the other side of the house from the room where you and he sleep."

Bentresh nodded slowly. "Yes, and there is a

doorway near there where someone could slip in and out."

"But what of before?" I questioned, "when we were yet traveling and dwelling in tents?"

"Oh, those were the best times. Father himself would lift me from my bed of warm furs, draping the top one around me, and carry me to his tent where Mother waited. She would open her arms . . ." Isabel shook her head to dislodge the tears that were pooling in her eyes. "We must have spent hours together, singing and laughing, until at last I grew sleepy and cuddled against her, burrowing like a small animal. Do you remember the scent of her skin, Bentresh, a mixture of cloves and sweet lime? That is how I remember it, though I could not have named the fragrances then."

"What things did you speak of?" Bentresh asked, and I thought her voice sounded tired, almost hollow.

"She would often tell me stories of when she was a child."

I could not help gasping a little. "Such as?"

"You know them. She spoke of harvesting the ripe figs with her father when she was young, of walking knee deep in the juice of them. The fig and the olive, the sweet chestnut and the grape—" Isabel's eyes grew dreamy. "I could almost taste their goodness from the way she described them. She told of the warm springs she visited with her mother and the strange, exotic peoples she saw there. Then the story of her pet lamb who was lost on the cold mountainside in winter." Isabel shuddered and her dark eyes grew soft. "I both hated and loved that story, for she always ended it by saying, 'That was such a bitter loss to my young heart. If I had known then that I would one day lose a far more precious lamb in this far-off place.'"

She shuddered at the memory. I stared at her, wide-eyed. "She told you these things?"

"And many more." Confusion was beginning to creep into the young voice.

"What did she say of herself, of the fact that, for all intents and purposes, she was no longer a mother to you?" Bentresh kept her voice level, almost wooden.

"She gave an explanation," Isabel laughed lightly, "that I suppose only a child would accept. She said that soon it would be necessary for her to leave me, for she would be going where Omni had gone, to live in heaven with Omni and with her beloved parents." She paused and scanned our faces; I nodded for her to go on.

"She made it sound wonderful—something to be desired. But she said she was worried for me. 'It will be too painful if you simply wake up one morning,' she said, 'and find I am gone. So I shall prepare you now, to make it easier when the time comes.'"

"That was all?" The question was blunt, but I could not help it.

"No. No, she used to say also that her heart was too sore . . ." Her voice had dropped, and Isabel stared at her feet now, as graceful and white against the tall grasses as those of a young marble sibyl. "She said the light of day was too harsh for her, that she could not take up the burden of her sorrow where all eyes could see. So she had placed me into your gentle keeping." She glanced up at Bentresh with a winsome expression in her sad eyes. "That is how she put it," she added, as if by way of defense. "The days would belong to you and Rensi, but the nights would be ours."

We sat in a silence so deep that we seemed to hear the small water insects skitter across the calm surface of the pool. Bentresh's voice trembled into a sigh.

"Rensi knew then—from the beginning?"

"Yes, Rensi knew. Rensi and Father. No others, I suppose. Though I never gave it any thought. I merely accepted it, Bentresh, as children do."

"Why not us?" Bentresh no longer attempted to conceal the hurt she was feeling.

"She would not have it so. She said it was our secret. I suppose she must have had her own reasons . . ." Isabel's voice faltered.

"Hush, Bentresh," I chided. "The child has done us no wrong."

"She would not have it so, she would not have it so!" Bentresh chanted. Isabel's eyes sought mine in perplexity. So it would be my task to try to explain.

"We had no idea, my dear," I began. "Mother left us to believe, well, from the way she behaved and from what we could tell, we thought she had ceased to care for you, ceased to care for any of us!"

"I believe that she did, at least in some ways. Even Father felt of her coldness. But in those night sessions with me it was as though she could pretend, as though everything else fell away from her, and she was truly herself again—" Isabel could not go on. I opened my arms to her, but Bentresh was before me. She gathered Isabel close to her breast and hid her face against the girl's raven tresses, which smelled of lime and cloves.

This is as it should be, I thought, watching them. But the sorrow that was wrenching through Bentresh had not left me untouched. *The child had more of her than Bentresh and I put together.* The realization was sore, yet for Isabel's sake I was satisfied. It could have been no other way. It was of no use to dwell on the tragedy of what had been withheld, no use to dwell on the loss.

We three walked down the gentle hillside together, swinging hands like young girls. *Isabel is wise for her eighteen years,* I thought decidedly. *She has drawn into herself much of the meaning of life.*

I felt lighter in heart after that, more prepared to lose her and let her go. Though I found myself often during the next months going to the bed of my own sleeping daughter and gazing down upon her in wonderment. Awhere was five years old, the very age Isabel had been when my mother began her strange ritual. I could not begin to imagine the anguish, nor the strange ecstasy that must have existed between the two of them. But I treasured up in my heart all the feelings, all the stirrings of my own soul. I wrote some of them down and gave the lines to Isabel, but I believe that I wrote them more for Bentresh and myself.

> *She is dead, who was my mother here on earth,*
> *Who walked amid the silence of her soul,*
> *Unheard among the tumult of our days.*
> *My soul walked blind to hers,*
> *Behind her eyes her secrets sat protected.*
> *I will praise*
> *The gentle strengths she masked,*
> *The pure desires*
> *Which rose above her weaknesses and pain.*
> *A mother's heart,*
> *Oh, surely God regards it,*
> *Oh, surely He will bless her in her need.*
> *No man can pierce the depths of woman's longing.*
> *In our aloneness, bless us,*
> *In our joy, consecrate our desires.*
> *Raise us, God,*
> *Unto our greater selves,*
> *And sanctify*
> *The soul which suffers, and yet longs to lift.*

ᠻ

My father died as he had lived—a noble patriarch. He took his leave of this life with the dignity of one who knows he has lived well and goes to a place of honor and rest. He went down to his grave with a prayer on his lips for the living and words of praise to his God.

He had placed his hands—not so powerful and large now as they once had been—upon each of our heads and bestowed upon us his last, parting blessing. Looking back on it now, I can see that he held on until Isabel was safely married before he allowed the vigor to leave his frame. It had become difficult for him to walk, and his eyesight was failing. It must have been with relief that he let the flesh have its way with him, granting his spirit that longed-for release which would reunite him with her whom he loved more than any thing, any person he was leaving behind.

As I bent to kiss his sunken cheek for the last time, I whispered, "Give Omni my love. You will do that? And Mother. Tell her . . . tell her I wish I could have talked to her as a woman, just once."

I could not bear to watch him die, and yet I sat there until the last breath shuddered through his large frame. I could sense the spirit leave; I could almost see it. I wondered if Mother were near—his Hannah, the way only he remembered her—and wished that I could feel her presence. Who would be there to meet him? Surely Omni, and his own parents—and Ishmael who had died in the wilderness—perhaps even Lehi himself.

I bent my head until it came to rest on the broad expanse of my father's chest. But there was no longer a heart beating there, no longer the warmth and pulse of blood driving through his veins. I closed my eyes and let the quiet, lonely tears come.

My father was buried with honors, and great was the mourning of the people when he was gone. The city of the dead here is growing in numbers. In time these dark, mute memorials will dot this land, like our cities—our cities which grow daily in wealth and splendor—and will be passed on from hand to hand, seemingly mindless and careless of those who shone once as splendidly as they do, but lie now in the grave.

So brief is the life of man, so weak are his ways. And

yet to think what one man, my father, had done! He lived a noble and influential life in Jerusalem, with comforts and commodities which we cannot imagine. Then, when it all fell apart and he feared his own life was in danger, he followed the voice of conviction and turned to face the unknown without murmur or petty complaint. His was one of the strong arms which Nephi came to rely upon.

Now he had helped to found a city, build a temple, and establish a way of life better than that which he had been born to. What a feeling that must have been! He had sacrificed and suffered, but he had never wavered. Now he possessed a goodly posterity, and the people of Zoram would increase in the land; his spirit would live on in the least of them, and that was good.

Man is nothing of himself, but with Jehovah's help, see what can be done. Every righteous desire of the heart, the Spirit whispered to me. I pondered long in the cool evening stillness beside my father's grave, and he seemed as near to me, as real to my mind, as if he stood by my side.

At last I rose, numb from sitting and chilled by the damp earth. "I must go, Father," I murmured. "I have much to do. My work is not yet done." To my amazement the words, spoken aloud, tasted good on my tongue. A sense of purpose and an awareness of my capabilities spread through me.

"Go, Father," I whispered. "We will carry on here— in your name, and God's."

Nefer

Chapter Nine

A chocolate plantation?"

"Does that sound strange to you, Nefer? I would be but an investor." Himni rubbed his cheek with his forefinger, something he did whenever he talked about business and profit.

"The returns should be high, the risk minimal."

"And your partners?"

He grinned at me.

"One partner. A good man, a very competent farmer. We have together purchased a strip of land where several large cacao trees—good harvesters—already stand. We plan to sow several acres, begin a plantation, then hire workers. In very little time, you will see—"

I was beginning to guess. "Rensi?" I clapped my hands in delight as he nodded. "I am so happy, Himni. This is a good fortune he is deserving of; he will not fail you."

"Yes, yes, I know that." A small frown played across his forehead. "You are very fond of your brother-in-law."

"Yes, I am. But in no way that should distress you. He is like a brother to me. That, and no more. You remember how it was when we were children in Bountiful."

I spoke without thinking. "I remember, Neferure."
He regarded me thoughtfully, his finger still rubbing his
cheekbone. "Do you think of Shemnon often?"

My heart began a sudden painful throbbing against
my chest. I had not heard those syllables spoken out
loud for years. "Not often," I answered honestly.
"Though it is impossible to not think about him at
all."

He said nothing, but continued gazing upon me,
and I could not read the thoughts his eyes veiled.

"You would not have been happy with him."

"Himni, really!"

"But, are you happy with me?"

"I am happy." But even as I said the words, the
incompleteness of the statement glared at me, like
morning sun reflecting off the glaze of still water.

"What makes you most unhappy about me—about
our life together?"

Himni had never asked me such questions before.
Did I dare hazard an honest answer?

"The fact that we have not had more children," I
began gently. "The fact that you spend more time with
your business concerns than you do with your family,
and that you spend even less time pursuing your reli-
gious obligations."

"That was a quick answer. Have you held it ready
and waiting?"

"You know how I feel."

"I provide well for you, Nefer. I am highly respected
among our people, and my influence is widely felt."

"To be respected among the people is good, Himni.
But what of our God? It should be his respect, his
approval we seek for."

"I do not understand you! Am I a wicked man? Do I
cheat my neighbor? Do I fail in my tithes and offerings?
Even the poor receive alms from me!"

There was no talking to him. "There are deeper things of the Spirit—ways of thinking, ways of—"

He made a short, impatient gesture. "You live in your own world, Nefer. I do not know what you want."

I could never compare him openly to Rensi; he would be too threatened and mistake the lesson which otherwise he could profit by. Rensi lived his life under direction of the Spirit: day by day, decision by decision. He feasted upon the sacred writings and upon the words of our leaders; they were like the manna in the desert to him. How can one explain it? His heart was different—his intentions, his desires belonged to God. Himni wanted this world, as much as he could amass of it. Rensi lived for a better world, the world Nephi told us of. It seemed real to Rensi, more real than to most. I too wished to purify myself, to become godlike. But I was not as consistent as my brother-in-law. I could not always keep hold of the iron rod, as Lehi had taught us. I could not always remember. Most of us were weaker than Rensi—but if I could be convinced that Himni truly cared! He took care that all the out- ward signs of piety were there, but he showed no sign of any interest beyond what would assure him of sta- tion—proper station in the eyes of his fellows and of the church itself.

Such thoughts wearied me because it seemed they went nowhere and left me with a discontent that was tenacious and nasty. At such times I took solace in my children or, from time to time, in my writings. Life is fickle and frustrating at best. Bentresh possessed little comprehension of the deeper things of the Spirit, and was largely unaware of the depth and power of her hus- band's spirituality. She profited thereby, but she did not understand; therefore, she did not share with him, any more than Himni shared with me, the inner realms of the soul. Does each man in this world walk alone? I often wonder. Is the loneliness of self unavoidable, and the only solution for it communication with God? I clothed my hunger with words, but I showed the words to no one, though the writing of them soothed my heart and made it a little easier for me to go on.

> *There is none but Thee, O God.*
> *Each walks alone,*
> *Unknown except to heaven.*
> *The arm of flesh*
> *Is insufficient:*
> *Wisdom is not ours,*
> *Nor might, nor beauty.*
> *Clumsily we crawl,*
> *Grieved and wounded.*
> *Only in thy light*
> *Can healing come, and peace,*
> *And strength anew.*
> *There is none but Thee, O God:*
> *The solitary soul*
> *Finds not its own*
> *Until it comes to Thee.*

༄

As the shifting of the winds o'er the land, as the movement of the sun through the heavens, as the inevitable progression of night following day in an endless, unchanging pattern do our lives wear away. The hours of an individual day may pass slowly, but the years melt from us, like the frost before sun. Isabel had married in the year 565 Before Christ, when my own daughter was five years old. Now, three years later, the chocolate plantation is thriving and my son, Seth, and Bentresh's son, Jarom, who are young men of sixteen, work with the laborers their fathers have hired, hacking the ripe pods from the trees with knives attached to long poles, then cutting the pods open and scooping out the precious beans. They place the beans in small piles

which they cover with banana leaves so that the leaves
will ferment. Not until then are they dried in the sun
and roasted, ground, and blended in preparation for the
market. It is tedious and at times difficult labor. But it is
good for our young sons to be given the responsibility
of it. They work hard, anxious to bring honor to their
fathers and to learn the ways of grown men. Rensi is
concerned about Jarom. He is boisterous and rowdy,
and he loves nothing more than a fight. He can hold his
own, though he is young, and once the men learn this
they grant him a grudging respect. This is a heady thing
for the lad and whets his appetite further. Seth, on the
other hand, is still drawn to book learning and the
things of the mind. He works with skill and discipline,
but his heart is not in the work. He laughs at his bold,
more active cousin. There exists a strange understanding between the two.

"They cover for one another," Rensi explained.
"Have you not seen it before? No bully dare touch a
hair of Seth's head for fear of having Jarom to deal with.
And likewise no teacher dare shame or demerit Jarom
for fear of Seth's brilliant wrath."

We laugh when we discuss it. We are pleased by
their closeness, but it frightens us a little bit too.

"Jarom and Ethem are brothers," Bentresh sighs,
"but one would not know it. Ethem must find his
friends elsewhere, for Jarom's devotion to Seth leaves
no room for him."

We shake our heads and wonder, and watch our
sons with more care than they know.

One day Seth approached me with a request that
took me by surprise.

"Jothan, one of the men who works for Father, is
soon to head an expedition, and he has invited us to be
part of it," he began.

"Yourself and Jarom?"

He nodded.

"And why is that?"

"The man has surveying skills. He values Jarom's brawn and my intelligence—that is very much how he put it. Mother, he is to survey sites for a city—a new city. Imagine it!"

I smiled wryly, but he did not notice.

"I am on fire to go. You can imagine it—discovering places no one has ever seen before, being the first to lay out a city, to choose and designate—it does stir the blood, Mother."

"Of course, it does."

"I may go then?"

"What does your father say?"

"Father approves of it. 'It is right that you should rise in the world,' he said. 'You have learned discipline working in the fields. Now your mind will have a chance at it, as well as your muscle.'"

I nodded silently after he had quoted his father. It was not easy to hold my tongue, though in one respect my unwavering prayers had been answered—Seth seemed to possess none of the pride and sense of self-importance which was his father's greatest weakness.

"Your son is like you," Bentresh told me when we discussed the proposition. "But where did my Jarom come from?"

"Some ancient warrior," I mused, "who brought honor to our line or Rensi's."

"But he is like neither myself nor his father," she lamented.

"Then try to enjoy him for what he is."

"You sound like Rensi now," she teased. "And I get full enough of such counsel at home."

So our sons left us, to be gone for months, whither we did not know. Our people are builders of cities, and it is Nephi's intention that we spread and grow stronger and inhabit the land. In this way too do we hold back the threat of the Lamanites, who are thieves and marauders, who will gladly reap what others have sown and lay waste the tedious, hopeful efforts of years.

I had my gardens, my weaving, the running of my household to keep me busy, and Awhere's antics to delight me, but I missed my young son. I sensed what he could not see yet—and what was of no concern to him—that I was losing him, step by step. Each year he forayed further into his own world, of necessity leaving me behind. Watching him, I realized that I was not ready yet, and I disliked the isolation, the sense of stagnation I felt.

"You are but thirty-three years old," Himni reminded me when I complained to him. "A woman reaching the height of your powers. Your handsome and clever son brings but more honors to you—and increases your own appeal."

He drew me into his arms. "I love the touch of you, Neferure; I love the scent of your skin." He kissed me, again and again, and his ardor surprised me. "When you walk by my side other men turn to look at you. I see the envy in their eyes, and I enjoy the feeling it gives me."

I shivered as his lips touched the soft hollow of my neck. "Of all the grand things I possess, Neferure, it gives me the greatest pleasure to know that you are mine."

His lips were insistent and I gave in to his caresses. I was his wife and he loved me. Was I foolish to look beyond that?

Our people are a people of ritual, and for us religion is a way of life. Nephi had ordained his younger brothers, Joseph and Jacob, to be priests and teachers over our people. Other wise and good men were ordained to join them so that we, as a people, might remember our God. Nephi pled with us in all of his teachings and all of his sermons to reject the pride of the world and seek those things which will last. In our temple the priests performed sacred and holy ordinances. But Nephi often reminded us that each heart must become a temple wherein God is enshrined.

"And now, my beloved brethren, I know that unless a man shall endure to the end, in following the example of the Son of the living God, he cannot be saved. Wherefore, do the things which I have told you I have seen that your Lord and your Redeemer should do; and then are ye in this strait and narrow path which leads to eternal life. And now, my beloved brethren, after ye have gotten into this strait and narrow path, I would ask if all is done? Behold, I say unto you, Nay; for ye have not come thus far save it were by the word of Christ with unshaken faith in him. Wherefore, ye must press forward with a steadfastness in Christ, having a perfect brightness of hope, and a love of God and of all men. Wherefore, if ye shall press forward, feasting upon the word of Christ, and endure to the end, behold, thus saith the Father: Ye shall have eternal life."

In this manner did Nephi teach his people. And in this way did Jesus Christ come to be the mark and standard we looked to as we sought to perfect our lives. Faith in Christ and enduring in that faith—enduring to the end. Himni had been right. I was but thirty-three, and a child in my understanding of what life and life's trials might be.

And it came to pass that Himni rose in position and power, and the chocolate plantation prospered, as did all things which came under his hand. And it came to pass that our sons, Seth and Jarom, returned to us, preserved in safety by God's mercy, wiser in the ways of the world than they had been when they left.

Onihah, husband to our Isabel, continued also to prosper, and to increase in boasting and pride. He enjoyed flaunting the beauty of his wife whenever he had occasion, dressing her in rich, sometimes gaudy, attire and taking care to attend every social event for which he could negotiate an invitation, and hosting many large, elaborate parties of his own—as many as, and more, I would suppose, than his purse could afford.

People humored Onihah because of his charm and his pleasing ways and winked at his minor indiscretions or lack of manners. Onihah liked pretty women but possessed the wisdom to flatter all females, so that the opposite sex flocked to him—women of all ages and all kinds. Isabel smiled with that same indulgence others seemed to extend to him.

"It is his way," she would say, in defense of him. "Am I not always beside him, shown off as proudly as he shows off himself?"

She was young. The attention and admiration were sweet to her. "Besides," she would sometimes add, "Onihah flatters men as well as women. I fear he has discovered it is a good way to reach his desired ends."

And his desired ends kept shifting and rising, his aim reaching higher and higher. There was always someone close by to help him, some shoulder offered for him to climb upon, some helping hand. With a canny sixth sense he was meticulous in returning favors, at times extending some that, upon maturing, would turn to his own advantage.

Himni was one of many who freely and openly assisted him, as charmed by the lad as any of the others.

"That one has a good head on his shoulders, and what's more he has a nose for a deal like I've seldom seen!"

"Keep an eye on him, will you, Himni?" I asked.

He gave a short, surprised laugh. "It is difficult to keep an eye on someone who's running as fast as he is."

"Oh, come now," I protested. "The boy cannot be all that brilliant."

"Just watch. It will not be long until you see for yourself."

So we went on about him; Himni amused and impressed, myself concerned and uneasy. But then, I have never pretended to understand a man's world, or the strange workings of their ambitions and desires. As long as Onihah did not get ahead of himself, or veer off the right path, as our people are wont to say, or let flattery and ambition turn his head and confuse him. As long as—oh! there was so much to worry about! As long as our little Isabel was well-cared for and happy and loved—then perhaps everything else would work out all right.

Nefer

CHAPTER TEN

It came to be that forty years had passed away since Lehi came out of Jerusalem. And our men prepared to go to battle against the Lamanites. My eldest son, Seth, my only son, prepared to go with the warriors, being eighteen years old and well trained in the skills of warfare which Nephi had instructed be taught to our young men. And his cousin Jarom prepared to go with him. Their youthful hearts rejoiced at the prospect before them, but we, their parents, did grieve and pray unto God for their protection.

I remember the day when Seth stood before me, clad in his battle accoutrements, the finest and most costly which his father was able to provide. He wore a tunic reaching down to his heels, closely woven and thick in order to deflect the sharp edge of enemy swords and lances. This tunic I had embroidered in a dozen deep shades of yellow and violet, red, blue, and brown. He wore a breastplate over this and a helmet fitted with bright feathers and covered over with gold. He carried a richly worked sword and a cimeter, which is a curved, axlike weapon carved of wood and fitted with an obsidian blade. At his side rested his steel bow and a quiver of strong, finely shaped arrows, in the use of which Seth was well skilled. He looked the young warrior, his body lean and well-tuned, his square jaw set with determination, despite the slight flush that brushed his high cheekbones. His generous mouth was the only feature of his face taken from his father, and even it was more finely drawn. His hair was thick like Himni's, but brown like mine, not black like his father's. He had Zoram's rich, resonant voice, so that when he spoke he seemed older and wiser than his years. He took most things about life—and therefore himself—very seriously; in this too he was like his mother. Yet he derived a great pleasure from life, from all things he learned, from the accomplishments of those he cared for, from the beauty he responded to in thought and in form. He had maintained much of the curiosity he had possessed as a child, and this quality frightened me. In the coming conflict, where would his curious nature lead him? Especially since he would have the bold, even rash, Jarom beside him. I trembled as I gazed upon my son. My mother's heart longed to protect him; aye, even to prevent his going—rushing forth as he was to meet that life which would surely come to him quickly, and painfully, enough. I loved him to the point of distraction, as all mothers love their firstborn. Yet it was my part to suffer in silence, to stand back, to let him go.

Himni seemed taken only with the glory of the moment, the possibilities for advancement and advantage couched in it. But Rensi felt much as I did. Our concerns were the same, but my anguished fears were the same as my sister's. Indeed, Bentresh was pale with fear and had become so distressed that she could neither eat nor sleep.

"This is nonsense," I told her. "You do Jarom no more good than you do yourself. You must contain this terror which would eat you up from the inside out."

"I cannot. It has such power over me. I know my son's reckless ways, his love of the difficult and dangerous."

"He will have Seth there to work as a leavening influence."

The eyes she lifted to me were dark with misery. "Aye, and what if it works the other way round?"

I put my finger to her lips. "No! You must not think so, much less say it!"

"But, Nefer, I do not understand! Here there is so much space. Every time our parties of explorers go out they find more. Land and water, fish and beasts, fruits of the field—all in abundance!" Her chin was quivering.

"I know. Have we not all thought it ourselves a thousand times? Why will the people of Laman and Lemuel not allow us to dwell here in peace? Why must there be wickedness and deceit, even bloodshed?"

"Rensi says—"

"I know what Rensi says." I smiled at her. "But his answers are no consolation; the truth is no consolation. Our sons are imperiled because of the wickedness of others. Has it not always been so?"

As I spoke the words I remembered without thinking those days in a world which had at one time existed, but was no more. *You would punish Shemnon for the sins of his parents!* I had once said to my father. Even in remembrance the agony was terrible. Could I live through it once more?

Rensi and the others like him had planted their crops in the spring months, when the fields had been cleared and the refuse and rubbish burned. Then came the rain and the wet summer months when the crops are watered, and at times washed away, and the intense sun raises steam from the moist earth, and you can almost see the corn grow. Harvest takes place in the dry, mellow autumn months even into the very last months of the year if the yield has been abundant. Thus the fallow time comes in late autumn and early winter, and how do men fill it? By going to war.

The boys' fathers blessed them before their departure.

There was some comfort in that. Rensi was deeply distressed, and perturbed with himself for being so.

"My feelings are too tender," he complained to me.

"Think what understanding it lends you. Is not God himself as tender toward his children as a loving mother would be?"

He winced; I had too clearly revealed my understanding of him. "At times I would rather be more like Himni," he confided. "He is a man of the world, with a man's skills, and is able to hold his own there."

"No," I said firmly. "No, do not say that. The world may need men like Himni, but the kingdom needs men like you." I kissed his cheek and his slow smile started, until at last he looked as much a boy as those two who were preparing to go off to battle.

But reason and courage could not so easily win over my sister. She wept bitterly all through that last night—sometimes in my arms, sometimes in Rensi's, but found little comfort—because she would not be comforted. As the long hours wore themselves out, Himni kissed me on the cheek and said, "I am going to bed. Your sister enjoys this ritual in her morbid way, but I do not. And I have important work in the morning."

His words stung—all the more because they had a strong strain of truth in them. But I remained, because Bentresh would have it so. At length I sent Rensi off, too.

"He will be exhausted tomorrow," I told my sister. "Let the poor man get some sleep."

"You are so kind to me, Nefer, as though God appointed you to watch over my life."

"The great God Jehovah," I echoed. "He made us sisters, just as our namesakes, the Egyptian princesses. And what tie is stronger?"

Reflected in her eyes and mine was the answer, the haunting answer: the tie of a mother to child. *God made that, too,* I thought, *and bound us to our offspring with cords*

strong as steel; otherwise, we might run away from the terrible
pain of our task.

I stroked Bentresh's soft, fine hair and sang the
songs I sang to Awhere, until at last exhaustion claimed
her and a kind of comfort set in, at least a stillness in her
soul that allowed her peace for the few remaining hours
before the dawn broke.

Our sons marched proudly behind their captain of
fifty, Seth himself having been appointed captain of ten
young men such as himself. Thus have the armies of the
Israelites organized themselves from the time of their
exodus out of Egypt, with captains of thousands, hundreds, fifties, and tens, there being also a chief of all the
captains of the host. Our men did also march under
flags or standards, each with a different symbol or
device. And they did swear a solemn oath of loyalty
which imposed penalties upon them if they were to
defile their pledged word.

It was not a large army which marched out this day,
but a moderately sized group sent to quell the arro-
gance of the Lamanites who had been setting upon our
merchants and traders, killing innocent men, and then
robbing them of the merchandise they carried or the
profits they had earned. Succeeding in this, they had
waxed even bolder, destroying fields and outlying
granaries and barns belonging to our people. This was
petty guerilla warfare, and they would not agree to a
declared battle, as our people are accustomed to doing.
Thus our men were to march south, along our own
roads, toward the place of our first landing and the
strongholds of the Lamanite peoples, and bring the
battle to them.

"They will capitulate," Himni assured us, "once
they see our numbers, once it is their fields which are
burned and their houses destroyed."

It was a dispassionate statement. But homes and

fields meant innocent women and children and a kind of suffering I did not wish to think of. Himni, watching my silence, mistook my thoughts.

"He is there somewhere, Neferure. And, knowing his nature, would you not guess him to be in the thick of things?"

He rarely referred to Shemnon directly by name.

"I was not thinking of Shemnon," I replied, speaking the syllables distinctly, "but of the women and children which a war of this nature might harm."

"Lamanites," Himni responded, "no matter what their age or sex may be."

"Meaning?"

"Meaning whatever, Nefer." He was disgusted with me. But I refused to allow him to draw me out where Shemnon was concerned. In all these years I had seen or heard nothing of him. At times I had asked myself, *Would he come up to battle against us? Would he take up the sword against me and mine?* But I knew it was not that simple. I knew his ways would be different; the expectations placed upon him would take precedence over time-worn memories and loyalties. I knew all this, but I could not picture it, could not make it real in my mind. I could not see him with a coppery-skinned wife. I could not see his face fixed in a grimace of hatred, his body painted in grotesque and gaudy patterns as he fell upon our people with the sword. I could not see such things at all.

So when my son marched away to do battle against the Lamanites, I closed my mind to certain possibilities, to certain unthinkable things.

"Leave all in God's hands," Rensi said. Rensi always said that, and he could do it better than I. However, even he was finding it difficult this time, with his own son, with so much at stake—something so very precious to be placed in God's keeping. But then, what better place? How foolish and narrow we are to fear and hold back.

Shemnon

CHAPTER ELEVEN

It has been a fair day for a battle—a cool wind blowing in from the ocean and a blue sky overhead. No rain, and the dense, heavy heat that accompanies moisture in this place. We of the Lamanite nation relish going up to battle against our sworn enemies, the Nephites. We have increased greatly in numbers and power since our people first came to what we then called the Promised Land. But we have gone one way, and our brethren have gone another. And we, because of the simplicity of our habits, and also our warlike nature, have drawn the native peoples of this land to our standard. In this manner have we become stronger than the Nephites, who establish cities, stay in one place, and spend their riches erecting temples and costly buildings and fashioning ornaments with which to decorate both their buildings and their persons. They have grown dependent upon their storehouses and their factories; the years our people spent wandering in the desert are but a memory to them. We of the Lamanites have remained true to our heritage and are wanderers still, and dwellers in tents. We move swiftly and freely, as our own will takes us, and we prefer it that way, though the Nephites look down upon us and pity us because we are not as they are.

In the years since our two peoples have become separate, we have contended often with the Nephites. Such contention is a way of life for us. Of the many mighty warriors who exist among us, I am one—Shemnon, son of Simon, son of Ishmael. I have been a skilled warrior since the days of my youth: strong of body and lithe of movement, with an eye as keen as the hawk's and a tread as soft as the leopard's. Skills such as mine are greatly prized by my people, and I have fared well. At least for the most part. At least to all outward appearances.

On this, one of the last days of autumn, in the fortieth year since our coming out from Jerusalem, I went forth with my comrades to meet a small army of the Nephites who had come on an errand of revenge, intent upon punishing us for harassing their borders and assailing their merchants, the same merchants who deal unjustly with us and who tell tales of our fierceness and unreliability so that our own trade is spoiled. Thus do they deal with us, but they see no harm in their dealings because of our "uncivilized" state.

On this day I had my three sons beside me: Geb, Saul, and Emer. All were fine warriors, but only Saul excelled and showed the promise of becoming like his father in time. We moved easily, our bodies oiled, painted, and taut with expectation. The thought of battle always brings a high, singing ring to my head and a taste like the salt of brine tears in my mouth. The Nephite army was not large in number, but they were determined in purpose. As is their custom, they had sent messengers ahead to decide upon the position and time of battle. Indeed, they did offer terms of peace before they launched an attack, which somehow is a point of honor with them. But in the thin, misty hours of early morning our two armies came together in a clash that flushed the birds from their nests in the marshes and set the squirrel and rabbit scurrying. It is an unholy sound, the sound of battle, but one that sends a thrill through every inch of my frame. We were situated in a long narrow valley near the foot of a hill, and it was our intention to push the armies of the Nephites up that slope where the growth was but sparse and scattered. For our people knew that a large cleft, hidden by a thick growth of trees, cut the hill in twain, and it was our intention to drive our enemies against that yawning cavern and then down to their deaths.

Thus we did attack fiercely with volleys of stones and arrows until we did maneuver them, inch by inch, toward that rise in the ground. And their captains did believe that they might take the hill and place themselves in a position to fire down upon us, after they had encamped themselves amid the strength of it, while we yet remained exposed on the open plain. Thus did they position their men to work out their intentions. As soon as we saw this, we did pretend to contend for that coveted slope, struggling tooth and nail for its possession.

With the skill of their bowmen did they wound and drive us. Once a slight height was attained, they did indeed have an advantage in firing upon us. But some of our warriors, those most skilled in the use of the bow, spread out on both sides to flank them; from trees and outcroppings of rocks did we aim our arrows into their midst, and many of our enemies did fall. And we exalted to see their fear and their suffering and to think upon what lay ahead.

Not until our supply of arrows was depleted did we fight man to man with our enemies, and in the last hours of battle many were slain by the sword. The Nephites fought fiercely, so we could not drive them to the height of the slope—to the line of dense trees which concealed the trap we had in reserve for them. If night fell and they camped on the hillside, we would be forced to bivouac, open and exposed. Thus we chose to encircle them and destroy as many as we could before the sun set and interfered with our work.

We fought to the point of exhaustion. When at last our forces retreated into the shadows, the remaining Nephites were huddled in a small, pitiable group only yards from the tree line.

"They will conceal themselves there this night," our commander guessed, "out of reach of our snipers. At first light they will slip away and head homeward." He smacked his lips. "We have given them a thorough whipping this time."

We agreed to dispense our men, let them melt into the shadows, so that the Nephite scouts could not find them. Some few would keep watch all night, prepared to pick off any Nephites who showed themselves by firelight or moonlight. I was assigned as one of these. I sent Saul and Emer back to the tent with their comrades, but Geb could not be found.

"Let me search for him," Saul pressed.

"I will be here," I reminded him. "And I can move more stealthily than the two of you put together. Do as I have said, and return here an hour before sunrise with the other warriors, to learn what our enemies will do." For there were many among us who believed we should not allow the Nephites to escape but should drive them into the chasm and destroy them altogether, despite the repercussions which might ensue.

My sons moved away and became part of the darkness of the night. I passed my hand over my face. I feared for the fate of my youngest; a tightness pressed on my heart, a sense of apprehension I had not felt in battle before. I determined to search once more among the bodies that littered the hillside before taking up my lone post.

A full moon cast a pale silver light over the landscape and I picked my way with ease; I am able to see

with the clearness of a cat's eyes at night. For long minutes, perhaps the better part of an hour, I progressed
from spot to spot. Then I became aware of a shuffling
noise off to my left, and the sound of muffled voices.
With no more than the tremble of a shadow I slid
behind a large rock and dropped to my knees. Several
feet away from me was stretched the body of my son.
He lay very still. I wondered if I had only imagined the
rise of human voices. Then a dark bulk detached itself
from the general murkiness and crawled slowly, clum-
sily toward the motionless form. I moved; I lifted my
sword above my head as the man approached Geb and
raised himself on one hand.

"Drink if you can. I have moistened your lips with
this cloth, but you must try to swallow."

My sword was in motion, inches from the man's
curved neck when the mumbled words registered in my
brain.

The warrior who had lifted my son's head and was
directing a trickle of water between his parched lips
wore the armor of a Nephite. His face, bare to the
moonlight, showed that he was no more than a boy. I
hesitated, and my sword trembled in my grip. The boy
shifted, releasing his burden to the ground again, and
his face turned to me, deathly white, the muscles drawn
tight with his own agony. What was it about his face?
Why did I turn cold—and then flush hot—at the sight of
him? I sank again to my knees, concealing my presence;
as I did so, the young man moaned and pitched forward, coming to rest within inches of Geb's body.

I sat back on my heels and gazed at the two of them.
Every instinct told me to smite the stranger and be done
with it. He was my enemy. I had never thought twice at
killing a Nephite before. Yet I sat hunched, rocking back
and forth, undecided. Clouds gray with rain streaked the
moon, and I shivered. *What was it about this young man?*

I rose and walked toward the two silent figures

stretched there on the ground. They had both suffered several wounds in the course of the fighting, and both needed care. Both. I stood over the Nephite youth. It was too dark to make out his features as clearly as I wished to, but the instinct that prevented me from slaying him was very strong. Without further thought I set about constructing a litter, tying sections of wood together with bindings from the length of leather I carried at my belt and cushioning it with strips of sod and moss I cut out with my knife. When the conveyance was prepared I placed the two boys upon it and dragged them some little distance to a hut I know—one I use from time to time on my hunting expeditions. They would be safe in this place.

I laid them on cots and covered their bodies with the skins that were stored for such purpose, then built a small fire and boiled water to use in attending their wounds. I moved swiftly, with the assurance of habit; I was performing tasks I had performed many times before. My son bore many slashes on his arms and his legs, and one cut along the side of his head that was angry and deep, but nothing more dreadful than that. I cleaned the injuries and prepared an ointment of the milk and resin of the mulli tree, which, used as a plaster over wounds, promotes healing. When he awoke I would administer datura, made from the leaf and flower of that plant, to grant him relief from the pain.

When I examined the Nephite boy I realized that he had suffered a deep wound in his left shoulder; this was his major injury, save the customary slashes and cuts. I cleansed the wound with ashes cooled from the fire, then applied white milk from the hoje tree to stop the flow of blood. As I worked over him, the young man moaned and his eyelids flickered, and the sensing of something familiar swept over me again. After the two were cared for and resting, I banked the fire and returned to my watch.

The storm which had been building broke with its
full force upon me, bending my back as it bent the trees
and the tall, supple grasses. Black rain blotted all land-
marks and left no delineation between land and horizon. The night was far spent when I arrived at the base
of the hill, only to learn that the bulk of the Nephite
forces, using the storm as cover, had slipped from our
grasp.

"That is well and good," I said to my friend Cohor,
who was captain of our forces. "I do not wish them to
come down upon us in a fearsome retaliation, a senseless spilling of blood." I squinted, trying to see past the
curtain of rain. The sky would not lighten with the dis-
solving of night, not while the storm kept its hold.

"We taught them a lesson, at least," Cohor growled
in a poor attempt to hide his frustration. "Perhaps they
will not be so eager another time to meddle in our
affairs."

"Yes," I agreed. "Will you give my sons a message
for me when they show up? I have found Geb and have
him in the small hut in the jungle north of the Sidon,
which I use when I am hunting. Tell them to return to
their mother and see to the needs of the household, but
to send Mara to me with food, medicines, and warm
clothing."

He nodded. "Is the lad badly hurt?"

"Yes," I replied, dissembling a little. "I do not wish
to move him as yet."

Cohor nodded again. "I will see to it." He scratched
his massive forehead with his thick forefinger. "We
should have stayed here and finished them."

"Well, there will be other times," I comforted him. A
restless need was upon me to return to the hut. I struck
back the way I had come, my leather tunic providing
scant protection against the wind-driven rain. I felt
haunted and fancied I heard echoes in the clamour of
the wind, and the shadows that skittered across my

path sent the blood pumping through my veins.

When I reached the shelter of the hut I slid in through the doorway, as silent as one of the shadows that had harrowed my path. I stood trembling in the dim, chilled interior. The still forms on the cots never moved, but I was aware of them—the small room seemed heavy with their presence. I sat back on my heels and built up a fire, only a small one. Then I crossed the room to look down once more on the Nephite boy.

The fire gave just enough light to see by, and in that glow the sleeping face appeared softened, the outlines less sharp. At once I saw it—in the set of the eyes, the shape of the bones, and the contour of the sweetly formed features—*this was Neferure's face!* I let out a cry, and the thick walls seemed to hold it, then send it back again, mocking me. I sank to my knees. Could it be so? Of course. I had half-expected such a thing to happen for years. We are not yet that great in numbers that we are able to avoid meeting old brethren in light of new circumstances. It is an awkward, often tragic thing: friend slaying friend in the name of nations and loyalties which had no existence scant years ago. A great sadness swept over me, more disabling than battle weakness and the wearing effects of the storm. I hid my face in my hands and remembered. And, with the remembering, I wept.

I acted the brave one, indeed, when Neferure left this valley, but I was existing on nerve and devotion alone. Once she walked away, everything inside me collapsed. I had told her, "Think of me as dead. Bury me in your heart, as though I was no longer living." But I had not known that I was, in fact, pronouncing my own doom. For I became dead to myself when Neferure passed out of my life. It was not a matter of succumbing or not succumbing, of behaving in a courageous manner—all that I was simply died and left nothing but an empty vessel, a void filled with pain.

I ran. In terror I tried to escape myself, ranging farther and farther into the wilderness where no living man could pursue. And there did I seek my own destruction—among the fierce, untamed beasts—doing all in my power to finish this death which consumed me!

I remained in the dense, uncharted forests, losing all track of time. If the creatures of prey stalked me, I did not see them nor hear them. No harm, no evil came near me. I had been fasting for days when at last the weakness of my unsustained flesh overtook me, and I sank into a stupor and supposed death was near. But the gods of fate, or the god of our fathers, or whatever power rules over us would not permit it to be. My father and his brethren who had been searching for me came upon me at last and carried me back, still gray with death, still emerged in that shadowy land where I wished to remain. And, while my mother and the other women nursed me back to health, Neferure came to me in a dream.

It was only a dream, but it had the strength of a vision. She smiled at me with those deep oval eyes, which are the color of doeskin when it has been warmed by the sun. She walked toward me with the suppleness of movement which characterizes her. Her hair was dark and dappled, like the rocks on the shore of Bountiful when they had been wet by the spray. And I could catch the fragrance of her as she moved closer and spoke to me, saying, "Shemnon, the love I bear you is stronger than the emptiness of separation, stronger than the span of mortality." Her voice came from deep inside my own being, and it both shook and soothed me. "Close your eyes, listen to the ocean, and I will be with you. I will always be with you . . . "

In this manner did she speak to me and release my

soul from that pain which is a living death. When I opened my eyes I knew the living would not release me, and I had nowhere to run.

So I lived, after a fashion. Upon the urgings of my father, I took unto me a wife, a woman of one of the tribes who live here, who have dwelt as fragments of broken civilizations for I do not know how long. They are a coarse, unruly people, savage by Nephite standards. She is comely to look upon, she is graceful of movement, but she is not Neferure. In the beginning I attempted to teach her of our ways, the settled skills of our women, even the reading of the old writings which exist among us. But she would not respond. She had her own ways, and she was content with them; she did not need more. She is loyal and hardworking and has borne me three sons and one daughter; in truth, I enjoy her companionship and the intimacy which marriage affords us. But it is not enough. My soul hungers for the things I shared with Neferure. I need what I had at one time tasted, the higher things of the Spirit which are with me no more. Thus, occasionally a loneliness creeps over my being, like a heavy sea fog, and I am frightened and ill-content because of these deep longings, which nothing can fill.

It is at such moments that I go alone to the sea and gaze out over the tide as it swells in great sweeps against our shore. I think upon the vast deserts of Israel where first we drew breath, and the land of Bountiful where the grace of God was upon us, where Nephi built a great ship—such a ship as our people had never seen before—a ship that bore us over the sea and planted us here, where two children who loved one another believed they would dwell forever in peace.

I think thoughts which my brain is too narrow to handle, and the loneliness grips me, and the sting of the spray dims my sight. Then I close my eyes and listen to the music that the sea makes, and I hear the sound of her voice. Her voice surrounds and lifts me, and I feel her presence as closely as if she stood at my side. Thus I draw the strength to go back, to continue. I am not content, but I am fed, sustained in some way by Neferure's spirit. In truth, she is with me yet.

Shemnon

CHAPTER TWELVE

The boy awoke fighting, as though he sensed his position and knew he was a prisoner of the enemy. I had to constrain him before he did harm to himself. I found myself explaining to him, in simple terms, why he was here, and alive.

"You would be sleeping with the rest of the slain," I told him, "if I had not seen you rendering service to my son."

He turned his head in Geb's direction. "It was I who wounded him," he replied, "but when the battle left us both helpless on the field, I considered my duty as an enemy to be over." His face relaxed a little, and the expressive mouth almost smiled. "We were both two young men, that is all, hurt and in need of succor."

"And you felt this then had become your duty."

"Yes," he replied. "Yes. You put it well."

"Not many young warriors feel as you do. I warrant it was your mother who taught you to view life that way."

He looked at me more sharply. He really was like her, a mixture of the wise and the impetuous. "What is your name?"

"Seth," he answered.

"And have you brothers and sisters?" I felt the pace

of my pulse begin to quicken as I asked the simple question.

"One sister, much younger. Her name is Awhere."

I nodded. "Good Egyptian names, names your mother was partial to." I drew a deep breath that seemed to burn in my chest. "How does your mother, Neferure? And how fare Rensi and Bentresh?"

His mouth twitched at the corners. "You were a friend of my mother's?"

I sidestepped his question. "I would be glad for news of her."

He considered for a moment just how he ought to answer the question, how much he ought to say. "She is well."

I did not attempt to hide my disgust. "Really. And what does she do with her time now as a matron in your fair Nephite city?"

His frustration was showing. "I am not really certain, sir. She has her gardens and the care of the household. My aunt lives just across the way—"

"Ah, so your mother is still looking after Bentresh."

Seth glared at what he considered my insolence. "And?" I pressed.

"And . . ." He was thinking, groping for anything. Young men are seldom aware of either the every day activities or the inner, private lives of their mothers, and Seth was no exception; such things are of little import to them.

"You are close to your mother." I made it a statement. "You two get along well."

"Yes," he answered grudgingly, knowing he was giving me the response I desired.

I left it at that, for Geb stirred on his cot, and, at the same time, the low door of the hut was pushed inward and my daughter, Mara, entered. She has inherited from me the skill of moving both swiftly and silently. In the

space of a breath she stood beside her brother and
placed her hand on his brow.

"He is burning with fever. It is well that I brought
the bark of the Cinchona with me, for none grows near
here." She dug into her bags, her long slender fingers
searching; it was like Mara to set to work at once. She is
but fifteen years old, yet she thinks and behaves like a
woman. Nefer was little older than this young girl
before me when Lehi died. She seemed woman enough
to me, and yet we were both pathetically childlike in
our expectations. I shuddered, and Mara felt it and
turned.

"You are chilled by your soaking in the rain. I will
brew some tonic for you, Father, mixed with vanilla and
honey, the way you like to drink it."

She hummed under her breath as she concentrated
on her labors, and, while she worked, I observed her for
the first time as a young man might look upon her, and
I did not like what I saw. She has skin as fair as the
white doves our people prize, and her hair is the color
of dried corn husks at harvest, with the shine of the ripe
harvest moon woven through the long tresses. Her eyes
reflect ever-varying shades of green and blue, as the
lights and shadows play through them; she was born
with sea eyes. That frightened me as I glanced up and
saw the young Nephite watching her. I remembered the
legends about such maidens, whose souls embody both
mystery and constancy. I know little of the genealogy of
her fathers, which has been passed on to her by her
mother, and so at times she has seemed mysterious even
to me.

At first Mara was unaware of the strange man's
presence. Not until she had satisfied herself that her
brother was comfortable did she release her mind from
its concentration and expand her attention. When her
wandering gaze rested upon Seth, she took a step or

two backward, fury in her eyes—cold fury, much like that of the seasoned combatant.

"Who lies here, Father? This warrior is not of our people."

Seth met her seething gaze with composure, and I remembered the first words he had spoken to me, his captor: "It is I who wounded him." Chances are that I would have lopped his head from his shoulders right there, and well he understood that.

"He is here by my permission. That is all you need to know, child."

My imperiousness had no effect upon her. She placed her hands on her hips—light, slender hands, so amazingly capable. "He performed some good office to you or yours, or he would not lie here, still breathing, and staring brashly at me." She walked deliberately closer to the wounded man. "What is your name?"

He told her, with a gracious gesture of his handsome head which, I noted, was not wasted on her.

"What say you to recommend yourself?"

He grinned a bit impertinently. "I am a skilled warrior and an honest man."

She stared, unimpressed.

"And my mother raised me up to be virtuous."

"Words," she responded. "What deeds have you to show?"

He had not taken the measure of her; now he realized that. "I did wound your brother, Geb, with my sword, and then did tend him on the battlefield. Your father, in search of his son, had pity upon both of us; thus, I am here."

She laughed aloud, and her indigo eyes shimmered. "Anyone who could fell Geb is indeed a warrior of some merit!"

Her words were light, but she was observing him closely. "Does anyone besides yourself know that he is here, Father?" She glanced at me, then met my eyes. "I did not think so." Annoyance accented her words.

"I am much stronger now. I can leave and rejoin my people," he offered nobly.

"I think not, Seth," I replied. "A few more days."

"But how in the world can we hide him? This is an untoward thing you do, Father." Mara's voice held a tinge of disgust.

"I have my own reasons, daughter."

She pressed me no further; she was, for all intents and purposes, a dutiful daughter. But she did have a mind of her own, and a freedom of expression—a leniency that I myself had given.

"You will be my liaison with the others, moving back and forth, bringing food and medicines. Tell your mother I hunt for game and will return when Geb is strong enough to be moved."

"And if Mother or the boys choose to come to you, or if any of your war companions stop here in passing, desiring a bed and a fire, and company?"

"I shall deal with those things, if they happen." I set my jaw firmly. "We will manage it, daughter."

She glanced again at the stranger, her curiosity growing. Why would her father, a sworn enemy of the Nephites, risk so much to assist one? She knew the reason was worth telling, and she wanted to know. But Seth had sunk back upon his blankets, his face gray and drawn.

"Food, Mara," I said gently, "talk later."

She complied, but there was an unease between us, a tension woven of various strands that seemed to snap through the room. Geb said little, but I felt he resented the Nephite. They might have parted friends on the battlefield, after the strange camaraderie that had passed between them. My interference made the difference, and my deference to the enemy—something my son had not seen before.

We ate in silence, the boys both too exhausted for much speaking, and Mara stayed the night with us. She would stay for two days, then return to her mother's tent to secure further supplies.

I arose early, just as the fingers of dawn were beginning to streak across the ash-colored sky. I would indeed go hunting for fresh meat to help build the strength of my weak lads. I walked out into the stillness, which is not really silence. The sounds of the earth and its creatures awakening came to my ears. At such times I was not an intruder, but part of the system of nature, in harmony with it.

I stayed out for most of the day, bringing home a brace of pheasants and a young stag for Mara's table. I took a certain pleasure from the thought of providing sustenance for the son of Nefer. I foolishly imagined her near me, walking with her chin up, the way she used to, her perceptive eye picking out spots of beauty I would have passed right by: a splash of orchids in a damp nook, a swallow's nest, half-hidden, a low blackberry bush dripping with ripe fruit.

Her presence, even pretended, had a soothing effect upon me. When I pushed open the door and scanned the small room with my eyes, I realized at once that it held only Geb; both Mara and the Nephite were gone.

"She helped him walk out to that sunny spot on the stream bank," Geb muttered, in answer to my unspoken question, "at least three, four hours ago."

I scowled as I set down my things. I should have expected this: I myself had already seen the first signs. I had already field dressed the deer, so I hung it in the small clearing to the back of the hut and prepared the pheasants for the pot, pacing myself purposefully. I wanted nothing more than to go after them. I knew the nature of my daughter; I knew what dangers I broached. Did young Seth share his mother's passionate nature or was he like his father, cool and meditative,

weighing all things to his own advantage first? I
remembered Himni from the days when we had played
by the seashore. We had never liked him as much as he
had liked us and had wanted to join in our sport. He
was older than we were and lonely, and thus he was
usually kind—but his kindness was to achieve his own
ends. Well, he had done that! Bile rose in my throat at
the thought of it, and I stomped out in the near dark to
bring the two in.

I had to nearly carry the boy, spent as he was, the
last few yards. "'Tis an untoward thing you have done,"
I hissed at my daughter as I deposited him with little
ceremony on his low bed.

She smiled back at me—and her smile was radiant. I
knew I had lost already, and the son of Himni had won.
*You must not look at it that way. You must remember who he
really is,* I chided myself.

The remaining hours were tight and ill-fitting, as
they had been the previous night. Mara was devotion
itself, making up for her indiscretion by nursing both
boys to distraction and preparing a meal so enticing
that even Geb was drawn out. After the lamps were put
out and the breathing of the two boys became steady
and even, I pushed at Mara's cot with my toe. She sat
up at once, and I could feel her luminous eyes upon me.
"Tell me something of Seth," I demanded. When she did
not deny me, I knew all over again that she was won.

"He is a young man," she said, "with dreams and
ambitions." I could feel her shrug in the darkness. "But
he has a good head, and much experience behind him."

"Experience in what?"

"His father is a goldsmith, but he also owns a chocolate plantation. Seth has worked for him there."

"He does well, this young man's father?"

"He is wealthy and cares much for money, and he
possesses many fine things."

I thought of Nefer in one of the houses I had heard

of, with finely worked wood and polished stone floors, with fountains and gardens—things I could not give her. Had Nefer come to care for her things? "What does Seth care for?"

"He says he is more like his mother and cares for the things of the Spirit."

I drew my breath in sharply and she paused. "Father?"

"Continue."

"He reads much. He would like to be a teacher among his people and guide their thoughts and their hearts."

"Ah," I replied. "Did you tell him that you too are a reader and are hungry for words scrawled on parchment?"

"I told him," she said solemnly, "and it moved him deeply. He caught my hands up and gazed into my eyes. 'Your soul has been waiting for my soul,' he said."

"Think not upon it!" I hissed. "You could never dwell with the Nephites."

"I could dwell wherever I had a mind to, Father." She moved, crawling forward until she knelt beside me. "Go to sleep," she murmured. "It was you after all, my dear one, who brought him here." She touched my hot forehead with the coolness of her slender fingers and smoothed the skin at my temples, as she had done since she was a child. "His mother too is a writer of words. Did you know that?"

I was grateful for the darkness that concealed my suffering.

"Would I like Seth's mother, Father? Tell me this, true."

I choked on her question, yet I could not dissemble. "She is a woman much like yourself, Mara; strong minded yet easily moved, one who feels deeply, holds deep convictions, and expects much out of life." I drew a ragged breath. "You would either love her—or hate her."

"I would love her, because Seth does so un-ashamedly—and because you still do." She planted a kiss on my cheek. "Sleep now, dear heart," she urged, as she crawled back to her bed.

But there was no sleep for me, not while that long night lasted. Memories and longings tormented me, and I was seized with a bitter regret for what might have been.

The second day proceeded in much the same manner as the first, but when evening fell a restlessness came over me; I knew with that same sensing which serves the wild beasts that something was amiss. I slipped out, disappearing behind natural barriers, melting into the shadows as I listened and watched.

I caught the young giant unawares and had his hands tied behind him before he could gather his wits about him. I dragged him back to the house and deposited him before the fire, prey to Mara's stares and Geb's pokings. But Seth dropped down to his knees and clawed at the ropes.

"This is my cousin, Jarom. He is like a brother to me. Unloose him, please."

Geb spat into the hot flame. I could see the gleam of the knife he held close to his thigh. "I say split his skull right here and roast him over the fire! He is a Nephite spy, Father!" The battle lust darkened his eyes and twitched in his muscles.

I had gagged the boy's mouth with a handful of moss. I leaned down and scooped it out now. "Speak for yourself, lad," I said.

Geb lunged forward, but I caught his knee with my foot and he fell, sprawling and gasping a little. "Speak," I repeated.

"It is true. I am cousin to your prisoner."

"And his self-appointed guardian angel?"

The boy nearly grinned. "Something like that. I was

nearby when you took off with him, and followed as best I could."

"You did not try to join the others?" He shook his head. "That was your duty."

"I have a sworn duty to Seth that comes first."

"You must leave, the both of you," I said, rising to my feet.

"Yes, we must," he agreed. "I spied a small detachment of your men heading this way—"

"Friends, most likely."

"They could be here any time."

"Yes." My mind was thinking, moving forward. "There is a way I could direct you which—"

"Father!" Geb ground his teeth in frustration. "In the name of your own honor!"

I turned on my son. "You know nothing of honor, you pup, especially honor among friends." I closed my big fingers around his neck and held him, forcing him to look into my eyes. "This man's father was the first and the best friend I have ever known in my life. I honor him in my heart as I honor no other; indeed, I would sacrifice my life to ensure his safety. Surely his son will not fare ill at my hands—not this day, not ever!"

I released Geb and he fell back, gasping for air.

"Mara, food for the journey. At once!"

She rose noiselessly and set about her duties. "I will go the first few miles with you," I said, "until I know you are safe."

Our scanty preparations were soon completed. I looked at my daughter. Her face had gone pale. Her sea eyes had no lights in them. "A few minutes only," I said, and nodded curtly. She slipped out the door, pulling Nefer's young son behind.

I know not what they said, what all passed between them. But I know that when I stood on the bare, rounded knoll with Seth and Jarom and pointed out the path of safety to them, I said, "Do not come back. I cannot make a habit of this." And there was no jest in my voice.

"God willing, I will not come back as a warrior," Seth replied. Then he drew himself up to his full, slender height and looked into my eyes. "But I will return, sir, I will return. You can count upon that."

Then he did a thing I had not been prepared for. He drew me into his arms and embraced me in the way of the desert tribes which we come from. I could smell the scent of Neferure on his skin, and the tenderness that welled in me was nearly too much to bear.

Then they were gone, and I was watching after. That was many weeks ago as we count time. Now it is spring and the crop of corn waits to be planted so that the warm rains may water it. Now is the time. Now I wait, to see if the son of Neferure is truly a man of his word.

Nefer

Chapter Thirteen

I thought I had tasted the full bitterness of suffering; I truly believed that I had. But on that chilly, overcast morning when our warriors marched into the city, hailed on every hand—when men left their fields and shops and women ran out of houses wiping their hands along their aprons—upon that morning I knew anguish of a kind that was entirely new to me.

Seth's face was not among those I searched with anxious gaze. Neither my son nor the son of Bentresh was anywhere to be found. I was stunned. The cry of lamentation for the dead was already rising into the thin, misty air. But I could not join the grieving mothers and widows. *He is not dead.* The thought came unbidden and would give me no peace, until it became almost as cruel and haunting as a mourning for his death would be.

The survivors came and found their ways to their various homes and families. But we went home empty-handed. The emptiness which follows expectation—how bitter it is! Himni took his grief out in anger, directing it upon anyone unfortunate enough to get in his way. He spent the whole of the day seeking "official redress"—someone to blame for overzealousness or underzealousness, for insubordination or vain self-

seeking. His efforts came to naught in the end. He wore
men's patience thin; he wore even their sympathy thin
before he was through. When he returned, haggard and
tight-lipped, I fixed him a soothing tonic and bathed his
sore feet. But he was far from ready to let go yet, even a
little. The sharpness of his chin and nose seemed more
pronounced as he sat, staring into the emptiness, but his
full mouth hung slack, hinting at the defeat which he
would not admit.

"Seth is not dead," I said.

He jerked his head round to glare at me. "Do you
know this, Nefer?"

"Only in my heart," I replied.

He made a deprecating sound deep in his throat,
dismissing me.

"I would know if he were dead," I maintained, not
meaning to put it quite so sharply.

"All mothers feel thus," he countered, his tone
slightly contemptuous.

"But this feeling," I persisted, "this assurance came
from somewhere and will not be denied."

He shrugged his shoulders. "The captain said Seth
was wounded. He saw him go down. But no more. He
thought the boy was alive still, yet when they searched
the battlefield he was nowhere to be found."

I swallowed against the tightness in my throat.
"And Jarom?"

"Even more unaccountable. No one seems to know
what happened to him. There were heavy casualties—
too heavy, considering the nature of the action. Smacks
of neglect, if you ask me. Military incompetence! Seems
the Lamanites trapped them on the side of a slope and
drove them up to the peak where the mountain was
cleft in twain and a large cavity opened up. They meant
to drive our warriors into it—the confusion must have
been terrible!"

I covered my face with my hands. "Himni, *please!*"

He paused to really regard me for the first time since that morning. "I'm sorry, Nefer, but I've just got this deuce of a notion that the two lads got themselves into some sort of mischief, probably out pursuing one of those scatter-brained schemes of Jarom's. Seth could never deny him, you know that. He never seemed smart enough to resist following his cousin's foolhardy lead, despite—"

"That's not fair, Himni."

"Fair, Neferure? It is most certainly accurate. Come now, you must agree with that."

I rose from my chair and walked to the window. I did not wish to have this kind of a conversation right now. I wished for a man whose wisdom and strong arm I could lean on; I did not wish to discuss petty things, to tie up my grief with knots of triviality and blind pride.

"I think I shall go check in on Bentresh."

"By all means, do so." He was exasperated with me now. Perhaps he was even afraid to be alone with his own grief.

"Bentresh needs me," I said.

"Bentresh has always needed you!"

"Yes, she has, from the very beginning—and, from the very beginning, you knew that."

"And what of me? Do you ever think I might need you?"

I lifted my eyes to look at him, and my gaze must have been terrible, for he appeared to shrink from it. I wanted to say: *We are not good at meeting one another's needs, are we?* Instead, I answered softly, "I can do nothing for you, Himni—not right now."

He let me go, as I knew he would. I walked through the moist darkness, aware of my aloneness as I was aware of the night. *My firstborn, my only son—would God take him from me?* The thought came again, with the clarity of a voice which is spoken aloud: *Your son is not dead.*

I fought down the impression; I did not wish to have faith in it. I did not want faith to disappoint me, and, in my ignorance, I believed that it could.

I met Rensi outside the house.

"I saw you coming," he said, "and wished to speak with you first."

"I also," I responded, and then I told him of the unusual sensations I had had, not thinking until I had spoken that the strange assurance did not extend itself to his son.

Yet he was glad for me. "God is speaking to you, Neferure. Listen to him. Do not run away this time."

"I am so afraid."

"Yes, I know." He was being very gentle with me. "But God cannot work through your fear. He will save you from the terrible pain of it if you will let him."

"And yourself? Have you found this peace of faith which you speak of?"

I was not as kind as Rensi, but he seemed unmindful of that. "I have felt it, but I cannot always hold on to it." His voice faltered a bit, and I put my hand on his arm.

"Forgive me!" I cried.

"Hush, hush," he admonished. "We must go inside now. You can see for yourself that Bentresh is resting peacefully. The physician has given her a draught made from the leaves of the coco bush which has calmed her and made her grow sleepy."

"This is good," I said.

I went in to my sister. She looked as white as the newly spun cotton that was twined round her loom. Her eyes watched me enter, but they registered nothing, no expression at all. I sat on a low stool beside her and took hold of her hand. It felt as slight as a child's hand, as the hand of my own little Awhere, who was only ten years old but already able to respond to the faith in God which I tried to instill in her heart. I felt a longing to gather my sister up and hold her against me—tightly, fiercely—as perhaps I would never hold my son to me again! I wept softly, my head bent above her. I wept for her pain and mine, and I wept for our lost, perhaps suffering, boys. But Bentresh said nothing, nor did her fingers move in my grasp, nor did her eyes come alive. I was as alone as I had been when I first walked out into the night.

"Rensi has suggested that we fast three days for Seth and Jarom," I told my husband the following morning.

He looked up from the plate of food he was eating. "Rensi has suggested, has he? The self-appointed spiritual head of the tribe of Zoram." He bent once more over his guanabana and papaya, and I turned away, refusing to be baited by him. His anger had not run its course yet and in this, as in most things, he had not turned to heaven for strength but had drawn within his own self. Perhaps he was lonely, as I was. But I could not reach out to him, nor did he try to reach me.

We did fast, all of the family of Zoram and many of our close friends beside. Amon and Esther were awkward in their grief; their abundance in the face of our diminishment created a reserve which they felt more than we. The fasting helped, but it provided no answers, no resolution, no comfort. Were our sons indeed dead, slain by the hand of a Lamanite in a place and a manner which we never would know? To have certain knowledge of their fate would have been a blessing—no matter what that fate was. Hope as slender as ours merely kept the pain fresh, self-renewing. We could not resign our sorrow to rest. We could perform no proper mourning. We could in no way lay down our burden of grief.

Himni raged, or rather the pain raged in Himni. It

had sunk its sharp teeth into him and would not let go. He blamed every person, every circumstance he could discover, until at last he blamed God. "How could God allow this to happen to me?" was the refrain of his days. After all, he was accustomed to an unusual degree of control in the affairs of his life—and he felt he had earned blessings from the hand of Deity. Oh, vain, foolish mortals that we are to view ourselves so! I was not one to judge my husband in this matter for, within my own heart I too harbored a child's sense of betrayal that God could allow such a heavy burden to be placed at my door. As with Rensi, there were times when faith came to my rescue, when I could see with an illumination which filled my whole being with light. At such moments I knew that all that matters is what we carry inside, the eternal part of us which is unconcerned with the common comings and goings of mortal life. Even those terrible sufferings which tear us apart here lose much of their sting when viewed with an eternal perspective. A moment's separation—and then enjoyment unhampered by the ills of our present state. Such realization brought the peace I longed for and enabled me to lift my gaze upward. But oh, to hold on—to hold on was such a difficult matter!

Awhere was my sweet comfort, and I hers, but my sister Bentresh drew inside herself while pretending that naught was the matter. It was chilling to see. I could not soothe away her fits of tears and trembling as I was accustomed to doing. This time she shut even me out, and I was reminded of our mother, which, of course, made the whole thing even worse than it was.

So early spring came, time to prepare the fields for the corn crop. Rensi labored day and night working his own farm and overseeing the chocolate plantation. He could have used two extra pair of hands and two strong young backs now. But no one mentioned the loss. Profits were high, and that was something to be grateful for.

I spent many of my evenings with Bentresh, while Rensi bent above the furrows and Himni bent above his work-bench carving gems and hammering pieces of gold for the prosperous among the people of Nephi.

My sister and I worked silently, with the ease of much practice, dyeing yarn and then weaving it, or sometimes spinning the soft, naturally colored cotton which our people grow. We worked in an atmosphere of harmony, despite the strain her denial imposed upon us. But never was their presence not with us: the two fair lads, so different, each with his own unique promise of great things to come. Our mothers' hearts closed pro-tectively round their images, round their memories, round the joy we had had in them and the hope we cherished for their futures. No word had to be spoken. We suffered together, we longed together, and our hearts went out to one another in a compassion that was all-encompassing and unqualified.

Shemnon

CHAPTER FOURTEEN

With all my anticipating, as it happened I was not prepared for the young Nephites when they came. It was a dark night, a night of storms and forebodings, and I should have caught the vibrations. But I had been ill, beset by the achings of old wounds, so that the needs of the flesh overshadowed the impressions of the Spirit.

The first thing to alert me was Mara's behavior. She came into the room where my wife was carding llama wool and said something which made her scowl and begin to scold her daughter. I looked up from the weapons I had been polishing, but Mara would not meet my eyes. Her face appeared flushed, and there was a color staining the pale skin along her cheekbones which was not commonly there. I had seen this singular expression, this mood upon her features, but one time before, and well did I remember the time and the circumstances. *So it has come,* I said to myself, and I could hear a hot ringing inside my head.

"Mara has broken her loom again," Rachel sighed, "and my aunt is the only woman who has a replacement spindle. I am the only person she might possibly relinquish it to—and the beseeching for it may take me half the night."

She rose from her stool, casting a disgruntled look

upon her daughter, who at once rushed forward and planted a kiss on her cheek. Then did I know past any wondering or doubting, and I too rose to my feet.

She followed her mother's departing figure with her eyes, but once Rachel was safely away Mara slipped noiselessly into the small room at the back of the tent which she had claimed, as the only daughter of the household, as her own personal place. I followed behind her, but she did not prevent me. I saw at once that her personal belongings were tied into a bundle, to which she now added a few little things while I watched.

"Where is he?" I asked, half expecting Seth to materialize from one of the shadowy corners.

"He waits for me at the banana grove—"

"Where the foothills begin," I continued for her. "The foothills of the great mountain fastnesses wherein lie the strongholds of the Nephite people."

She still did not look at me. "Is Seth alone?" I queried.

"No. He has his big friend with him. He goes by the name of Jarom, and the two are cousins, remember?"

"Ah, then they never left these parts, did they? Let me guess. They have hidden out all this time, waiting for their wounds to mend and nursing their courage."

I could feel her smile, though I could not see her face.

"They have been more enterprising than you suspect, Father. For the last few weeks they have been employed by sea merchants, earning their keep— enough to buy food and supplies for the journey . . ." Her voice trailed off to a low, cautious note.

"Food for the journey and wedding cloths of gold and fine silk," I stated flatly.

At last her eyes lifted to mine. "Yes, that too, Father."

The radiance of her joy struck me more sharply than any sword edge. "You have little idea how different the life is which you are now choosing. Everything about it will be different—and difficult for you, Mara."

"Not everything, Father. Seth will be there."

"Love is not everything. The duty and drudgery of daily living makes up the greater part of our existence. Have you given thought to these things?"

"Yes, I am your daughter, Father, and I am given to overmuch thinking."

She smiled, and there was such tenderness in the expression that I had to cast my eyes down.

"You desert your own people to cast your lot with our enemies," I accused. I had to be sure.

"Yes, but you approve, do you not? Else we would not be standing here having this conversation, else the young Nephite would be cold in his grave—and unknown to me."

When she saw my body tense and then tremble at her words, she placed her hand on my arm—such a light touch, like a delicate bird fluttering its silken feathers over my skin.

"I will be fine, Father. I believe this is the life that was meant for me—my own fate coming to claim me."

"Yes," I agreed. "I too know this. I have felt it for years. Your destiny lies elsewhere. You are like *her*—you desire those things which I used to desire—"

Her fingers had tightened against my flesh. "You know my spirit! We are as one—you and I, Father. Oh, how shall I leave you?" she cried.

It was the nightmare, the exquisite agony lived over again. I had been required to endure this before, and it had broken my soul into little pieces and nearly destroyed me entirely. Could I endure it again?

I lifted her hand to my lips and kissed the sweet, slender fingers.

"You carry me with you," I told her, "in all that you are, all that you some day may be."

"Yes," she replied, almost fiercely. "I will be good for your sake. I will forget nothing you have taught me. I will be all you have hoped me to be, and I will honor your name."

I did not tell her that the world would be gray and colorless without her, that the pain of my loss was carving an emptiness in me which nothing could ever fill. I did not cry out to the deaf heavens against the blind indifference, the foul, unjust nature of life. The discipline I had learned through my many years as a warrior came to my aid, and I merely enfolded her in my aching arms and felt the pressure of her head resting against my shoulder for the last time.

"Father, may I take Tula with me? He is my pet; he would be lost without me."

She spoke of the young orphaned llama she had hand raised, and which followed her about much like a trained dog.

"Of course you may take him. He will remind you of home, and keep you company when your heart grows sore for us."

"As it will; as it will." She nestled against me, trembling a little. "You must give Mother a kiss for me and beg her to forgive me. Plead for me, Father, will you?"

I nodded, my fingers entangled in the fragrant strands of her hair.

"She is my mother, and I shall miss her sorely," she continued. "But leaving her will not wrench me, will not tear me asunder as—as—" She could not continue. I felt her chin tremble; I felt her terrible efforts to control herself.

"God go with you," I said, and the words tasted good in my mouth.

"Forgive me, dearest Father, for the terrible pain I cause you."

She lifted her face and I feasted my eyes upon the lines of her features, the glow of her anguished spirit exposed in its naked splendor before me. And, heaven forgive me, I thought of those other dear features which I had burned into my memory so long ago.

"You go to one who will treat you well," I told my daughter. Then, still looking into her startling eyes, I added, "Tell Neferure"—I struggled against the wild beating of my heart—"tell her that all that is left of me is in her safekeeping now."

We walked out together: I would see her safely delivered before returning to the wrath of her mother. The wind had dropped some, now only a hushed murmuring round our heads. Mara led Tula on a leash while I carried her bundle, into which I had placed a small knife of mine that she admired and often begged the use of for various of her household tasks. No stars broke through the wind-churned blackness, but we picked our way easily and moved with more speed than I would have wished. At times she would slip her small hand into mine, and the touch would sear through me like fire and nearly take my breath away.

It was not until we approached the ford over the Sidon, which is less than a mile from the meeting place, that I detected shadows which did not belong in the heavy woods we skirted. I said nothing to Mara, but I watched their subtle progress with a sense of foreboding. It might be nothing at all. Or it might be danger of one of a dozen varieties: thieves lying in wait for solitary travelers such as ourselves, a small band of wanderers, who hide under the guise of gypsies but are among the worst class of marauders, or it could be but wild beasts.

"Did anyone else know of your intended leaving, or guess at it?" I asked Mara.

"I have been cautious," she replied. "Seth came two nights ago, while you were off hunting."

"Ah, so he must have been watching, perhaps learning our habits?"

"I do not know."

"But you knew that your brothers would be leaving this morning."

"Yes. That is why we waited until now."

Her responses did not leave me easy; anyone could have spotted the two young Nephites the night they snuck into our camp. None of my people needed as much as half a reason to see their mere presence as excuse enough to attack them. If my own sons had been here—I shuddered to think! What guarantee had Mara that they would indeed be waiting for her?

"They will be there, Father," she said.

"Do my thoughts and fears show so openly?" I growled.

"Perhaps not to others," she replied. "But to me."

The two men were waiting. It was more difficult than I had imagined to set eyes upon them. "You keep your word," I said roughly as Seth came, almost eagerly, toward me.

"And, since you know this of me," he responded evenly, "then hear now my pledge. I will love and serve this daughter of your heart all the days of my life. I will protect and honor her and, God-willing, never give her gentle heart cause to mourn."

He looked into my eyes. "It is well," I said, after a moment, and clasped the hand he offered me.

For a brief moment I saw through a blur of tears— and it was that moment they struck. My eyes had wandered to the face of Jarom, who was grinning with pleasure at what he had just witnessed. Then his face began to crumple and, as it did so, an arrow whizzed close past my ear. Seth had already whirled round, with a terrible cry. I pushed Mara to the ground, half-covering her with my own body, as I reached for an arrow to fit to my bow.

Moments only. That is how it is in a battle. All is decided so swiftly, so irrevocably. When next I drew breath and took a sharp look around me the bodies of three men lay slumped and stiff on the ground, and Mara was bent above one of them, weeping bitterly, with her hands over her eyes.

I did not understand, not until I had taken a few steps closer. Then instinct, more than recognition, told me who it was that she grieved for, and I sank down to my knees. It was one of my own arrows that pierced Saul's throat. I tore it out with a howl that, even to my own ears, sounded inhuman.

I do not know how long I huddled over the body of my son, but when at last my brain cleared, I rose heavily, feeling that never again would I be agile and keen with life. Mara stood facing me, her face white and unreadable. "I will come back with you," she said.

"Impossible. Your treachery has caused the death of your brother. There would be no place for you now among your own people."

She hung her head and her whole body went limp. Seth came up behind her and steadied her swaying body.

"I will return with you, sir. I am prepared to pay for your son's life with—"

"No! No!" I cried. "What noble nonsense is this talk of sacrifice! Listen to me, both of you—you have all the more reason to go. Make something of your lives. Compensate for these senseless deaths with your virtuous deeds."

The young man, too, bowed his head before me.

"You must go quickly," I said.

"My dear cousin, brother of my heart, how can I return without him?" Seth moaned.

"Tell Rensi that I will give his son an honorable

burial and watch over his grave; tell my old comrade this."

"Father, is it ill to think of building happiness upon the ghosts of the slain and the cheated?"

"It is not!" I said fiercely, drawing her hands up in mine. "Fate and their own choices slew them. Do not carry their deaths like burdens to bow your strong backs."

Her haunted eyes stared back at me, and I shook her roughly. "I know whereof I speak! Live for their sakes—and mine—and sanctify any sacrifice here with your lives. There is no other way."

It was enough. She drew back, her eyes clear now.

Seth spoke softly but decisively. "We have made plans to join a large caravan of merchants and travel under their protection. One of the leaders is a friend of my father's, so you may rest your fears concerning us."

"It is well. Now, go quickly, my children."

They turned. The thick-growing trees made way for them, and soon the dark night swallowed their forms. I followed at as great a distance as I dared and watched as they were drawn into the warm circle of tents and wagons where an armed guard walked sentry. And then I turned back and retraced my steps more slowly, my spirit lagging as much as my feet, dreading the ghost-filled grove and the sightless, accusing eyes of the dead.

I washed the three bodies and placed those of Saul and his young friend in a shallow grave, then dragged large stones to place over them, thus assuring protection from the wild, roving wolves and bears. But I carried Jarom's body some distance up to a high, wind-swept peak I had discovered on one of my trampings. There I rested some time from my exertions before building a burial cairn for him there.

I had no written words to read over him, but I spoke what I could from memory and committed his spirit to

God. Then I knelt, weary and aching, and prayed to that same God whom my fathers had rejected. And, as I prayed, I felt the strength of my trembling muscles renewed. I am a warrior. I do not speak of such things lightly—the effect on my body was real. And as I descended the mountain, wondering what I would say to the woman whose life I was about to destroy, peace, like a warm mantle, folded around me. I knew in my heart that the words would be given to me—as well as the strength I would need to bear the terrible onslaught of grief and reproach.

I walked beneath the cold fingers of dawn, but I did not walk alone. Do not ask me who it was that accompanied me; I do not know. But I knew that my own strength was not sufficient, and some kind hand was upholding me, in much the same tender manner that I had upheld the body of the slain Nephite as I carried him up to his grave.

Nefer

Chapter Fifteen

We gave up hope—is that the way to say it? There seemed no reason to think that the fate of our sons would ever be revealed to us. It was as though faith had perimeters; we had set our own limits of time and credibility. Then the caravan came.

I am not one to watch the comings and goings of merchants about their business—my own work keeps me busy enough. But Himni, whose shop is located in the center of the city, observed the arrival of the travelers, with the usual crowd which they draw. Recognizing an old friend of his, he sauntered over, and Sebus promptly waxed effusive in praise of his clever son. Himni went pale, they later told me, nearly fainted in the street, and had to be helped to a chair. But when his son stood before him he rose to his feet to embrace him, and all the crowd cheered. And when he would have Seth explain what had happened to him and the boy tried to demur, he called out in a loud voice that he would have satisfaction for the resurrection of his son from the dead.

"There is cause to mourn this day," Seth said finally, "not cause to rejoice. For I come without him who was brother to me, who laid down his life for my own."

Then the crowd hushed, and even Himni sat silent

while Seth walked back to the still-loaded caravan to claim what was his. But he did not return past the city street where his father waited. Rather, he led Mara upon the back of a llama, past the thoroughfares where men do business, to the silence of the cornfields and vineyards; he led the girl home. And I, kneading dough for bread, felt their presence before I saw them and went to my doorway to look. When he came near with her, I knew without asking whose daughter she was. And I cried out in my heart, though my tongue was silent, at the pain and joy of the sight.

They came to me slowly, with a reluctance that was grievous to watch. At last I crossed the distance to meet them and take the girl into my arms, her burnished hair fragrant against my cheek.

"You have Shemnon's eyes," I said, "and I am glad of the sight of you."

Then she pillowed her head against my shoulder and wept like a child. At length I sent Awhere to draw a cup of cold water for her and cajoled her into the cool recesses of the house. Even in her grief her steps slowed as her eyes wandered over the fine murals painted upon the smooth stucco walls. The patterned stones at her feet, the heavy rugs and intricately worked tapestries, the gleaming candlesticks and urns and figurines of Himni's designing—none escaped her keen gaze. She tried her best to conceal the astonishing effect they had upon her, but in the end she gave up with a sigh.

"Such riches are undreamed of where I come from. Such order and splendor." She looked up and met my eyes frankly. "Did my father know this was what I was coming to?"

I shaped my lips into what I hoped was a smile. "He could only have guessed. But he wanted it for you, did he not?"

"Yes, he did. He wished me to be with you—he

wished for me to become like you, I believe, and was
willing to sacrifice his own happiness that this greater
purpose might be brought forth."

The pace of my pulse was dizzying. "It is not the
first time he has made such a sacrifice," I replied, not
even attempting to stop the tears that slid down my
cheeks.

"Mother," Seth cried. "Shemnon's is not the only
sacrifice. Jarom lies dead! He fell because I would have
my desire—despite risk or cost—and he has bought my
happiness with his dear blood!"

He buried his hands in his face and wept as only a
man can weep, and it was a terrible thing.

A horror had come over me at his words; Mara read
it in my face. "I will tell your sister," she said. "You
should not have to do it."

"No. There is no one but I. I am the shield that separates her from the full force of life's blows; it has ever
been thus."

"So my father said. But I would spare you that suffering if I could."

With those words, Mara became my own daughter,
as surely as if she had been born of my flesh, as surely
as if she had been born of the dreams her father and I
had cherished when we were her age.

Seth at length determined to go himself to Rensi's
fields, in search of him. I too thought this the best plan.
Rensi, though broken by the news, would endure it; he
possessed inner resources to call upon. It was not so
with Bentresh.

Then came the question, after he had gone and left
us together: should I go to my sister, or should I take
the easier path? Rensi could handle it. I had every right
to impose it upon him; he was her husband, not I. But it
was my son she would hate with a vengeance—and

this pale-faced girl who sat gazing so solemnly into my face.

"I must go. I must face her now, and pray that I can find some way to keep her from holding this grief inside, for if she does, she will hate both you and Seth, and that hatred will be the first thing with power enough to come between us." The realization, spoken aloud, chilled me to the bone.

"I do not know how to pray, or I would pray with you."

"You are praying in your heart," I replied, kissing her soft cheek, "though you know it not."

I found Bentresh in the sunny, south-facing portico, resting in her favorite low chair, a little pile of worn clothes sitting in her lap to be mended. She often came here to escape the noisy confusion of a household full of young boys. She missed Isabel's company and the gentling influence of having her about the house.

She looked up when she heard my step, but she did not smile. "You bring ill news, sister," she said.

I started at her words. "Why do you say so?" I demanded.

"Nothing more than the simple fact that I can see it in your face. You are an ill concealer of emotion. It has always been so."

I sat down beside her but could not hold still, so I rose to pace the narrow strip of flooring. Bentresh put down the hood she was working on and folded her hands in her lap. *I must be swift and merciful, but not so abrupt that I shock her reason into madness.* With this thought, I plunged into the deep waters ahead.

"There is tragic news now. Certain word of . . ." I could not look at her, "of Jarom's death."

She nodded slowly. "I knew all along, Nefer. Only you and Rensi hoped."

"But you do not understand. He has not been dead these many months."

"What do you mean?" She leaned forward, an unconscious response she had not thought to check.

"Bentresh, my dearest! I am the one who must tell you . . . somehow . . . what . . ."

My voice was trembling. Her expression grew gentle, but I could see the wariness sitting behind her expression.

"Yes, it is as horrible as it appears—as horrible as your imagination could conjure—and I must tell you quickly or lose the strength to do so at all."

I watched her face as I told the tale; I watched her features tighten and close in upon themselves until I thought I would scream. I wanted to shake her. *Cry out, Bentresh. Strike back at me. Do something!*

"I did not understand him," she said under her breath. "I had no—what would you say—sympathy for the things he wanted from life. For that matter, neither did his father; though, of course, Rensi showed more patience with him." She shrugged her shoulders, thin beneath her light mantle. "Perhaps God took him from both of us. Perhaps he is better off where he is."

She picked up her mending, ignoring my open-mouthed stare. "Bentresh!"

"Hush, Nefer. No more of this. What good will words do?" She did not look up; she was shutting me out still. I dropped to my knees by her feet and placed my hands over hers, but she shook them gently off again. "Seth has returned with the Lamanite girl, you say? Well, I wish him joy with her."

There was no bitterness in the words when she spoke them; there was no emotion at all. But I went cold with the force of the unacknowledged horror of her mis-felt guilt, her resentment and pain.

"She is the daughter of the man you loved," she

mused aloud. "There will be trouble with Himni; you can be certain of that."

"Then I will need you. We need one another, sister!"

Bentresh bent over her sewing and gave no reply. At length I arose and walked stiffly along the dim portico, back the way I had come.

My sister was right. There was trouble with Himni on every possible point. When he found that his son had come directly home to his mother, he felt both hurt and angry. He had wished to brag about the boy and his miraculous appearance; his son's narrow thoughtlessness had cheated him. Then, when he learned *why*—when he saw the reason for all the trouble, the inadvertent reason for Jarom's death—he hardened his heart to the girl, and that was the end of the matter. It did Seth no good to attempt to explain that her father had been the direct means of saving his life.

"To what end?" he would say. "To what end, Seth, I ask you!"

And Seth would make no reply. And I, seeing the tight pain in his features, in the very set of his body, would suffer with him, over and over again.

At last I tried myself, though the task was both unpleasant and awkward.

"She is *his daughter*," Himni would snap at me. He never shouted; he was too quiet by nature for that.

"Why will you so rarely name him? What are you afraid of, Himni?"

"Do not be ridiculous! Why do you say such things, Neferure?"

"Because you act irrationally and will not even show compassion upon an innocent child."

"Innocent child!" He molded his full mouth into a pout. "Open your eyes, my darling. She is a young woman, with all a woman's charms and powers."

At such points I always turned away, for I had not the heart nor the stomach to go further with him in such a vein.

For whatever reason, perhaps as penance in their own eyes, both young people displayed an uncommon patience and forebearance. I knew both were suffering, though in slightly differing ways, for Himni's barbs had cut deep.

Then the inevitable happened. Himni came home from the marketplace one evening spouting cruel remarks and insinuations, spoken to me but of course heard by the entire household, as he intended they should be.

"We harbor a Lamanite girl whose family is responsible for the death of one of our noblest sons."

I ignored him with cool indifference, continuing my concentration upon the sweet potatoes I was scrubbing and slicing.

"People are talking, Nefer, and soon it will go farther than that."

"It need not. You encourage the commotion, Himni."

"Encourage!" He was infuriated with me. "This whole affair is harming our reputation! My business is beginning to suffer! I ask you—"

"Hush!" I hissed at him. "The children come near."

"The children!"

I disliked how easily he used sarcasm with me these days. "Yes, the children," I emphasized, "my little Awhere among them. I will hear no more of your selfish rantings right now."

He seethed, but he did not oppose me. And, when actually in Mara's presence, he retreated somewhat, unwilling to display his emotions in so forward a manner. But my heart went out to the girl. She was a prisoner here for all intents and purposes. And I knew such conditions could not forever be borne.

Then a few evenings later Seth and Mara came in to me, holding hands, looking like children only half their age.

"We have decided, Mother," Seth began. "And you cannot dissuade us."

"Yes?" I looked up into their faces—so intent, so filled with the trustful assurance of youth.

"We will go away together. Father is right; we have imposed upon you in too many ways."

"Ah! And where would you go?"

"You remember my friend Jothan? He has helped to survey a new settlement not ten miles from here."

"And how would you live?"

"He has offered me work with him."

"And what of your studies?" I saw a shadow cross Seth's features; I knew his dreams too.

"They will wait."

I shook my head. "Nothing waits, especially not when you are taking your life in a wholly different direction. You wish to survey plots and roads or work on a chocolate plantation for the rest of your days?"

"He wishes to be a teacher," Mara said. Her eyes met mine, and a perfect understanding passed between us.

"Sometimes one must do what is expedient," Seth stammered.

"You are right," I agreed, "and I will tell you what is the expedient thing."

They lifted their faces to me and I thought: *They want me to deliver them, despite their fine young bravado. They are still very young and afraid.*

"This child you love," I said to my son, "is just that—but something of a child still. And you have already required much, very much, at her hands. Too much. So, at least for the present, Mara will stay here with me. I will care for her; I will raise her as my own daughter."

Seth nodded slowly. "But then, I shall be considered an outcast who has killed my cousin, disgraced my father, and proved himself unworthy to claim his bride."

They were solemn words, earnestly spoken. I rose to my feet, went to my son, and folded my arms around him. "Your heart is so sore, my dearest. Would to God I could lift this terrible burden from you and bear it myself. No, I have already arranged for you to live at the school where the learned elders will teach and prepare you for the work you do best, the work that God made you to do."

"Mother," he replied, "I did not seek what has happened."

"Indeed. How seldom we seek the things which come to us in life. Lehi did not seek the incredible task heaven thrust upon him. He sought only, I suppose, to do his duty and be faithful in serving his god. But that same god marked him for other things, greater things. And so he has marked many of us who came with him here."

I looked into Seth's eyes. Could I go as far as my thoughts took me? "Perhaps he marked Jarom for death. So his own father believes, Seth. Such a purpose seems unclear, even cruel to us, but that is because we see darkly and for the day of this life alone. Your cousin's death was not of your doing, nor Mara's. You must let it go!"

I glanced at the girl, who had been watching me closely. "I believe it was meant for Mara to come back with you here. Her father and I loved one another so desperately when we were young. The happiness you two shall know was denied us. Yet, in your lives, our own youthful desires shall blossom into beauty and fulfillment and our souls be woven together as heaven intended they be."

They understood, as much as they were capable of understanding. But I still had Himni to deal with. That very night I sent the young ones on a long walk and cornered him where he reclined on the low bamboo couch where he liked to relax of an evening.

"You spoke harsh words the other night," I began, "concerning your son and the daughter of our old friend. Harsh words achieve nothing, so I have taken the matter in hand."

He glanced up, interested despite himself, and wary, of course, of what I would do. "Well, you are good at that, Nefer, taking people's affairs 'in hand,' as you put it."

"Thank you," I replied, refusing to be drawn out and thinking to myself how much I would rather he assume—in justice and wisdom—many of the tasks that fell on my shoulders. I started by telling him of the arrangements I had made for Seth's education: he could not help but be pleased; indeed, it seemed too good to be true, and he did not ask how I had won my son's acceptance and compliance.

"And what of the girl?" he asked, his eyes and voice wary again.

"Mara will stay here with me. We will raise her as we would our own daughter, until she is of a marriageable age."

"Should she not be returned to her family, Nefer? They are both young. Time and separation may very well change their feelings for one another, and then where would we be? It could prove awkward, my dear, very awkward." He liked his own arguments and the clear reasonable logic of them.

"The girl's family would not take her back; you know that, Himni. She is one of us in spirit and deserves to stay here. Would you deny the blessings of the gospel of Christ to one of his daughters?"

"When she is a Lamanite and determined to drag my son into an undesirable marriage . . ." He left his cruel words open ended.

"Undesirable from no one's point of view but your own," I replied evenly, though I was hot and trembling inside. "And they will marry, Himni. Time and circumstance will not change that."

"They changed things for you," he said bluntly. "You did not marry where you first thought you would. It is madness to resign ourselves—"

"It may be beneficial for you to resign yourself to things you cannot change," I interrupted, "as many of the rest of us do."

His generous mouth tightened into a pout and his eyes narrowed until they appeared like small, sharp stones in his head.

"Hear me out, Himni," I said, "and hear me well. You have what you desire because of the sacrifice and deprivation of another man. That man now has nothing—not even the daughter he adores." Himni's pout tightened into a scowl as I continued. "You and I together will honor that sacrifice, and we will honor our commitment to God in doing our duty by Shemnon's daughter. Do you agree?"

He would not speak, but nodded his head curtly, and I noticed how beautiful his black hair was, long and thick still despite his forty-five years. I was surprised to see misery widen the dark eyes; not anger, but misery. And though I knew it was his own suffering which consumed him, not the suffering of others, I felt compassion for him. I walked over, bent down low and brushed my lips over his, then left the room quickly before he could weaken his commitment to my position by more discussion or argument.

In the quiet of my chamber, I wrote down the thoughts of my soul.

> *I loved you well,*
> *But, through no sin of mine,*
> *I was denied.*
> *And thou. Life parted us.*
> *But Love did not forget,*
> *And in this child*
> *That love has found a purpose and a peace*
> *My doubting heart ne'er dreamed of.*
> *In her eyes*
> *Thy tender spirit shines*
> *And I am blessed*
> *Twice-over by thy love.*
> *I will serve thee,*
> *Dearly remembered,*
> *By serving her,*
> *Love thee by loving*
> *This enchanting girl*
> *Who bears on her heart*
> *The impress of thy soul.*

Nefer

CHAPTER SIXTEEN

As soon as the change took place, as soon as Seth was out of the house, things improved. The boy himself was much happier: he had something to consume his attention besides his own misery, besides the perplexing problems he had no way of solving. Mara also relaxed. She was no longer expected to carry the burdens of the past and of the future upon her narrow young shoulders; she could be a girl again, indulge in youthful dreams, play games with Awhere, and grow up slowly and at her own pleasure.

Her company was pleasant for me, taking me back to the time when Bentresh and I were girls sharing our hopes and disappointments with one another. Everything with her was for the first time, since she was older than Awhere; I had never raised a daughter up to this point before. I often found myself trying to remember what it had been like when Bentresh was raising Isabel; not that long ago, really, yet how dim those days had already become. I longed to turn to Bentresh for her counsel and opinions, but there was no chance of that. Since Seth's return she and I talked of nothing but mundane things.

Rensi, on the other hand, I could approach. Soon after my scene with Himni I sought him out and informed him of the decisions which I had made. He listened intently, as was his habit, but his delicate features relaxed in the listening, as though he had all the time in the world for what it was I needed to say to him. He allowed nothing to distract the attention which was rightfully mine.

"You have done well," he pronounced at last. "I suppose you do not recognize the differences which are plain to my seeing?"

"Not at all." I shook my head at him. "You talk in riddles; you always have."

The corners of his mouth lifted just a little. "This is the first time, Nefer, that you have come to report something which is already resolved, decided. Always you ask my counsel, which is all right, but this time you have moved out with the strength of your own will and wisdom, and that is good."

I blinked back at him, and his smile became real. "A nice revelation, don't you think? You are growing, Nefer, and I know that pleases you well."

I went home and, for the second time in months, I took up my pen. I had not been able to write during the time that Seth was lost. I had felt too empty inside and was able to draw nothing from that vast emptiness. But now the words poured out of me, or through me—I do not know which. And, as always, the words themselves were a healing for me, and I wondered how it was for the others: Himni, weaving tight nets of resentment, yet strong enough to hold back the pain. Rensi, able to say of his son, "It would have happened much this same way, sooner or later. Better now, in this manner and for this cause, than afterward in some senseless slaughter that would bring forth no good at all." And Bentresh, who, in denying her sorrow, had to deny life itself and become a stranger to the very fabric of her existence.

I went in to my bed sobered by all that was befalling our people in this new world. Nephi still counseled us, as did those whom he had appointed, but we had become much preoccupied now. Where were our thoughts? Upon what did we place the desires of our hearts? Himni lay waiting for me, and I closed the disturbing reflections out as with a thick door. It would not do to lay with my husband with such thoughts between us—that would not do at all.

Himni was right about one thing: the people of Nephi did not take kindly to a Lamanite girl. The fact that she was beautiful to look upon and possessed a pleasing, respectful demeanor worked, sadly, to her disadvantage: her critics could discover no real reason to disparage and censure her. The facts concerned with her coming we kept as well concealed as we could; indeed, some thought her a victim of the same deceit which had killed Jarom, as, in some truth, she was. A few of the older people, displaying a condescension liberally sparkled with disdain, took pity upon her—pity from their high pinnacle, which was better than nothing at all. But, by and large, observers wanted nothing to do with her, save for the very curious, who are the worst kind of all, who would prey upon her as though she were a freak from some other world to be stared at and whispered over.

I was inexperienced in such matters. I handled the situation largely by ignoring it. We kept very much to ourselves, Mara playing with her pet llama and learning, with my help and Awhere's, what is expected of young Nephite girls. We were fortunate that Awhere took to her, indeed, that they took to one another. And of course there was much I could teach her concerning the household duties of women in a society such as ours.

"You have more work to do than our women," she told me one morning as we were cleaning vegetables freshly dug from the garden.

"And why is that?" I asked.

"Because you have so many things"—she struggled for the right word—"so many possessions to look after. That is part of it. And you have more clothes to wear, to be woven on the loom and sewn together, to be cared for and cleaned." She bit into a juicy slice of guanabana. "And you have more foods to eat—but less fish. I like the fresh foods the sea offers, and I like the taste of red meat." She wiped away the juice with the tip of a long tapered finger. "My father is the best hunter among the men of our village. Many of the women envy my mother because of that."

Some expression on my face must have given her pause, for she clammed up suddenly and said no more of her life. I knew she missed her home and family with a pain that was as wearing and constant as a bad toothache. One day I asked her how it was that she had come to be so close to her father when she was the only daughter in a household of boys.

She colored a little, looking like a blushing sunset with her cinnamon, smooth skin and her golden-hued hair.

"Go on," I urged. "It is all right to speak of him."

"He always told me I reminded him of someone. 'Your brothers are wild like your mother's people,' he would say, 'but you are different. You are like the gentle women of another race which I used to know.'"

I looked away for just a moment, and I felt a touch on my shoulder from her cool, slender fingers. "I understand," she said. "If he did not love my mother, it would be different. But I know that he loves her, and so . . ."

"What existed between us," I tried to explain, "was a fine and good thing, built upon trust and the endearing affection of our childhood. That some fragments remain does not mean—"

"Yes," she said quickly. "Yes. I told you I understand."

Thus we felt our way, solitary, shunned somewhat by others: she bereft of her family, I bereft of my sister, both of us missing the young man who was behind all of this. We saw Seth only occasionally, and even then he did not stay with us but returned to sleep in his room at the school. I knew she missed him, but at the same time she treasured her maiden freedom. She too was busy learning, and not only the skills of homemaking. I had hired tutors to teach her reading, basic mathematics, and music. She possessed a quick, pliant mind and was eager for knowledge, soaking it up as do the dry, cracked highlands after months without rain. I loved her: in part for her own sake, in part because the son I loved loved her, in part because she was Shemnon's child.

The tutors made the difference. I discovered that if one wanted a friend, if one wanted kindness or companionship, the secret was to ask others for help. Bentresh and I had always been so close, had turned so much to each other, that I had never discovered this simple fact. Now offers for assistance and counsel came from the wives and friends of the teachers. All I had to do was mention something, express my frustration or consternation, and they were right there. Many of these were customers of Himni's, who took the occasion to praise his work to me. Thus I had an excuse to draw him in to the success of what was happening, and this pleased me well.

"Now the tables have turned," I told him with proud delight one evening as we walked out together under a low sky sagging with stars. "She has become 'our little Lamanite,' and our friends are vying to help her, to share their talents and insights. Do you know that many of them admire us, Himni, for taking her in! Perhaps they have thought so all along, but ignorance and fear diverted them."

"Fear, and a fair sprinkling of pride. Now it has become fashionable to coddle the little stranger. That is all the difference, my dear."

"You think ill of the people with whom you associate?" I questioned, stunned by his attitude.

"I simply know them for what they are, Nefer. I do not live in the unrealistic idealism of your world."

His words stung me to silence. I gazed up at the stars and tried to calm myself. *What a base world this is,* I thought. *We must shame the pure lights of heaven by the cruel, petty sights which we show them.*

"She is a choice girl, Himni, with many fine qualities and an abundance of love in her nature. People are drawn to her by what they see in her."

He stared straight ahead and laughed roughly. "It makes them feel good to so regard her, Nefer. But she is a Lamanite still. Is not her mother from one of the savage tribes which roam here?" He made a sound deep in his throat, and the contempt in it crawled over my skin like a loathsome insect. "She may be *his* daughter, but even that cannot save her. When will you open your eyes, Nefer? Even *he* carries the blood of traitors and reprobates in his veins."

"He is called Shemnon," I cried, but Himni ignored me and continued with his venomous attack.

"And what do we know of the wild, ignoble blood of this girl's mother? Seth is our only son. In the name of common sense, woman, do you really want his blood mingled with hers?"

"It is the mingling of spirit with spirit which should be our concern here, Himni."

He laughed rudely and I fell silent again, bruised by his hardness, as though his words had been stones.

"You fancy you still love him," Himni growled, startling me. "Foolish woman that you are to hang on to your girlish fancies. He could not have given you the life I have given you, or paid for your son's fine schooling, or even hired tutors for this Lamanite intruder in our family. He could never adorn you like this!"

With one thick finger he lifted the strand of gold at my throat wherein were woven many fine gems, as dazzling in their radiance as the white stars that danced overhead. "Do not waste your thoughts upon him," he hissed, his face close to mine. "You are so exquisite, Nefer, with your white skin and your elegant neck, and this mass of hair like spun silk!" He lifted its weight in his hand and let it run through his fingers, and I was reminded of the white sands of Bountiful and the laughter of children's voices.

"Come to me, Nefer," he moaned. "Your thoughts keep me miles away from you." He pressed his lips to my neck and pulled me closer.

Husband, I cried to myself, *it is your thoughts I desire, a generous integrity and a loyalty to something beyond your own needs and ambitions.*

It was then that I knew in my heart that he and I, though we traveled together, did not walk the same road, did not seek with watchful mien for the same things along life's way.

Among those who came forward to help were Esther and her daughters. Hannah, her oldest, was of an age with Mara—both were sixteen. She was a pretty girl, having inherited her mother's best features: the honey-white skin and brown hair all warm shades and lights. The two girls got along well and began going places together; often they were seen about the city and commented upon. I was glad of the association until one day Esther herself came to see me, much distraught.

"Walk alone with me, Nefer, will you?" she asked, taking hold of my arm. I left Awhere with her Sariah, who was just a year older, and led my friend up the same pathway Bentresh and I had traveled with Isabel on that memorable day when we thought we would be surprising her, and it turned to be the other way round. At a certain point I veered to the left, down a steeply banked incline to where a warm stream bubbled forth, flanked by flowers in every shade of the rainbow and a thick carpet of grass. Here we sat down and she pulled her knees up to her chin so that she looked like the girl I once knew. From the dullness in her brown eyes I knew that she was greatly troubled.

"What in the world is it?" I prodded gently.

"I would be telling you nothing if it were not for Mara," she said, and I thought her words a bit strange.

"Indeed, I have been so happy over the friendship of our girls," she smiled warmly, "that I gave it no thought. Not until last night when Amon reminded me and thought it best I tell you."

"What in the world?" I repeated, feeling a sinking sensation in the pit of my stomach.

"It is our Hannah," she said. "Several months ago she became involved with a boy—a boy several years older than she is, and of the poorest repute."

"Involved?" I made of the word a question. She lowered her eyes with a sigh.

"She is our eldest; we had implicit trust in her. This boy made advances; you know, Nefer. He is very smooth and very handsome. She gave in to his persuasions and to her own desires."

"Enough to harm herself, Esther?" I felt a terrible tight aching around my heart.

"It is difficult to say. She has not confided in us. Once we discovered her involvement with him—once we got past the horror of it—we demanded that she sever all ties with him, that she never see him again—and she complied." Esther shuddered, and I put my hand on her arm. "But she suffers, and has grown very quiet of late."

"And what has any of this to do with Mara and their relationship?"

"My dearest, surely you see. In the first place, Hannah might exert an unhealthy influence upon the girl's own morals."

"I do not accept that as a risk, not for a moment," I responded, feeling to defend Hannah in my heart. "I have looked into her eyes; I see nothing to fear there, Esther."

Esther's own eyes filled with tears. "It is not that simple. Though her deception may not be intended, yet she has done sinful things, Nefer, and surely those things have changed her, have—"

I brushed her protests away.

"But there is more," she persisted. "Her reputation also has suffered, and that is no light thing. Now that the two are seen often together, Amon thought it but fair to warn you—"

Without thinking the words came out of me. "Does Himni know aught of this yet?"

"Not from us, but he may from other sources. Himni would act upon our warning, wouldn't he?"

"We will not consider what Himni would do. He does not feel as we feel, the Spirit does not speak to him as it ofttimes whispers to us." I leaned back against an outcropping of rock, my mind swirling in agitation and a dull sort of pain.

"So this is a kind of suffering Bentresh and I have not encountered yet," I said dryly.

Esther sighed again. "Yes," she replied, "and it eats up the heart. There is a shame here, and a loss more devastating than the loss of the physical body to death—" She put her hand up to her mouth, her eyes registering horror at the words she had spoken. But I reached for her hand and chafed it gently between my own.

"I believe what you say. Here we speak of the more tragic loss of the spirit, the loss of purity and chastity and power, the loss of oneself."

She began to weep gently, almost without sound. A terrible hopelessness came over me as I watched her and realized that I had no comfort for her, no solace for this kind of pain.

"God will help her," I said. "She is young. She can build her life again and put the mistakes of her youth behind her."

"Yes. They are sweet-sounding words, but bitterly hard in the doing. Yet I believe she can—if she will. *If she will!* If she desires to do so, Nefer!"

"We will pray for her, Esther. And I shall speak to Rensi. He will pray for her, too. Surely God will hear us; surely God will help her!"

We could only pray that he would, that she would allow him to enter her heart and influence her actions, for without her consent all would be vain. How often Lehi had counseled us, reminding us of that great agency which all men have "to choose liberty and eternal life, or to choose captivity and death, according to the captivity and power of the devil; for he seeketh that all men might be miserable like unto himself." It sounded cut and dried, but in reality there were so many shades in between. Humans are complex creatures, with strands of good and evil, strength and weaknesses all intertwined. Only with God's help can we disentangle it all and weave a fabric of goodness and beauty to bring back to Him.

Nefer

CHAPTER SEVENTEEN

As Isabel walked toward me, I scarcely recognized her. She had grown thin and wore her black hair piled in a thick coil at the back of her head, making her appear taller and more sophisticated. I reached for her hand.

"It is overlong since I have seen you, and yet you look younger and more beautiful than the last time."

She did not smile at my praise; in fact, I had a sense that it pained her.

"Mara is waiting," I said.

Isabel had made plans to take the girl with her to the city and show her the impressive buildings, art pieces, and wares of the finest shops. Her young husband, Onihah, was like Himni, possessing the skill to turn to profit all which his hands touched. Isabel usually dressed in rich cloths which clung to the lines of her body, or hung loose, revealing the smooth white skin of her arms and neck. This is how Onihah wanted her dressed, so that others might admire his wife's beauty. There were no children as yet, though the two had been married for over five years.

I thought as I watched her showing the intricate embroidery work on her new sandals to Mara: *She talks little of her life. I do not know what fills her days, or whether she is happy or not.*

"You are not hurt, Nefer, that I leave you behind this time?"

She had also invited Bentresh—coaxed her, really—to take this excursion with the two of them. "No," I hastened to reassure her. "You have achieved a miracle, and I am grateful and happy."

Indeed, the day did go well. Bentresh relaxed in the company of her affluent sister whose beauty made people's heads turn. So they repeated the outing the following week, and the following. And each time Isabel would report back to me, pleased by the progress Bentresh had made. But she began adding, "Your young Lamanite makes quite a stir in the city," winking as she spoke toward Mara, who would blush at her words. After the fourth week she said, "Many men admire this young lady. Seth may discover that he has incurred competition when he finally asks for her hand."

Something in Mara's eyes alerted me, and I took occasion to question her later that night. At first she hedged, not wanting to answer my questions. Yet, rather than reluctance, I sensed a yearning of her spirit toward mine.

"You fear hurting me, do you not?" I guessed. "Do not let any fears mar the open trust we enjoy."

Then she told me how Isabel had introduced her to her husband, Onihah, and his young friends—bright men making names for themselves in the business districts of town. These young men said certain things and made certain advances which embarrassed her, and disturbed Isabel, she was sure.

"Have you spoken of this to anyone else?" I asked.

She shook her head. "Not even to Hannah, though she would be one of few who would understand."

"It is wise. Fears and suspicions expressed seem to grow of their own accord. Speak to no one," I entreated her. "Does Onihah do nothing to stop them?"

She dropped her eyes, staring hard at her hands

folded over her skirt. "Onihah is one of the worst."

Fear stabbed my heart, and unaccountably I wanted to sit down and weep.

"I am sorry," I murmured, "that you have been submitted to such treatment." I hesitated. "Does Bentresh do nothing?"

"They are careful to conceal the things they do from her eyes."

"And Isabel?"

Mara's sea eyes darkened. "Isabel tries . . ." The dull eyes swam with tears. "Isabel can do nothing."

You feel for her as I do, don't you? I said in my heart.

> *Must it be so?*
> *O Savior, who knows all,*
> *Must we learn by the things we suffer?*
> *Redeem us still,*
> *Caught in the snares of mortality,*
> *Helpless, ashamed.*
> *Must it be so?*
> *O Savior, who loves us,*
> *The path is hard,*
> *Pity us when we stumble and lose our way,*
> *We reach through the mists*
> *To find Thee,*
> *To feel thy grace*
> *Fold like a mantle around us.*
> *O gentle Man,*
> *Sustain us amid our sufferings:*
> *Forget us not.*

The following week Isabel sent her young serving girl over to say that the weekly outings must be discontinued for a season; her mistress was not feeling well. I thought it only a convenient excuse to end what must be ended, until Esther expressed her concern for my sister. "I think Isabel may be with child," she said.

Embarrassed by my thoughtlessness, I went myself to visit her. And, indeed, Esther's suspicions were true. But the girl was so ill that she could take little pleasure in the contemplation of future happiness if the path she must travel to get there was this.

"It will be worth all this, and much more," I assured her. "And you will forget—oh yes, you may not think so, but you will forget."

She looked down at herself, thin and wasted, and placed her hand on her belly. "I will become swollen and shapeless, and Onihah—" She stopped herself just in time.

I pretended not to notice the sudden catch in her voice, the high color in her cheeks. "Children are a source of great joy; they are a comfort to mothers," I said.

"Truly? I do not remember it being so when we were young."

She could not disguise the intensity of her own longing. I sighed. "Mother bore us during the days of our people's wanderings," I reminded her. "Those were difficult, unusual times." I smiled. "And she was a difficult, unusual woman." Isabel smiled a bit, too. "I do believe that she derived more pleasure from her love of us than we ever knew. Think of those nights when she sang you to sleep, dear."

Isabel nodded slowly. There were tears in her eyes. "That will be something to look forward to," she said. And I felt that her words were a prayer, uttered from the depths of an aching and lonely heart.

It should not have happened; none of it should have happened. Shortly after Mara's trips into the city with my sisters, I began to notice that Himni's attitude toward her had changed. Alas, not for the better. He began making bold insinuations concerning her that both hurt and confused me.

"Your sweet Lamanite has made quite a stir in society, Nefer. Did you not know?"

"I have heard certain things," I replied, knowing my husband was unaware of Mara's concerns. "What do you refer to, Himni?"

"She is canny, that one. She could have Onihah and his bunch eating out of her hand, if she so desired."

"She cannot help being young and attractive; it is no crime on her part."

"Indeed, I am beset by my clients who have heard talk of her charms and request that you and I bring her to the best galas to show her off—bedecked with gold jewelry and costly gems of my making, of course. 'What an advertisement she would be for you,' one of my best clients said. 'Imagine the hue and cry for your wares then.' Curse the woman's audacity!" Himni trembled with annoyance at that which was an offense in his eyes alone.

"You are usually eager to turn anything at all to your financial advantage. Why should this be different, Himni?"

"Because it is *her*. Because it would acknowledge my tacit acceptance of her place in my family, her worthiness as the wife of my son."

I stared at him. *He is envious of her*, I realized. *He has made of her some sort of symbol to which he attaches every greedy desire, every sense of inadequacy, every harbored grudge, every need for power and ascendancy.*

"You exaggerate both in concept and in interpretation," I told him.

He stared back at me. "Do not speak in riddles," he growled. "And do not play holier-than-thou with me, Nefer. I know whereof I speak, and I will hold to my opinions, thank you."

"Be that as it may," I replied. "Only be sure you hang on as firmly to your pledged word. For I intend to hold you to that."

"I expected no different from you," he retorted. "You see everyone's viewpoint, Neferure, before you choose to see mine."

Perhaps he was right, in a way. We seemed at odds about most things these days. I could not look at people and issues the way he did, try as I might. So perhaps in his eyes I appeared always unsympathetic, which was no way for a righteous wife to behave. I sighed as I left him, seeing the problem but having not the slightest idea of how to remedy it.

Bentresh came to me. She walked into my kitchen and tugged at my apron. "Come quickly!" she cried, her eyes terrified as a frighted doe's. "It is Isabel. Help me, please!"

Even in the madness of confusion and concern I felt a sweet flowing of joy. Her spirit had reached out to my spirit, and that had not happened for months.

We raced to our sister's house, arriving breathless, hearts beating. An old midwife sat at her bedside in a room that was darkened, and she hushed us as we crossed the threshold, though Isabel attempted to raise herself on one elbow and insist that she would be fine— and that she did not know what all the fuss was for.

We soon learned from the reluctant midwife, who shooed us out and then shuffled after in her own good time, that Isabel's body had threatened to miscarry the babies.

"Babies!" I breathed, catching the word.

"I believe there are two. Her body is weak, the birth pains come early. She must do nothing at all. Otherwise, she may bleed to death, and we will lose both Mama and the little ones."

There was no need to say more.

"We can take turns," I assured Bentresh.

"I should like to come together," she responded quickly. "I do not wish to come here alone."

"Very well. One of us can sit with her while the other cleans her kitchen and prepares her meals. That would work nicely." I kept my words simple, though my heart ached and I longed to gather my frightened sister into my arms. "We can do it, Bentresh. Together we will help her—and her babies—come through."

As it worked out, we had help which we had not anticipated. For the next seven weeks Esther and her girls, as well as Mara and Awhere, joined their efforts to ours. We were a family pulling together. Never before had we come to know each other so well. Now, mingling our skills and resources as well as our hours together, we learned the small, endearing things which bind heart to heart. Isabel was restless, bored with the inactivity, haunted by her own fears. Esther's girls entertained her with games and stories. Mara told her of life in her village, and brought her llama, Tula, for petting. Awhere made a doll of dried husks, with a painted face and a dress of dyed linen to keep Isabel company until her own children should come. We laughed together, ate and worked together, sang together, and felt the sweet flowing of sisterhood, binding our spirits with those gentle ties which womankind alone understand. Bentresh came more and more out of herself, until one day she embraced me and whispered against the damp tendrils of my hair, "You have never forsaken me, Nefer. I want you to know that I know this." And in those words, she said all.

Our days held a higher purpose now, and our hearts responded to it. The giving fed all of us, and each felt an investment in the children who grew in the silence of Isabel's womb. I could not help thinking of these spirits who were being sent to fill up this new land. What did God have in store for them? What would life here be like as we moved into the third and fourth and fifth generations, and on, and on?

As we worked one with another I noticed that Esther's Hannah often held back from the others and was silent, at times even taciturn. When I questioned Mara about it, she said, "Hannah is not at peace with herself. She is obeying the restrictions her parents have placed upon her, but in her own heart she yet hungers after the companionship of her old friends and the light-hearted ease of their ways."

"It grieves me to hear this. She isolates herself from all that is best around her."

"She no longer sees it that way. She feels inadequate and unworthy when she is with the rest of us."

"We must change that!" I cried.

"Dear Nefer, you would make all people happy and whole, if you could." Mara kissed my cheek gently. "We can pray for her and love her—little more beyond that."

I smiled at her wisdom. "Pray for her, Mara?"

She blushed gently. "I have learned much concerning your ways these past months," she said, "and much concerning your God. I like to pray. On the days when Seth comes we pray together."

"I did not know that," I replied, unable to conceal my pleasure.

"You see," she hesitated a little. "I pray for my father and mother each day. I believe—and I know you will not scoff at this—that my father prays also for me."

"If you feel it, then I am sure you are right," I said. "When he was a young man he knew how to pray. He once heard the mighty prayers of Lehi, our father, and of Nephi, his son. His own spirit responded. There is no reason not to believe that he lifts his heart in entreaty to heaven on behalf of his well-loved daughter."

"Yes," she murmured. "Yes. I too believe it is so."

Thus the weeks passed, and my hands and thoughts were so busy that I did not see certain things which were right under my nose. I did not see Himni's

resentment growing, spilling over in petty criticisms
and insults which Mara took care to conceal if she
could. He complained when she spent too much time
on her lessons, neglecting to help about the house, as
was her duty; he complained when she helped too
much, making a nuisance of herself. She could in no
wise please him, try though she may.

Then came an afternoon when Mara, Awhere, and I
fought our way home through a cold cloudburst that
soaked us all to the bone. The swollen stream boiled at
our feet, and the ferns dripped like weeping maidens
bent over with grief. It had rained off and on all through
the day. Knowing we had to get home some time, we
had ventured out during a dry spell, but then the low,
leaden skies had opened in torrents again. Torrents in
summer are common, but the wind had a bite to it that
felt like autumn. We shivered as we stepped into the
house, water trickling from us into little pools at our
feet. Isabel had been better that day, and in a hopeful
state, and I remember that the three of us, hopeful and
feeling better ourselves, laughed together, drying one
another's hair and drinking chocolate, hot and sweet-
ened, to warm us. I remember too that Awhere offered
to take our wet, muddy shoes out to the small store-
house, leaving them to dry in the warmth there, at the
same time fetching the vegetables from the granary
which we would need for the evening's meal. She skittered through the puddles, beneath a sky that was only
dripping now, and when we heard her frightened
scream tear through the stillness it raised the very hairs
on our heads.

Mara and I raced through the yard to her, only to
see at once what had caused the child to cry out. The
soaked, stiffened body of Mara's young llama hung
grotesquely before our eyes. Mara put her hand to her
mouth and swayed a little, and I put my own hand out
to steady her. It was obvious that the poor animal, teth-

ered to a post and exposed to the weather, had attempted, probably over the course of several hours, to free itself, but had instead become entangled, had by some cruel quirk formed a noose in the rope. Then, in his struggles—tugging and side-stepping and prancing in circles—he had pulled it tight enough around his neck to become a cruel death trap. I could not bear to think of the gentle creature gasping for breath and perishing there, alone.

I was sick inside and could only imagine what Mara felt. I put my arm around her shoulders. "Come inside, dear. Himni will cut the poor thing down for us when he—"

"No, not him!" she cried. "Do not let him touch Tula, please!"

She pulled away from me and went to the animal herself, kneeling in the wet earth and attempting to work loose the knots and tangles in the long, woven rope. I started after her, but Awhere placed a hand on my arm and led me aside.

"You must understand, Mother. It is Father who placed Tula here. He complained that, being a pet, he was too skittish to be placed with the other beasts."

"How so?" I blinked stupidly.

"I do not know, Mother. Something about the production of milk and tender, not stringy, meat." She leaned closer and I could see that tears wet her lashes. "Mara begged him to wait just long enough for us to build a little enclosure for him. But, you see, we have not had time. And . . . Father would not wait."

I put my hand to my stomach. If I had felt ill before, it was as nothing compared to the bitter weakness that engulfed me now. "Can you manage to help her?" I whispered hoarsely. When Awhere nodded, I turned and stumbled away from them, toward Bentresh's house.

I found Rensi in his workshop at the back of the

house, a small room which reminded me of that place in
the old settlement where he had pulled me in and
talked about Shemnon and the future, and had told me
for the first time that I could do anything—endure anything—with God's help. *He will not leave you comfortless,*
he had said.

Now he looked up as I entered, and at once saw my
need.

"Sit down, Nefer. Look—you are all wet and shaking. Cover yourself with this, and tell me what it is that
has brought you here."

He handed me a finely woven blanket of Bentresh's
making. I wrapped it around my shoulders and began
to tell him my story—going back, far back to all the
things that concerned me, that alienated me from
Himni, and ending at last with the pathetic death of
Mara's young pet. He listened patiently, with that calm
which has never ceased to amaze me. I could not dis-
cern any of the emotions which may be moving him,
save for the tightening of the muscles of his face and the
intense concentration of his gaze.

When I at last fell silent, worn out by my own
words, he did not speak for a moment, and by that I
guessed that he was deeply moved and did not yet trust
his response. For a moment, guilt washed over me as I
watched his solemn, tired face and thought of the burden I had so willingly laid at his feet.

"No, Neferure, it is right that you have come here.
We are a family, are we not? And there are certain things
that men, men holding the priesthood, ought to take
care of. This is one."

He rose, his agitation showing now in how he
rubbed his hand over the piece of polished wood he
had been working on, again and again.

"There is much I could say to you. But I have said it
all before, Nefer." He smiled kindly. "And much of
what I have said to you is written in your own heart."

He caught up my hands and pressed them between his own. "Go home to your children, my dear. God will take care of you—and I will take care of Himni."

My astonishment must have shown on my face. He laughed gently. "Never fear, I will waylay him before he gets home. And we will talk, as we should have talked years before now. Do you doubt me, Nefer?"

I looked down at my feet, discomfited by his discernment. "Why can you read my thoughts so easily?" I complained.

"I do not read your thoughts, sister, so much as I see into your heart."

"But will he listen, Rensi?"

"He will listen. Have no doubt of it, Nefer. Now, go home! You are tired—go at once. And God go with you."

With a soft push of encouragement he sent me out into the dusk, Bentresh's blanket still wrapped around me, the stars piercing through the stormy sky like warm, friendly lights overhead. *Have I done the right thing?* I wondered. *What will he say to Himni?* I had no idea at all. But I trusted Rensi, and I trusted that Power which I knew he relied upon—and that would have to suffice.

Nefer

CHAPTER EIGHTEEN

I never learned what passed between Rensi and Himni, but it clearly was something of import, for there was a discernible change in my husband from that moment forth. Unfortunately, though the onslaught of insensitivity was checked, much damage had already been done. Mara avoided him as much as she could, and her pain still transmitted itself to me. I knew things could not go on much longer as they were. Shemnon's daughter had been a part of my house for a year, and even Himni had not been able to suppress the joy which I took in that. Now and again I could not keep myself from wondering how her father fared, if he regretted the decision he had made when he helped her. I did not like to think of any man having to tell a mother of a loss such as he had been forced to report.

Once, without intending to speak of it, the words came tumbling out. "Your mother must hate me," I said unexpectedly, and Mara glanced up, startled by my suddenness.

"She will know little. My father will tell her little," she answered quietly.

"But, what of her pain?"

Mara's mouth twisted in her attempt to control herself. "I think of this often, too, and pray that one day she may forgive me. But it would take understanding for such a thing to happen, and I do not see how it ever could come to pass." She sat in silent contemplation for a moment, then added, "But I do not regret what I have done. God intended that I live the life I have found here; I could never have been happy living as my mother lives." She smiled sweetly. "Yes, I am fortunate, I know that." And I wondered what she had seen in my face.

The time was approaching when Seth's schooling would be completed and he would have earned the right to be a teacher, instructing others in the history and poetry of our people, reading and writing both in Hebrew and in what we term reformed Egyptian, which is using the Egyptian characters or script to express Hebrew words. And, in much the same season, if all went well, Isabel's twins should be born.

Thus it came to pass that we planned a wedding for my son and his bride. All the best of our old lace and our old silver was brought out, and Himni—without complaint—fashioned new ornaments of gold: delicate rings, armlets and bracelets, and bells to be sewn round the hem of her garments, candlesticks and finely beaten basins, small animal figures cast in gold, golden sandals for Mara's feet, and a tiara with intertwining designs to place round her head. My mother's dress, fragile with age now, was carefully cleaned and prepared, and once again in this new land the ancient rites of our race were observed.

Himni played more and more a leading role in the government of the city, as the elders or heads of the most influential families are expected to do. He shared with Rensi and my brother, Amon, the distinction of heading the tribe of Zoram, but Rensi was retiring in nature, and my brother possessed the soul of an artist; Himni alone savored business and reveled in the intricacies of social and political favor. But, what a city ours

was, set in the clean, blue mountain air with wide
paved streets and plazas gay with gardens and fountains; large public halls supported by graceful columns,
finished inside with fine gems and ivory worked into
mosaic patterns; gold, silver, brass, and rich woods,
intricately fashioned. And, surpassing all, rose the
temple, its walls covered with thinly beaten gold plate
so that their shining, beneath the rays of the morning,
put even God's sun to shame.

Here amidst the beauty and splendor of the City of
Nephi Seth and Mara were united as man and wife—
line joined to ancient line, seed mingled with seed: the
future embodied in two young souls drawn to each
other in love.

I wept to see it. I wept to think of that future in which
I had no part, save as a vague whisper of memory, a
name on a page of those who had gone before, but had
no relevance now. I felt alive—so keenly alive in this pure
land where God had placed us. I wished to go on, and
on, and see what would become of our people; I wished
to belong to it all. Mortal life passed so quickly. A shiver
ran over my skin as I thought of it. To let go, to pass to
these eager spirits what was so jealously mine! I sighed.
So it had been from the beginning; I must reconcile
myself to it somehow. I was thirty-six years old, a mature
woman, and Himni was forty-four. We had nearly as
much to remember as we had to look forward to.

But for the moment . . . for the moment I could take
joy in my son, noble and modest and filled with high
intentions, and this gentle girl, gracious and discerning,
willing to mold her desires to the dictates of God. For
the moment nothing else existed beyond the hope in
their eyes, nothing mattered as long as such young
people existed for the God of Israel to lead.

In the eleventh month of the forty-second year since
the departure of Lehi and his people from Jerusalem,

Isabel was safely delivered of twin sons, whom her husband named Kimnar and Kumen. They were strong babies and finely favored, and Onihah was pleased and boasted openly of that which heaven had done for him. And my sister relaxed and drew joy, as women do, from her children. But the ordeal of their birth had told on her, and the demands of their care made it more difficult for her to recover and gain back her strength. After a few weeks Onihah tired of the schedule which kept his wife in the nursery and never out by his side. He wanted this wearisome business over and done with. And, even though she had a wet nurse and other household aid to assist her, this was not sufficient for him. Yet still Isabel basked in the tender pleasures of her new motherhood—and did not see the signs. No one saw. None of us was close enough to them, none of us had eyes wide open, searching for trouble before trouble came. No, it is hindsight alone which torments our sensibilities, when all is too late.

Three months passed. Seth and Mara had left us to make a home of their own; close by for the time being, though he cherished hopes, I knew, of starting a school in one of the new cities which were being surveyed, where colonization was just beginning. Isabel's babies were growing, Bentresh and I were talking again as sister to sister, on intimate terms. It was the season of winter when all should rest and lie fallow, but men's greed and ambition know no such restrictions. Our men went to war, for what seemed to me countless petty reasons, against our brethren, the Lamanites. Himni took issue with me concerning the need of such conflict in our lives.

"It is the struggle of evil and good, which has been with us since time began, Nefer. God himself sanctions battle when the cause is righteous enough."

"If men could but love, if they could deal justly with one another—"

"Perhaps even the worst among us could be constrained to do that," he conceded. "But the Lamanites do not see things that way. They are predators, Neferure, and nothing can change that. If God led the Nephites away from here, our brethren would still be violent and warlike and prey upon others as they have upon us."

I knew he was right. I knew I could not speak of the things that troubled me concerning the weaknesses of our own people; I have seen how men prey on each other in the name of profit, in the name of power, and no blood is lost—only the heart is wounded, only the spirit suffers, only a man's integrity is spilled in the dust.

Then one evening Himni came home late and tired, and I sat beside him while he ate a late meal and bathed his feet in a basin of cool, scented water.

"I saw Onihah in town," he said, "with a woman on his arm—a very young, very attractive woman."

I clutched at the carved arms of the chair I sat upon. "You could not have been mistaken?"

"Heavens, no. I have heard rumors, Nefer, but this is the first time I have seen for myself."

The shame of it washed over me, as if it had been my own pain. "Why have you not told me before?"

"To what purpose?" He reached for my hand and rubbed it gently. "You and I can do nothing, you know."

"But, Himni, you are a man. Could you not speak to him, confront him directly?"

He smiled grimly. "You know so little of the way of things where men are concerned, Nefer. He would probably admit it outright and then tell me to mind my own business. My opinion is nothing to him."

"And Isabel's?"

Himni bit at his lip as he fashioned an answer. "He would rather that Isabel not know, but more for his own sake than hers."

I was shaking my head. "You are right, I do not understand."

"Nothing will make him stop," Himni added, seeing the look in my face. "It is how the man is constituted, my dear." He shrugged his shoulders and began drying his feet.

"Then, what are we to do?"

"Isabel will have to live with it, or leave him."

"It is not that simple. Now there are children involved. And her own feelings . . ."

"She will have to weigh everything and decide for herself."

"And what of Onihah? He is responsible before God and before the law."

"So it would seem. But he is powerful. The law will not touch him. And, as for the spiritual . . ." He looked up and met my eyes squarely for the first time.

"Do you think that is right?"

"What I think makes no difference."

"But, Himni, does it not grieve your heart? Do you not tremble because of the sins of our people?"

He gently lifted my hand up again. "It has ever been thus—men are carnal creatures—"

I tore my hand from his grasp. "That is too simple an explanation! We are a chosen people. We have had concourse with the very God of Israel himself. And this is what it all has come to in less than a lifetime, less than fifty years?"

"You see why I do not wish to bring such things to you, Neferure? I bring information, simple facts of the day, and you use it to drive a wedge between us." He rose from his chair and walked in the direction of our small, enclosed arboretum where a pale, milky moonlight broke through. I turned my own way and slipped out into the moonlight where I could nurse both my anger and my pain. Why must mortal life be so difficult? I walked quickly through the gardens out toward

the pale fields and a line of black trees. I was torn apart
by a morass of emotions which clogged my spirit as
surely as thick spring mud clogs one's steps. I trembled
with womanly weakness at the shame and agony Onihah was willing to inflict upon my sister. Yet part of me
rose up in indignation at the hardness of men who, for
convenience' sake, shut off their spiritual perceptions. I
had wanted Himni to weep with me, to share the
oppression of concern I was feeling, but he was not
hampered with such inconvenient reactions and expectations.

Under the glare of the white, harsh moonlight every
outline was relentlessly drawn, and I felt my own soul
exposed, etched in stark, bold lines. I felt myself shiver
as a wandering wind touched my skin. And suddenly I
longed for the strong support of my father. What would
he have said to this thing? He had been a powerful
man, yet more gentle in demeanor than many women.
How would he have handled Onihah: Would he have
put the fear of God in him if he could not engender any
finer emotions within him?

"We are a passionate people," my father had more
than once told me. "All we do, we do with our heart as
well as our head. Even in the worship of our God we
ascend to heights of feeling which other races are ignorant of."

Our strength, and our downfall, I thought. *The God of
Israel wants not blind obedience; he desires men's hearts.
Therefore, when we turn our powerful emotions to carnal
uses, how rich in iniquity we become!*

Esther's Hannah, and now Onihah—not one among
us is safe from the misery which mortal sin brings,
bound as we are by ties of love and kinship, of religion
and race.

The shadow of night had spread like a stain, dulling
the purple sky to slate. *There must be many,* I thought,

who live and die without this knowledge we have, this grace from heaven which lifts us out of the shadow and into the light. I walked beneath the shadow as I thought of my father's courage and wisdom, of the silent despair which my mother rose above in her own way. *I am a daughter of Israel. I carry the light within me,* I realized, and the realization was good. *The shadow will always be there as long as I dwell in mortality. But it need not obscure the light, the light within and which is fed from one source only. God is the light, and, just as Rensi had often told me, he gives liberally to his children if only they will hold out their arms, and open up their hearts to receive.*

Nefer

Chapter Nineteen

The days passed, the weeks passed. I could not bring myself to it; I said nothing to Isabel. Nor did I speak of Onihah's betrayal to any—even those closest to me—lest I breathe further life into both the realities and the rumors that surrounded his name. How is it that life goes on seemingly the same, no matter how much we suffer inside? Now that I was looking, I could see small but distinct signs of Isabel's suffering: the far-off look she would get in her eyes when she thought no one was watching; the fact that Onihah was seldom with her; the tightness that came round her mouth when anyone mentioned his name; the anxious way she plucked at her skirts when she spoke of the weight she must lose now that she had given birth to the babies. My heart ached watching her, and I know Bentresh was suffering, too. And though we two once again spoke of many things together, we did not speak of this.

Meanwhile my own daughter grew old enough to worry over, though she was a sweet, compliant girl—all the more so, I had remarked, since Mara had come to our household. A sister, and such a sister as Mara, had helped Awhere to blossom, awakening to her own possibilities and to the whispers of tomorrow which only young ears can hear. And Mara herself was soon to become a mother. I could not imagine that. I was too

young for life to take such a turning; it seemed strange
enough to see Isabel nursing her little ones. But Seth,
with a child of his own!

Near the end of the year 557—counting six hundred
years from the time of our leaving Jerusalem until the
coming of Christ—Mara gave birth to a son. They called
his name Shemnon, after his mother's father. Himni was
wroth with both of them and would not be reconciled to
this thing they had done.

"It was not meant to insult you, or even to annoy
you," I argued. "She was very close to her father—it is a
natural thing."

He glared back at me, his lips extended and pouty.
"You take her side as always. You allow her to ridicule
me!"

"Himni, have you been listening at all?"

He would not be persuaded, nor would he acknowledge his grandson in any way—at least not privately.
He would not hazard his public image to suffer, so he
played the pleased and doting grandparent, but the
deception cost him dearly, and he was not at peace.

For the most part, the rest of us ignored him, the
only alternative being to let him disturb our peace as
well. We took delight in the child—his beauty and intelligence. But sometimes it smote at my heart to see how
much he resembled his mother and the man who was
his namesake, with his sun-washed auburn hair and his
sea-shaded eyes. *He has both our blood running through his
veins*, I would think, as I watched him. *If Shemnon and I
had wed, might our own child have looked as he does?* They
were natural thoughts—unavoidable, really—but I tried
to keep them, and all others they might lead to, firmly
in check. The boy Shemnon and the girl Neferure were
mere shadows from a well-loved dream which I was
struggling to put to rest. The aching inside came less
often now, and I knew how to ignore it and count my
blessings, which were many. What might have been has

nothing to do with what is, however we might wish it so. I was content with my life, despite the things about it which were disappointing and less than I had wanted or had hoped for. I liked where I was, in this land of mist and mountain, of curving blue sea—this land of jungle and forest which God had prepared. I could not imagine myself a desert dweller. Though my own memories were dim, the stories of life before the great voyage still persisted among us; though, as year followed year, they began to take upon themselves the characteristics of legend. I had written stories myself of what I remembered, of what I had felt during those consummate days. For, such they were. We had then something to live for, something so overwhelming that nothing in day-to-day life seemed ordinary. How soon we forget. How easily did our people fall into the pattern of mediocrity, obscuring all that was rare and singular, reducing it to a level not worthy of the chosen people of God.

So I mused during those days when the spirit of a newborn hallowed and lifted our hearts and enriched our awarenesses. Precious and brief they were, for life does not hold still, nor go back, nor allow us to rest from the struggle nor turn aside from the race.

Three months after the birth of Mara's Shemnon a scandal broke out in the city: Onihah was part of it, and, in her own way, Esther's Hannah was too.

It seemed there was a loosely woven group who had been living immorally, supporting one another in their loose, wanton ways and disregarding the words of Nephi, Jacob, and the others Nephi had appointed to preside over us. The young man Hannah had been involved with came from among them, and Onihah was one who urged her to run away with this man to one of the new settlements where she would be out of her parents' reach.

Amon, not Esther, came to tell me the sad news. His face looked ashen, his eyes beaten; it horrified me to look into his eyes.

"I cannot bear this pain, Nefer," he confessed. "She was our firstborn, a tender girl with so much promise . . ." He seemed to choke for a moment, and put his hand to his throat. "Esther is heartbroken—though you know her strength, Nefer."

"And that strength is her very curse now, for she needs to mourn as only a mother can mourn."

He looked at me closely. "Will you come, Nefer? I fear that I am so little good to her."

"Of course I shall come. You need not have asked me."

"I know that, I know that." He put his hand on my arm and gazed with doleful eyes—kind, gentle soul that he is.

I patted his hand. "But I cannot be to Esther what it is your place to be, my dearest. Now is the time—you must step into the forefront and be a strength to her. She has led so long—and so well."

He nodded, his eyes moist and red-rimmed. "Indeed, Nefer. I know you speak true."

"God will give you the strength," I encouraged. "Go to her, Amon. It will not be so hard as you think."

"Oh, Nefer." His voice held chagrin, like a bitter taste in his mouth. "Think you I know not how you have been the strength for our father's family these many years—and Esther the beauty and strength of my own family."

I leaned closer and spoke softly. "God has given you an opportunity now, through this terrible thing you are suffering. Use it as he intends."

He nodded again. "It is so easy to take the way of least resistance."

"I know, brother, I know. That is simply mortality—

and God intends us for so much more that we must break out of our weaknesses which clutch our spirits like bonds."

His lips parted and his expression became as sweet as when he had been a boy, and I was transported for a moment to the white sands of Bountiful, soft as rose leaves against our bare feet, and his anxious face bending over one of us who was hurt or had been lagging behind. Ready, ready always to help and lift us—but now that boon had been denied him, and he must watch his own daughter suffer without aid.

"If I did not have you, Nefer, how would I manage?"

"How would we manage without each other?" I whispered, my voice hoarse with emotion. "We help one another. That too is God's way."

I thought of the many times Rensi had comforted or enlightened me, I thought of my sweet concourse with Bentresh, and I knew how true my words were.

I went to Esther. I still thought her lovelier than any of her daughters, with ivory skin, like smooth honey, stretched over such a delicate frame. Her fig-brown hair was still lustrous and luxuriant, though she was now thirty-six years of age. But this day she looked ten years older, shrunken and haggard, which is what pain can do. Her eyes too looked haunted. I gathered her into my arms, and together we wept.

"You did all you could do, and more," I said. "She is in God's hands now."

"Ah, did I? I think of dozens of times I might have helped her, might have handled things differently, might—"

"Stop it, Esther!" I begged. "To torment yourself is meaningless, and will help neither Hannah nor yourself—nor anyone else."

"I know," she conceded. "But sometimes I cannot help it. And to think of her, Nefer!"

I let her talk of the precious child she had nurtured, had filled with the beauty of her own soul, the beauty of God's sweetest teachings, and now had lost.

"We know not God's times and seasons," I said carefully. "Perhaps it is merely that—a season only, and she will return—to you and to the ways of her fathers."

"Perhaps . . ." Esther tried to smile, but her lips trembled and curled into an expression so wistful and vulnerable that I nearly cried out.

"You must remember and think of her in God's hands," I repeated. "For I believe that she is. He knows your heart and Amon's. Besides, she is His daughter, too. He loves her, yearns over her, and will not leave her friendless." I covered her small hands, so cold and trembling, with mine. "We will pray and hold a family fast for her. God will heed our entreaties, Esther."

"Yes," she answered in a voice so low that I had to lean forward to hear. "But he will not take her agency away from her for the sake of our pain. And this life she is choosing is what my Hannah has wanted for a very long time."

She gazed up with stricken eyes, and her trembling ran like a freezing current through my own veins. "Have you been to see Isabel?" she asked. I cringed inwardly and shook my head, feeling miserable and cowardly. "You must go," she said, her voice low still, and persuasive. "The child is in torment and yet insists on closing her eyes to that which is destroying her."

"Perhaps there is no other way." I spoke without premeditation, but I could read the agreement in Esther's eyes.

"Nevertheless, she needs you."

I smiled resignedly. "Yes, dear sister, I know."

I kissed Esther's cheek and left with such a weight upon me that I felt bowed beneath it. I could not face my baby sister, not yet. I went home, fed my family, and played with my grandson gratefully when Mara came by for a few moments. She was a transformed creature, Mara. She dressed in soft muted colors, and the gowns she selected for herself draped in modest, elegant lines a body which moved with the suppleness of a forest creature, a trait she undoubtedly inherited from her father. She was kindly and gracious of speech, with impeccable manners which she had largely taught herself from observation and imitation. One would never know that she had not been born a Nephite and been one of us from her infant days. She appeared totally content now that she had her child to nurture and her own household, free of awkwardness and constraint.

"It is better than I had anticipated," she told me once, coloring just a little. "With Seth and me, all things are sweet and harmonious."

"This is because your own spirits are in harmony with that which is good."

"You judge well of us," she replied, smiling and kissing the tips of her fingers to me.

This day I drank in the sweetness and goodness of her nature, like one parched with a thirst which cannot be filled. When she left I sought out my husband, restless still with the lonely burden of grief and sympathy which pressed on my soul. I told him briefly of my visit with Esther. Though he listened attentively, after the telling he merely shrugged his shoulders and replied, "It is a shame. But all people seek their own level. Look at our Seth."

It was a comment meant to sting; he was always narrow and caustic after Mara had been in the house.

"What is your level, Himni?" I asked a bit pointedly.

"You ask this to insult me because I have angered

you," he bit back, drawing himself up as he faced me. "I am a successful and respected member of this community, who has amassed great power and influence. All men know my name. Many men serve me. I bring honor and wealth to your house." He struck his fist against the table, making the golden candlesticks clatter. "I am respected by all, Nefer—all but yourself! You will never consider me good enough for you, no matter how much I do." He was sniveling now, deploring his condition. I watched him as from a distance, as though a great barrier that swallowed all sound and sensation had suddenly been cast up between us. "You will never give me . . . you still love that savage," he growled, "who never was half the man I am!"

I stared back at him, unable to make any reply.

"I love you!" he cried. But the words were an accusation, not an avowal.

"I have loved you," I replied. "Do you diminish that love by pretending it does not exist, by accusing me of falsehoods, by breaking your word to me and behaving in ways that you know will wound me?"

I was referring to our son and his wife, and he knew it. But he chose instead to be hurt.

"I can never do enough; I can never please you. Others praise me, Nefer, but never you."

I turned away in sadness. Perhaps there was some truth to the bitterness he nursed in his heart. Many women would be pleased, even honored, to be Himni's wife. Perhaps they would praise him and fuss over him as he desired, content with his success in the marketplace and the power and pleasure it brought. I could not help that I wanted different things from him, that I longed to share the holy desires of my soul with a man. He paid lip service to a religion which had become a way of life to me. He did what was necessary—and he did it smoothly, with great persuasion, so that he shone fair in men's eyes. But I knew his heart; I knew the God of Israel had no more place there than I had.

I went to my bed in silence, and I lay awake a long time, grieving for the hardness of my husband and the solitary desolation which seemed my lot.

I visited my sister the next day. Himni's unkindness had freed me, somehow, strengthened some core within me, when I had feared the very opposite might take place. He was penitent as well, in a way I found pathetic—bringing ripe fruit and freshly picked flowers in to me, kissing my neck as I was bent over my combs and brushes and face powders. It was as though nothing had happened between us, and he wished to keep it that way. Pretense was as important, nay, more important to him than reality, for in pretense he could achieve what he desired with no effort—and no guilt.

He took his leave of me, but I did not watch after him, as a woman might after a man she loved well, a man who stirred a tenderness in her which nothing could quench. And, knowing this, I grieved for both of us as I sat alone, bathed by the unheeding sweetness of the new morning air.

Though I had gone to see Isabel with a sense of uncertainty, I could see at once that she was glad of the sight of me, and, though her eyes were shadowed, she smiled with a warmth that bewildered me.

How could a man be in any way unsatisfied with such a beautiful woman? I thought as I followed her into the pleasant, open room where she did her spinning and weaving. The two babies lay on llama rugs at our feet, and we knelt and played with them for a few happy moments. Such beguiling and innocent creatures! Then she sent their nursemaid away and turned to me, her hazel eyes light, almost colorless in her white face.

"I know why you have come to me, dear sister," she began. "But you must not distress yourself. I am all right."

"Isabel, really! You are not all right—I can see that. I know you too well."

She waved a long slender hand at me. "I do not wish to discuss it."

"Isabel," I pressed. "If you allow Onihah to treat you thus, it will only grow worse. And now you have these two precious sons to think about."

A faint smile played at her lips. "Yes, and I shall do that. I shall pour my love and energies into them."

"It is not enough."

She blinked at the seeming cruelty of my blunt words. "I have raised a child to adulthood. You must trust my judgment: it is not enough." I leaned close and touched her smooth raven tresses. "You have a life of your own. You cannot ignore it and hope to be whole."

She turned slightly away from me, her thin body rigid. "I know all these things which you say to me, Nefer. I know! Yet I also know that I love the father of my children. So, tell me, what choice do I have? I could push him away from me, rise up in righteous indignation and assure myself of an existence without him, spurned and pitied by men and women alike. I ask you, is that any kind of life for my sons?"

What could I reply? What arguments could counter her reason? "Isabel, Isabel," I murmured in agony. "Cannot something be done?"

"Nothing. I see nothing at the moment, though I have lain awake nights trying to . . ."

She could not speak further. She bowed her head, as at the force of a blow.

"You could do something," she said, not yet looking up at me. "You could try to comfort Bentresh. This is harder for her in some ways than it is for me."

"Of course."

"She will not be reconciled. It is as though she torments herself with my pain."

I grimaced inwardly. "Do not judge her harshly. A mother's love cannot often reason its way calmly through such matters." I spoke ruefully, and she touched one of her babies' cheeks and said, "Yes, I suppose you are right."

"But I shall do what I can," I added hastily. "Believe me, I shall, for your sake and hers."

Then we spoke of other matters, eventually taking our noon repast together. I know that my presence strengthened her, and the hours spent together were precious to us both. A sisterhood of spirit which is sanctified by suffering embodies intimations of that higher world we left behind, and hope once more to inhabit. Thus it was with my little sister and myself, and I felt to praise that God who had designed his plan so that such priceless moments might be in it to bless and hallow our lives.

Nefer

CHAPTER TWENTY

Bentresh would not have done it; despite her moody, excitable nature, she would have remained in control if one thing following another had not pushed her too far.

I could do little with her where Isabel was concerned. "She is a master at concealing how she suffers! That cruel young man, in satiating his wicked desires, has brought shame and grief on us all."

She would grow pale as she spoke, and her hands would flutter like small, frightened birds. "I wish Father were here. Rensi will do nothing and Himni cares not at all. And Amon—because of what his own child has suffered—I believe he fears, if he lifts a finger, for what he might do."

"Isabel has made her choice. We must find ways to support her."

She brushed my gentle suggestion aside. "She is incapable of saving herself! Thus, that task becomes ours, Nefer. Do you not see?"

So she would go on and on, working herself into an anguish that was truly frightening, so that Rensi began to fear for her health. And Onihah, the smooth and handsome, the seduced and the seducer, went on his way, with none but God to call him to an accounting.

As all this boiled in its mighty cauldron, near to
overflowing, Ethem announced to his parents his intention to become a great warrior and avenge the death of
his brother. Ethem is Bentresh's second son, born nearly
five years after Seth and Jarom, so that he now was
eighteen years old—exactly the age Jarom had been
when he was slain by a Lamanite arrow. Despite this, he
proudly revealed to his mother that he had been receiv-
ing instruction secretly and that his skill with eye and
hand could match his brother's. Oh, the sad blindness
and vainglory of youth, that he expected his parents to
take pride in this and support a desire which struck terror into their hearts and called up every ghost of the
past to haunt and torment them!

"I have failed somewhere," Rensi confided. "If
revenge has become a vital part of my son's makeup,
then I have failed in some way."

"Motive is not so direct, so easy to isolate with children," I reminded him. "I believe he has been influ-
enced by Bentresh's anguish. Perhaps his childish heart
responded to seeing his mother suffer in ways which
you could not have known."

He nodded. "You have become wise in your own
right, Neferure."

His words gave me inordinate pleasure, though I
brushed them aside. "I am merely beset with more and
more experience, so that I learn without wishing to."

He nodded sadly again.

So things teetered precariously on the brink of disas-
ter, though we could not see this, nor realize it was so.

One day, early, Bentresh had gone into the city to
make some purchases. Contrary to her usual custom,
she went alone. And there, passing boldly down the
wide, main thoroughfare, walked Onihah, husband to
the girl Bentresh cherished as both sister and child.

Beside him, with her arm linked through his, walked a lovely young girl, ornamented with fine jewelry and clad most immodestly. I am sure Bentresh did not think. She merely reacted to the unbearable stimulus before her.

As I have heard the story from those who witnessed it, she placed herself in his path and confronted him, in sight of all who happened to be near. And then she applied to him names which, though thoroughly justified, angered him. And he waxed rude and insulting in turn. A woman, an acquaintance of ours, who had worked her way close to Bentresh, said that she cringed before her son-in-law's maliciousness and, backing away from him, cried, "I will bring Himni to you. Himni will see justice done." Then she turned and began to scramble up the deep stairs that led to the building where my husband's fine wares were made and displayed. Onihah, not content to let her be, called an insulting phrase after her, and she whirled about to face him again, losing her balance and tumbling head first down the steps.

Our friend, who bent over her still, twisted form, said that there were tears on her cheeks, and she bade the watching crowd of people bear witness of what a wicked and disrespectful young upstart had done. And some in the crowd grew incensed and bore him away to the magistrate, while others lifted my sister's bruised body and brought her in sorrow to her husband, for there was nothing a physician could do.

Rensi sent Melek, his youngest, across the short space that separates our two houses. But I had sensed something before he burst in my door. At much the same time she was tumbling down the rough stones to her death I heard someone call out my name—so clearly that I lifted my head to give answer, but no person was near. The voice which entreated me had been tight with urgency, so that I sat long minutes staring down at my work, wondering what this might be. Thus, when Melek called out to me, I knew without asking. And my feet brought me slowly and unwillingly to Bentresh's house.

How can I tell what it was like to gaze down upon her sweet, lifeless face? To kiss the pale cheeks and try, once more, to comfort and soothe her, to no avail. Rensi was quiet; Rensi is always quiet. As soon as he could, he cleared the house of all the wide-eyed well-wishers who stifled our grief. Then we sent Melek with Awhere to finish the chores Rensi had been doing when they called him. Alone, the two of us began to minister to Bentresh for the last time: wash and clothe her body in the garments she would wear for burial, comb out her fine, tangled hair, prepare the balms and spices. But it was too early, too soon to do so unaffectedly. Our fingers fumbled, and then froze. I could do nothing but stare ahead, unseeing, unable to make my hands move. Rensi sank down beside Bentresh, buried his face in her neck, and wept like a child. And I could not comfort him. There was a great coldness inside me, spreading like a paralysis through my veins. I stood immobile, without response or sensation of any kind. Thus Amon found us, after the mourners had alerted him and he had come to our aid. He took up his vigil beside Rensi, and Esther half led, half dragged me to my own house, though I remember nothing—nothing of those terrible hours save my sister's dead face and the horrible keening of Rensi's sobs in that close morning space.

We laid Bentresh to rest beside our mother and father and her own infant son. The body of Jarom rested where only God and the heavens gazed down upon it. We were not ready—not one of us—to let Bentresh go. Even Himni had been consumed with anger at what Onihah had done.

"They must be taught a lesson," he growled, "these young men who wallow in pride and power before they have made even a passing acquaintance with judgment and maturity."

Esther was devastated. She had scarcely been able to manage Onihah's involvement in the corruption and loss of her daughter. But this was too much, beyond the confines of her compassion. And her pitilessness itself distressed her, drove the pain in further, like a shaft through her heart. Then there was Isabel.

One cannot describe pain such as Isabel must have suffered; one cannot even perceive it. She became like a cold, lovely statue cast in ebony and pearl. The cruel, intertwining cords which must have bound her—nearly strangled her—did not show. As to Onihah, what justice could be hoped for? Bentresh was dead, and Isabel's life lay in ashes at her feet. Nor could he be brought to any sort of trial without an accuser—her death was, by strict definition, an accident—and Rensi would not accuse. He would consider nothing by way of retaliation.

"'Vengeance is mine, saith the Lord,'" he would repeat slowly and patiently, shaking his head. "What good would further shame and suffering do any of us—especially that innocent child whom Bentresh loved so?" And, naturally, his words would silence us all.

There was only one who could in any manner release her, which, in his own way, he did.

Rensi seemed to turn ashen after Bentresh's death and shrink in upon himself, his already small frame becoming even more lank and sparse. Yet that control, that ever-present control, was still with him and seemed even more refined. A time or two I believe I glimpsed what it cost him, and then I felt shamed in my weakness. For weak I was. For years I had been the one others turned to: the strong, the patient, the untiring. But I could not sustain those exacting qualities now. Something within me had melted, run together, and hardened. I had not the power to bear what I before would have borne.

But Rensi. Rensi found the strength to go to his daughter and succor her pain. How—with what grace and what wisdom—I know not. But I know one thing he accomplished: he accomplished a uniting of their suffering, so that Isabel did not stand alone. She had someone to lean against and, for that matter, so did Rensi, and this made the unendurable bearable for them both.

As for myself, I continued to live in a stupor, a numbing shadow I could not dispel. I had never before realized how much time I spent with my sister, how much she had been a part of my every day. I had always pictured us going on and on together. This parting could not be so! It had happened so quickly that it seemed she had just gone away and would return any time now and resume life as usual. She could not be gone! That would alter too drastically my whole concept of the future, and dismal was the prospect of the years when our children were raised—I watching alone, without Bentresh beside me to sweeten the hours, to share the little failures and triumphs of which life is made.

I struggled on. Even Rensi was unable to help me. Day following day he would walk over on some little excuse and spend time at our house. If it was evening, at the end of his hours in the fields, Himni too would be there, and the three of us would talk more naturally than we had since we were children. Certainly Rensi was lonely, too. And lost. Bentresh had required much caring for; now those hours were empty, hours formerly spent in loving and sustaining her sweet spirit. I thought, not once, but countless times: *How foolish we mortals are to resent the hours of our lives spent on others. How better is our time used? Cooking food, cleaning clothes, washing dishes, weeding gardens—such mundane and mean-*

*ingless tasks. Whatever we do in the name of sustaining
another human being is ennobling and will outlive our mea-
ger existence. For such efforts build minds and hearts, and
support all that is eternal within us.*

Perhaps because of these thoughts I was able to
respond in a way I had not expected when Isabel
appeared at my door, alone, with her hood drawn close
to her face, her large eyes against her white skin as
green and fathomless as the sea.

I took her to where we could be alone; even then she
had difficulty speaking. "Is it Onihah?" I asked.

"Dare I speak of him to you, Nefer? I know what
Rensi would say. But I crave a woman's advice, and all
others spurn me."

I nodded, my throat suddenly dry. "You may speak
your heart to me," I replied, praying to God that my
own heart would be benevolent enough to respond.

"At first, following Bentresh's death . . ." she swallowed and her mouth began to tremble. "I do not wish
to speak of those days."

I knew for myself. Onihah had withdrawn in shame
and terror, hiding away, as it were, in the house of a
friend. I shrank to think of it: I could not have faced
Isabel either if I had been him! As the nightmare quieted, as he became assured that no malice was intended
him, he snuck out of his den—at first only in the dead of
night to visit his children, asleep in their beds. Beyond
that I did not know; I was surely ignorant of what had
passed between husband and wife.

"What I am concerned with is the last little while.
My husband has been coming to me, much disturbed by
his dreams. They have been filled, it seems, with dark
and hellish creatures, screaming with the terrible cries
of the damned. He has told me—not once, Nefer, but
repeatedly—that his taste for the pleasures which used
to arouse him is dead. He says that every time he looks
upon another woman he sees nothing but Bentresh's

face staring back at him—the same when he lifts up a
glass of strong wine, which before had the power to
obliterate all that harried or distressed him. Now he is
sickened with the thought of what he has done with his
life."

She sighed, her long fingers playing with the brooch
at her throat. "I know. It is not easy to believe him. He
may feel this way now, overwhelmed as he is with the
guilt and horror of what has happened. His old longings may very well return to him, as strong as before.
And yet—" She looked at me hard, her eyes piercing
through all my defenses. "And yet, he came yesterday
and told me of a dream very different from what he has
suffered before. In this dream Bentresh appeared to him,
Nefer, and smiled upon him, and he felt in his heart that
she has forgiven him. So he has come begging me to forgive him as well."

"Do you think it was a true dream?" I asked. "Do
you believe him?"

"I do," she replied. "For he seemed a different man.
His countenance appeared clean and open, as I have not
seen it—" she stumbled a little, "for a very long time.
He said that Bentresh's love had spread like a warmth
within him, making him feel strong and cleansed, as he
had never before felt in his life."

She was trembling. I longed to reach out and
embrace her, but I knew the time was not yet.

"Then, what cause have we to withhold our char-
ity?" I answered. "I know you love him." Her eyes filled
with tears as I watched her. "I believe that God has
allowed Bentresh to show us the way. Is it not, after all,
wiser to err on the side of mercy, my dearest?"

She was in my arms even as I spoke the words. We
clung to one another, overcome with those feelings
which only heaven can send us: so powerful, so
expanding that they weary our souls and leave us trem-

bling and weak, but renewed and reminded of that peace which is not of the earth and its ways.

Such moments do not last, but they remain with us. After Isabel had gone on her way I walked to my sister's house in search of Rensi. He was out in his fields. I found him repairing fences and called him to me. "You may relax now," I said.

He shaded his eyes against the glare of the sun, but he did not look confused as he returned my stark gaze.

"You have worn yourself out with praying and fasting," I continued. "But I believe God has answered your prayers."

I sat in a spot of cool shade and told him of what had passed between myself and Isabel. His face seemed to light up from within as I spoke. "Yes, indeed," he said quietly, once I had finished. "God, in his mercy, has listened to me. I am at peace now, Nefer."

I smiled a little.

"But you are not." He leaned forward, his eyes scrutinizing my features. "I am sorry. I would not have thought, even knowing both of you as I did, that this would be so hard for you."

"That is all right," I replied, trying to push him away from me; I wanted nothing of either his pity nor his discernment, though I could not have said why.

"I shall keep praying," he said with a wan smile. "You will not reproach me for that?"

I shook my head, and he let the matter lie. But I could feel his content, like a warmth spreading from deep inside him. At length I rose to my feet.

"I will see you tomorrow, Neferure," he said. "Go in God's care."

He smiled at me. I walked back to my house carrying the glow of his gentle smile like a light cupped in my hands, and feeling the dear, tender pressure of Isabel's young body within my arms.

O God, it is not in our nature to let go,
To forgive.
When cruelty tears us asunder
We cry for revenge,
And weep at the gates of heaven.
As children we weep,
Consumed with our own selfish suffering.
What use to us
The hard words of Nephi's counsel:
Love him who has harmed you!
Succor even that soul
Which has rendered your own heart desolate?
As children we grieve,
Slow to heed, slow to follow
Thy counsel,
And slow to be healed
By the power of thy love
Which nothing on earth can destroy,
Nor dim, nor diminish:
A constant though undeserved gift,
Offered freely to all
Who will open their hearts to receive.

Shemnon

CHAPTER TWENTY-ONE

A mother's love for a child is a terrible thing. I expected little quarter from my wife when I went back down the mountain to my tent and watched Rachel's face as I told her of the death of her son and the abduction of her daughter. Her eyes became live coals in her face, the skin across her high cheekbones pulled white and taut, and she struck out at me, like an animal in pain—needing to strike out at something—while a scream of anguish tore through her that shattered along my bones like the sharp tips of hundreds of arrow points piercing my flesh.

She refused to be comforted, and she would not allow me near her: I was not of her blood. But her two remaining sons were, and it was to these alone she clung during the first dreadful days. She knew in part my sympathy toward the Nephite boys; I do not know to what degree she and her sons discussed my madness, my cowardly weakness, as some of my behavior would be judged in their eyes. The fact that one of the enemy was buried on a high lonely promontory helped more than anything else. My son Saul, who alone of my seed promised to be a great warrior-leader, was laid to rest with a warrior's full honors, but the ceremony itself opened up wounds and rekindled the embers of passion. Rachel and her sons wanted revenge. They were all for desecrating the Nephite grave and carrying the dead boy's skull before them as they went to reclaim their sister. Not that she again would ever be counted worthy to dwell in honor among us, but so they might wreak vengeance upon those they hated and envied. Young men have such hot heads. They see reason as an enemy, and passion—with all its enslaving powers—as something to be desired, courted, and coveted.

I gave them a long lead and let them wear themselves out on it before I stepped in to be heard.

"We of the people called Lamanites," I began, "are fierce hunters and fine warriors, and we spill the blood of our enemies so we might live in the freedom we covet, after the manner we desire. We are dwellers in tents, as were our forefathers in the deserts across the sea."

My sons listened to me. By the orange glow of the firelight I could see their dark eyes, gazing up, sparked with interest despite themselves.

"We are a new people in a new country, and we walk our own way. But our roots are ancient, and our roots are the same as those of the Nephites whom we call foes."

There was a hissing sound as a log crumbled in the fire, and my listeners sucked in their breaths.

"We spurn them for their greed and their desire for gain; we spurn them for their hypocrisy and sham. But, in truth, we are their brothers and they ours, and we are bound with cords which are stronger than this life— stronger than all of us here."

I drew myself up so that the muscles along my chest and arms shone bronze and hard in the pulse of the fire. I could feel my sons' anger, like a cold touch on my skin. But Rachel sat unmoving and livid, like a small smouldering statue, and I could feel her wrath like flames lick at my tender insides.

"Your sister, Mara, is a gentle and virtuous woman, and she has gone to be the wife of the young Nephite willingly, of her own free will."

Rachel, without leaning forward, without seeming to move a hair, threw a handful of gathered dust and earth into the fire, where it sputtered and flared. I could see the cords tense in her neck, but she spoke not a word.

"Therefore, I say to you, as your father, as patriarch to this branch of our tribe, that you are to set this matter of your sister at rest. Allow her to go her own way, as you go yours."

There were dark, indiscernible mutterings then, from heads bowed and brows darkened.

"And, furthermore, I command that her name be held in honorable remembrance among us. That is my desire and my word on the matter."

"But that does not cover the whole of it, Father," Geb spoke out of the shadows, his voice as hard as the rock upon which he leaned.

"It does, so far as you are concerned," I answered. At my words they all leaned forward, like hounds on the leash held at bay. Even Rachel sighed, her eyes like two live coals reaching out for me.

"There is no need to avenge Kumen's death: he was your friend and joined in hostilities toward the Nephites of his own free will, knowing what danger he contracted in the doing. And Saul?" I drew a breath that spilled into my lungs like scalding water. "Saul was killed by my hand."

They did not believe me. My sons thought I was protecting the Nephites. I could see disgust stamp itself on their features. But my wife's countenance turned cold, stiff with a fury that froze every kindly emotion which had ever found place in her breast. I looked away from her, trying to shut out the malice which seethed in her eyes.

"I speak truly, as I ever have done, my sons," I continued. "It was my own arrow which I removed from Saul's breast. Such things happen when men set their hands against one another." I let my gaze travel the length of them. "Ask your mother, and know."

They turned to her and she hissed at them, eyes and breath, like an incensed Egyptian, and I could feel them draw back, instinctively.

"Therefore," I cried, "let it be. Such is my desire—and such is my command unto you." I fixed each with my eye in turn. "And you shall obey. If either of you breaks troth with me and goes out against these, he shall have to fight me in their stead."

The air was breathless. Rachel unfolded herself and stood, like a straight young sapling. "Who will avenge the betrayal of my daughter and the murder of my son?" she demanded, and her voice was like the north wind that bends the sturdiest sapling low to the ground.

The two boys stood and stared at her, until she cried out like a wounded fury, "Who will avenge a mother's black pain?"

Upon her words Emer lunged at me, catching me unawares with a clasp round my knees which brought me to the ground, but only for a second; with the upswing of the movement I was again on my feet, my hands locked on Emer's neck, lifting him clear of the ground. He gasped for breath, and his eyes bulged in his face and grew bleary before I hurled him to the forest floor and heard the crack of his skull against a protruding root. At the sound Geb cried out, and so I turned on him, pulling him to his feet, with one long arm twisted behind him, twisted high on his back, until I could feel the heat of his pain pumping through it. Then I dragged Emer to his feet. Though he was bleeding freely from a long cut on the back of his head, I could see he was fine.

"We live as wild men," I gasped, "and this is the price we pay. Have you had enough?" I growled the words at them, standing with my feet far apart and my head low. They nodded agreement. I glanced up at their mother, who had not moved. "We are a family," I continued more gently. "We may not agree, but we must stand united, no matter what sufferings attempt to bow or break us."

Rachel's mouth curled in contempt. Then she turned and, like one of the forest shadows, disappeared into the trees.

I did not follow her. I sat until the fire was no more than blackened sticks and gray ashes. Then I arose, my muscles stiff, my own heart ashen, and returned to my tent. She was gone, taking every trace of her existence with her. She had quitted the tent of her husband and gone back to her mother, and she would not return.

I dropped to the floor and sat cross-legged before the cold fire. I sat as one in a daze: emptied, like a cracked, discarded vessel which was of no further use but to be cast aside, trodden underfoot, and at last thrown into the furnace to be destroyed by that same force which gave it birth.

Thus did it come to pass with me and my family following Mara's departure into the land of the Nephites. I managed to subdue the wrath of my sons and therefore avert further conflict and bloodshed. But I purchased no peace. As the nights grew cold and the sea and land darkened at the touch of winter I took to walking the shore, thinking more on my beginnings than on my future. Even if I had succeeded in softening Rachel's heart this would have been harder than I could have ever imagined. Saul was precious to me; I had set great store by the promise I saw in him. And, though warriors die young, cut down in battle before their potential is realized, to die for no cause, in the manner my son died—I could not bear to think on it!

And yet, all my sons put together could not fill my heart as she did. An only daughter can do that to a man, they tell me; all I know is that Mara's absence was torture to me. I found myself repenting the steps I had taken to support her, wondering what madness had possessed me to deliver her into the hands of my enemies—for such they were. I entertained no fair hopes to the contrary. Only the worthy were accepted by God and his prophets, and I was not worthy in Nephite eyes. Would my daughter encounter only contempt and scorn from these arrogant people? Surely Neferure . . . I could not bring myself to believe ill of her, nor of Rensi, either. No matter what came to pass, those two would treat my young exile gently. But what of the rest? What had I done in urging her to follow the strange notions inside her head?

I walked the black shore and the sea birds were silent. Even the tide, cold and muted, spoke no comfort to me. In this vast space I was alone as I had never before been alone in all of my life.

The days passed, lonely and solitary. My sons kept much to themselves, and I did not press them. I had no dreams—of either Mara or Neferure—to console my heart. I cured the skins of the beasts I had hunted. I carved small things, and at length began work on a cradle, taking great care to use seasoned wood which was well cured and finely grained. I drew the pattern myself and carved the pieces which would fit into one another. It was a labor of love, and it occupied many long hours which otherwise would have dragged painfully on my hands.

The spring came, with its blustery winds and cold

rains, and even the forest pathways were soggy with mud. I had no desire to stir. The wild beasts were waking, and commonly a terrible restlessness stalked through me this time of the year. But all that was blunted. I sat in my tent, dirty and listless. Then one day the flap was pulled open and Rachel walked in. She glanced at me briefly, her eyes never meeting mine.

"This place is a shambles," she said. "You have not been living in a home since I left you."

"I know that," I said.

"Where is the fresh meat for the stew pot?" she demanded.

I grunted and rose to my feet, all my muscles stiff with disuse. "I am going," I told her, and I reached for my bow.

"This place will be clean when you arrive," she snapped, "and the fire will be waiting."

And that is how it came to pass that Rachel returned to my tent, and life began for me once more. And I was grateful enough that I put up with her moods when the blackness came upon her and she lashed out at me like a storm in its fury. I knew her impetuous, untamed nature must, from time to time, lash out at the pain which she was unable to explain or control or contain in any more civilized way. I understood that, and I felt a burden of guilt for her suffering which I was happy to bear—knowing what I know and being what I am. That she could love me once more—even in her fierce, demanding way—was a blessing I would never take lightly again.

The summons came. After the seasons had worn down our suffering and taught us the patience of continuance despite all, the summons came. A stranger approached me as I stood by the side of a large trading vessel which had just come in to dock. Her sides gleamed gray and green with seaweed; I thought the pearls of the ocean shimmered in her white nets. I remember thinking, *I could board such a ship and return to the lands which we left. See the vast, empty deserts, see the ruined temples and shrines of Jerusalem.* Then I felt a tap on my arm. I turned to see a stout, well-fitted Nephite merchant, with a round, kindly face.

"You are Shemnon the Lamanite?" he asked. "Father of Mara and friend of Rensi and Neferure, and the house of Zoram?"

My hand rested on the hilt of my sword. "I am the man," I answered.

"Then this is for you."

He held out a small scroll. I lifted my free hand to take it.

"Fear not, my friend," the stranger said, watching me. "The message consigned to the parchment will do you no harm." A smile lifted the corners of his small mouth, making his ample cheeks become jowly. "If you have need of aught," he offered, "this is my vessel, and I am at your service." He indicated the handsome ship with a wave of one arm, his fat fingers curling possessively, and a terrible envy shuddered through me as I nodded and turned away, seeking the quiet privacy of a damp, unused alleyway before I unrolled the scroll.

The writing was Mara's, as clearly hers as if her voice had spoken out of the silence I stood in: "Come, Father, and see the grandson who bears your name. Seth welcomes you, and my eyes long for the sight of you! You will be safe here, and need fear nothing. Come, I entreat you!"

I could hear the blood pound in my head and fell back with a staggering step against the support of a dark, damp wall. What madness was this? What pain her simple words had awakened within me. How could I do as she asked?

I stuffed the crumpled scroll deep into the leather pouch I carried and put her words from my mind. She knew not what she asked; her request was impossible! To travel alone into the heart of my enemies, to stand revealed, exposed before those who despised me! To see Himni and Bentresh—to once more see Neferure! And worse—to be seen of them, to be judged! It was not to be considered. It could not be endured.

A week passed, then another, and another. I did not return to visit the fat merchant; I did not return to the sea. But the discordant mewing of the gulls pierced through my skull, as though they had driven their sharp beaks into my bone. And the greens and browns of the forest fastness where I secreted myself could not obscure the haunting shimmer of sea-colored eyes which called from out of the depth of their loneliness and would give my spirit no peace.

At length one morning I arose long before the sun had dappled the damp forest floor with its light. And I knew, without making a conscious decision, that the sea eyes had won.

I cleaned and honed my weapons and packed what provisions I thought I would need for a long overland journey. I was not afraid. Nonetheless, a heaviness of spirit slowed my steps and clouded my vision; in truth, a sensation much akin to fear crawled over my skin. I would go forth and—whatever I might find, whatever might happen—I would be a changed man. It is this which frightened me, though fear is not the right word for it. Even Neferure, skilled in the way of words and their meanings, could not have expressed what I felt.

I began my journey during the time of harvest when the earth was gentle and pleasant and the rains would not hamper my way. Rachel knew nothing. I could not bring myself to tell her—perhaps when I returned. In the way of our women, she was accustomed to my long absences, only partly explained. We are hunters and warriors, and our restless spirits call no hearthfire home beyond the season of its usefulness, and then we move on.

I traveled with ease. I can walk for miles without tiring, and often I moved in harmony with the shifting blue shadows, unnoticed among the dense trees. And many times, in truth, I forgot my mission and the weight that pressed on my heart. Never before had I passed beyond the confines of that desolate land, beyond the tangle of forest and lush swamp which hugs our coast. Across the small neck of land leading into the north regions which the Nephites possess there stretches a wilderness, bleak and treeless, with the sea on the west and on the east. Here the earth is strewn with strange, twisted rock shapes, and yawning craters of fearful depth are torn out of the land as if in spite and anger. Here even I moved with care, and a grim sense of peril stayed with me until the land rose and I became immersed, as it were, in the very bowels of those mountains through which the Nephites have built their broad roads, always with an eye to safety and comfort—perhaps comfort first. If I, by some happenstance, had gone with them, I may have been part of this work; at least I would have been suited for the rough dangers which must have accompanied such a bold enterprise.

As I traveled I saw depths that could have swallowed a dozen giants and shown no sign of it. And I saw heights that stretched beyond the true scope of my vision, that seemed to dizzy the hawks that whirled and tumbled in the blue sky above. *The God Jehovah,* I thought to myself, *took great pains to separate his chosen from the heathen band left on the shore. All the distance—all this great, awesome distance. And yet, we found them at last, driven by the enmity which sits between us.* I shuddered inside. And, as each day passed, I was bothered more and more by the wonder of what I would find when I reached the Nephite city where my Mara dwelt, where Neferure lived a life which was foreign to all that I knew.

The sea, behind and on either side of me, sang its hushed song and was the only company I experienced, for I traveled often at night, at least when the landscape was tame enough to permit it—the moon silvering the long Nephite road, so that it appeared indeed like a pathway of the gods leading to regions above.

As I approached the Nephite fortress I observed on the hills great circular wind furnaces with the tunnel or mouth facing in that direction which would trap the strong air drafts necessary to obtain high temperatures—temperatures hot enough to mold swords of fine steel, those swords which Nephi was so expert in fashioning. And I remembered how Lehi and his people, as they journeyed, had camped by the fountain of the Red Sea in the Gulf of Aqabah where Solomon's great smelter had stood. Thus they had learned, every step of their journey, as God had intended them to—gaining in knowledge, in strength, even to the making of superior weapons with which to defend their own lives.

With an oppression upon my spirit I approached the city gates, still hearing the dull roaring of the deep Nephite river I had crossed earlier in my ears. It was evening, and the sun's slanting light fell like fire upon the gold-plated temple, the wide stone-paved roads, the roofs of shining metal and copper. Here was prosperity indeed, and opulence such as my eyes had never seen. The many buildings, though large and solid and fashioned of solid cut stone, possessed a symmetry of line, a beauty which made them appear delicate, almost ethereal in the warm evening light. I felt out of place with my rough serviceable clothing and my shaven head. I found myself in the middle of one of the large city squares where rose a fountain in the shape of a graceful robed maiden pouring water from a jug. Her white marble shoulder, the curve of her arm looked so real that I wanted to reach up and touch her. Instead I stood beneath the cool spray utterly at a loss, watching the people passing on every side of me, strangers and Nephites all. I would have to bring out Mara's message and show it to one of these strangers and ask of him where I should go—and for the first of many times reveal myself as the ignorant savage I am.

So be it. I had come of my own free will, knowing these things. Yet I lingered beneath the pleasant air of the fountain, looking up into the face of the marble maid who smiled back at me with her curved, laughing lips and her luminous but sightless eyes.

Shemnon

CHAPTER TWENTY-TWO

The gods were kind to me. I was not required to beg assistance. An old woman, gray-haired but unbent yet by age, approached me where I sat and actually inquired of my welfare as an obvious stranger in her city. It was not difficult to show Mara's writing to her and explain my purpose.

"Your daughter lives not far from my own home," she told me, "though the child is unknown to me. Come, I will show you the way."

We walked together, myself and this Nephite widow who labored in one of the mills where women spin and weave cloths of great beauty. To my surprise, she seemed content to be doing so.

"I have grown children," she explained, "who are good to me. My little garden produces in abundance. I have nothing of which to complain."

Her companionship had a salutary effect upon me which quieted my fears. When she slowed her steps and glanced up at me, indicating, with a nod of her head, a small stone structure, I knew what she meant.

"You will find your daughter inside," she said, smiling sweetly. "May you sojourn here happily, stranger."

Her kindness touched me deeply. I bent in a small bow of parting and turned toward the high door set in

the smooth white stone. I could not think of what I was
doing, or fear would o'ertake me again. With bold
strides I approached, remembering my prowess as a
hunter, my skills and renown as a warrior. I pounded
with my closed fist on the door. It opened nearly at
once; inward, with amazing silence. A young girl of ten,
perhaps twelve, stood before me. She had skin as clear
and white as new goat's milk, and the warm shades of
the earth in her hair. We stared at one another. I had a
disquieting feeling that perhaps I had seen her before.

"Is this the abode of Seth of the house of Zoram, and
of his Lamanite wife, called Mara?" I blurted out.

The girl nodded. Her eyes had gone wide and
frightened. But I had to be sure.

"Would you kindly tell your mistress that her—" I
got no further. Mara herself flew at me, and for a few
moments there was nothing but the pressure of her
arms around my neck, the smell of her skin and her hair
against my cheek, as it had been so often when she was
a child.

Drawing back at last, she surveyed me with shining
eyes. "Oh, Father, I knew you would come. Seth said
no, it would be too difficult, too dangerous for you to
make such a journey alone." Her lower lip began to
tremble as she spoke; she put her hand to her mouth
and her sea eyes swam in tears. "I knew you would
hear my heart calling to yours," she said, her voice a
hoarse whisper.

"Has it been so difficult, then?"

"No, Father," she hastened. "Not overly so. I would
not have you think . . ." She ran her small ivory fingers
through my hair, lightly, teasingly. "You are still shaggy
and strong, Father. I could not help but miss you sorely.
And, now that I have a son . . ." She allowed her voice
to trail off, and then tugged me by the hand toward the
place where the child, Shemnon, played on the floor.

The wide-eyed girl followed after us, and Mara smiled at her. "This is Ruth," she said, "daughter of Amon and Esther." I smiled at the child, knowing then why she had appeared so familiar to me. But as we entered the room I saw nothing but the shine of Shemnon's hair, and his pure, new gaze meeting mine. I have not the words to draw the sensations and emotions that were beating against the walls of my heart.

Thus began my stay in the household of the young Nephite whose life I had saved. Perhaps it *was* the God of Israel who led me to him and who stayed my hand that I did not rise up against him, even when he made claim to the daughter I loved. Perhaps it was the strength of the old affection which bound me to Nefer; I do not know. But to think of her blood and mine mingled in these two was nearly more than my feelings could bear. A burning desire to see her leapt up like a flame within me, and I think Mara saw the haunted look in my eyes, so that the day following my arrival she took me aside, into the small fragrant garden she had planted with her own hand.

"You do well here, daughter," I observed. "You have learned the ways of the people to whom you have bound yourself."

She smiled wistfully, much of the young girl yet about her. "I am happy," she said. "Seth is a kind, tender husband; you have seen that he is, Father. And the work which he does is both honorable and useful."

Some strain in the tone of her voice alerted my senses. "Meaning that this is not so with many of the Nephites who have created this city and the terrible wealth which it holds?"

Mara lowered her eyes. "Meaning that I am grateful Seth cares for the things of the mind and the spirit, and he shares his knowledge and wonder with me."

She was trying to tell me something. All my senses

were straining. I could feel her distress as surely as I am able to sense the distress of trapped or wounded beasts in the forests.

"You are telling me that Neferure is not happy as you are happy," I said.

She raised eyes heavy with misery. "I love Neferure like a mother. And, yes, I would wish for her more of what I have known through the blessing of her son in my life."

I turned away, my eyes fixed on nothing, my heart hammering, and a terrible sensation of tears stinging behind my eyes.

"Do not grieve for her, Father. Nefer is strong, and she has much to be happy for."

"Much that counts little beside what you have revealed." I growled out the words. Mara placed her hand on my shoulder, pulsing yet light as a small bird that had alighted for a moment to rest.

"I tell you this thing only so that you will not torment her, Father."

This brought me whirling back around to face her. "Torment her!" I blared.

Mara sighed, perhaps regretting what she had started. Yet she would not turn back. "I know your feelings for her—"

"You know nothing of my feelings!"

She tried again. "It would be easy for you to misjudge her, surrounded by wealth and beauty, as she is. You might easily shut your heart to her, and that would be terrible, for she needs tenderness now more than ever. Anything less from you would devastate her, Father."

I stared at my daughter, dumbfounded.

"You could not know that Bentresh is dead—oh, it is not my place to tell you!"

"It is not your place to deny me!" I answered, my voice so thin and hushed that I believe I frightened her.

So she told me the tale—fully, as she used to do when she unburdened herself to me as a child. As I listened my insides grew colder and colder, my heart more constricted. Unkindness, disloyalty, misunderstanding, greed, lust—they all tumbled out, and the misery Mara spoke of swept over me with such force that I felt weak, as though I had fought a great battle and expended my strength, and now lay panting, helpless and vulnerable.

Fool that you are! I chided myself. *What did you think? That the Nephites in their cleverness and power had created some magic barrier between themselves and this life? That they no longer shared the needs and distresses which are common to all mankind? That Neferure has existed all these years on some golden, sun-swept plain so pure, so elevated that you could never again reach her or speak to her heart?*

I trembled. Each word Mara spoke was as a blow to me. And, when she was through, I stretched out, drained and exhausted, at her feet, and she crooned over me as only women who have become mothers know how to croon. And I saw in her eyes what I had never suspected.

"You are like her," I said. "Spirit of her spirit, if not flesh of her flesh."

She knew what I was saying, but she did not understand.

"You brought me here more for Nefer's sake than for your own."

She colored a little and dropped her eyes again. "I love her truly," she said.

From that moment the words from my daughter's heart haunted me. When all in the house were asleep I went out through the garden, leaving the large front door undisturbed, and found my way to a hill—a gentle slope really—that rose beyond the stone houses and stood against the dark sky like a sentinel, unclaimed, unpolluted. Here I walked, taking long strides, breathing in the deep peace around me, cleansing my mind, and wondering what it was that the God Jehovah required of me. It was so long, too long, since I had given thought to him or considered those days when the life I hoped for— the life I had planned with Nefer—had a place in it for him. All was gray, indistinct. I could not remember what it had been like back then. Too many layers of living obscured the lost youth who no longer existed. Yet I must remember, I must! How else could I help Nefer? How else could I even meet her and face those eyes which had always possessed the power to see into my soul?

I remained most of the night alone on the hilltop. I did not see God nor openly commune with him, but I saw into my soul. And I remembered. Rensi and Nefer were with me, and so was the young man I used to be. The past became real again, and I came to understand that, for those I had loved, it lived on, running naturally into their present as a stream flows into a river, immersed and as one.

The hours of the next day I spent playing with my grandson and watching my daughter, talking with her and memorizing again the graceful lines of her face.

"I will leave in the morning," I said, "before the sun breaks over that hillside."

She nodded. "You should go to her now," she replied, "before Himni returns."

I shook my head. "That would compromise her in the eyes of her husband. But tell me where I might find Rensi."

I followed her instructions and came upon him as he labored in one of his fields. He embraced me and wept on my shoulder, and then we sat in the shade and talked of many things, from the tragedy of his Bentresh, the sin and sorrow within his family, to the workings of the Nephite city, their business, government, and reli-

gion. I found myself opening up my own life to him. He
listened, with that benediction in his gentle eyes which I
remembered from my young, willful days.

"Surely the Lord has been with you, Shemnon."

"I do not see this," I answered him.

"You have not been taught to recognize his presence. That alone stands between you."

"Between me and . . ." I could not finish the weighty
thought.

"Between you and your Maker," he said.

Then I remembered even more. I remembered that if
anyone could make God seem real, Rensi could. He had
grown during these years. I could feel the strength of
him, as firm and tempered as the cool rock we rested
upon. But his strength had not destroyed his gentleness
and the compassion of his nature. And at last it was
Rensi who spoke her name.

"You will go to Neferure?"

"I will go," I told him.

"God will go with you," he said. And I saw in his
eyes the knowledge that it would be so.

I had thought of warning her, of sending Mara or
Rensi before me. But, in truth, I wished to see the recognition in her eyes that foreknowledge would spoil.

Indeed, she dwells amid beauty, I thought as I walked
the short distance between her house and Rensi's, gazing upon the gardens and orchards which bore the mark
of her hand. I found her there, filling a basket with blossoms to carry inside. I spoke her name, and she turned
around slowly, so slowly that my heart stopped. But
when I looked on her face, all the feeling inside me
burst into one moment of ecstasy. Nothing appeared to
have changed. She stood before me as clear eyed, as fair
skinned, as filled with light as before. I drew her into
my arms and held her tight, as if holding her were the
key to holding the whole world together. I moved to

kiss the softness of her hair before I remembered myself. With painful clarity I recalled the fragrance of her skin, the soothing quiet of her voice, the sweetness of her smile, which seemed so familiar that I drew back, trembling, gulping in the still evening air as I gazed at her face.

She smiled gently, and her eyes were radiant, though darkened with tears. She could not speak yet, though her eyes told me many things which words cannot say.

The awkwardness did not touch us until she heard footsteps—before I did, with my finely tuned ears. She drew back a step, half turning toward the sound, and I saw for the first time that she was altered, not as slender and lithe as when she was a girl. Her thick hair had no gray, but the shine of it, the bright shadings were not so pronounced as they had been. And yet . . . and yet, something was added, some deep, mature enhancing of her beauty which the years had lent her, and which struck me dumb with admiration and desire. She put her hand to her throat.

"Himni approaches. He will not be pleased to find you."

"Do you fear him, then?"

Her lips tightened. "For your sake." Then she added, her doe eyes soft and open. "I feel embarrassment, even shame, sometimes at his behavior. But in his own way he loves me and treats me well."

It was a very difficult thing for me to raise my eyes to Himni, to acknowledge this man who possessed the one thing in life I had ever wholly wanted. He stood squinting in the slanted light, too dumbfounded to speak.

"You remember Shemnon," Nefer began smoothly. "It is many years since we have seen him. He has come to set eyes on the child, the grandchild which shall bear his name after him."

"He is not welcome here, not in my house."

Neferure ignored him and, taking my hand, led me past him and into the large, rich interior of the house where she lived. She showed me the rooms, describing their various functions, pointing out the murals and vases, the costly treasures with which she surrounded herself. Only in the small room at the back of her dwelling did I find aught of what I remembered of her. Here the walls were painted a warm shade, the color of sand in early morning, and many windows had been set into the wall so that she could view the garden beyond. Here her loom sat, with baskets of wool and cotton beside it, and large earthen pots filled with plants, so that the air was sweet with the scent of green things and newly washed wool.

"Yes," she said, watching me. "This feels right. The other is mostly pretense." She stood in thoughtful silence a moment. "Yet there is much beauty in my house, in my possessions, which you would not understand."

"I remember your need for beauty," I answered. "And I can only imagine how great that need would be now."

I thought she would drop her eyes before my blunt words, but she did not. She kept her gaze on my face.

"It is all right," she said. "I have not been so unhappy as you fear, not until Bentresh's death."

To hear her speaking to me openly, honestly, was like a precious gift to my heart. I drew the sensation into me, cupping it jealously. Then Himni appeared in the doorway, his full mouth drawn into a pout no different from that which I had seen often when we were children in Bountiful.

"You must go now. There is no reason for you to be here. Your presence can accomplish nothing." His voice was rich and resonant, and he spoke as one having authority, one accustomed to be heeded, obeyed.

I stared at this man for whom I had sacrificed so much, and said nothing. Neferure remained silent as well. The very room seemed to hold its breath, and I knew I would not allow Himni to order me to leave before I was ready to go.

Himni shifted his weight from one foot to the other. "I do not wish to be rude—"

"Of course you do not!"

The pleasant voice startled me. The corners of Nefer's mouth trembled into the beginnings of a smile. Rensi came up behind us through the open door that led to the garden. How much had he heard?

"Come in, brother," Nefer said, moving aside to admit him.

"That I will, thank you." He walked past us both to stand beside Nefer's husband. "I believe I will join Himni for a glass of that good blackberry wine of yours, Neferure, while you two have a chat."

As he spoke he linked his arm through Himni's and began to turn him gently toward the main house, from which he had come. Neferure was already poised in the doorway, only steps from the garden and freedom. But her husband would have none of it. He planted his feet firmly and scowled, the sharp line of nose and chin jutting unpleasantly.

"Rensi, you know I respect you. But you've no right to interfere here!"

"I have every right," Rensi replied, his voice unstrained and easy. "You forget yourself, Himni. Shemnon is an old friend of us all."

"Be that as it may, I will not leave him alone with my wife. Surely you—"

"Surely I doubt what I hear, brother," Rensi's voice had risen a bit. "It is through the courage and sacrifice of this man standing before you that you have Nefer as wife."

Himni glared, surly as a cornered bull, and shifted restlessly.

"You know this is true. He has come a long way. He has earned a few moments of this woman's company." He glanced back to where we two stood watching him.

"Fine. Let him come in with the rest of us!" Himni's words were a low, angry growl.

Rensi was no longer covering realities with the thin veil of his graciousness. He scowled back at his friend, the expression sitting awkwardly on his face. "You as husband ought to be able to vouch for the honor of your wife," he said sternly. "And I shall vouch for the integrity of Shemnon. Now, come and sit with me, Himni, and behave like a man!"

Nefer did not wait to see her advocate put his resolve into action. She slid into the shadows of the garden, and I followed.

"I have loved Himni," she said, without looking behind her. "But perhaps because he knows he has never received all of my love, he is yet uncertain of me—he becomes jealous where there is no need for jealousy, and he is often angry and insecure."

"I do not understand," I said. For, although I knew she still loved me, I could not see where her words led. I knew there was more, beyond the obvious meaning of her statement.

"I have loved you, and I have loved God, and he can understand neither. He is not a man of the heart. Reason rules his actions and his allegiances."

"You grow more and more like Rensi," I said, because the truth of it was clear to me.

"I have tried to," she said. "I realized early that life cannot be lived selfishly. If we do not get what we want, at least we can give, and in the giving find a purity that self-interest cannot know."

As she spoke, a warm sensation crept through me. It was as if I had heard her before. Her words sounded familiar, and they fell with peace on my spirit.

"Perhaps you have been with me before, Nefer,

speaking to my spirit, lifting me to a higher elevation. I feel it," I said.

She took my hand in hers. "God has been with both of us," she answered. "That is what you have felt."

"Not that only," I persisted.

"Shemnon!" The word in her mouth was like a caress. "You too have grown. Your native goodness, that which you were never able to recognize as I could, has flowered. You have become a strong and magnificent man."

I trembled at her praise, feeling confused and unworthy. And I could sense the sadness that my reaction brought to her heart.

"I have come to know you through the eyes of your daughter," she continued. "So, you see, I do not speak in ignorance. God has answered my prayers for you."

I touched her hand gently. "If only I could say the same!"

I could feel her smile in the growing darkness. "Shemnon, the discontent you feel in me comes from within my own heart. I am weary, and I am wounded. I have tried in my weak way to follow God's promptings in the lives of the people I love."

This I understood. "You were ever thus," I said gently. "Your generous spirit prompts it."

"My lack of faith prompts it," she countered. "I cannot seem to leave things to God, to lean upon his strength and wisdom, to accept—" She went on to explain to me the painful struggles she had been through with the daughter of Amon, the husband of Isabel, the loss of her beloved Bentresh. As she spoke she drew my heart out of me in sympathy, and yet at the same time I marveled at her wisdom and strength.

"You chide me unfairly," I replied at length, when she had finished and the silence of the garden enfolded us. "For you share my weakness."

"Shemnon, what do you mean?"

"You do not see yourself with any clarity, Neferure. You are good and gentle and also wise, and your strength is that of the tree which many storms have beat upon, scarred, bent, and stripped of leaves, and yet it still stands." Her hand, still in mine, tightened almost painfully. "No," I continued, "you are like the meadow flowers which bloom each season anew, despite the searing sun and the blighting frosts, and breathe forth their beauty and fragrance for all who have need of them."

She was very still as my clumsy words ended, and I thought perhaps I had displeased her. Then I felt the soft touch of her lips on my cheek. "God in his great kindness has sent you to me," she whispered. "My heart rejoices within me because of his love for us."

We sat in the garden for a long time, somehow knowing that here we were part of one another. I knew these moments would have to last me a lifetime. No vain desires could delude me into believing that I could ever belong in this place. I was a warrior and a hunter. I had sons who needed me, and a woman waiting, whose loyalty should not be betrayed. I had my own work to do. For the first time I knew this, and took some joy in it.

The last thing we did before going in to join Rensi and Himni was to kneel together upon the sweet grass and raise an entreaty to God, the God Jehovah who in his mercy had found room for us in his heart. I knelt and listened to Neferure pray for me, and I shall forever carry her words as a blessing within the depths of my soul.

I returned to Seth and Mara and shared with them much of what had transpired. Afterward I brought out the pieces of polished wood from my leather bag and put together the cradle which I had made for their child.

It was not easy to leave. It was perhaps the most difficult thing I have done, among the many difficult things in my life.

When the morning was yet but a promise beyond the horizon, I rose from my bed. The kiss I planted on Mara's cheek did not disturb her, but Seth opened his eyes.

"I will care for her," he said, repeating his old promise. "All the more tenderly, now that you have been here. And my son shall know of the noble father whose name he bears."

Who can fathom the patterns of life, the unexpected blessings which rise, like the phoenix, from the ashes of despair?

I made my way homeward without any mishap; indeed, a peace and benediction seemed to rest on my soul. It was with joy that I contemplated mingling with my sons and my wife once again as I saw the sea rise before me and heard its murmur, as sweet as the hum of angels, in my ears.

Nefer

CHAPTER TWENTY-THREE

Time hung on my hands, like the twisted and clinging tatters of an old dress from which I could not dislodge myself. Himni lived in his own world, to which I had little access. Awhere was at an age where she too had a world of her own. Seth was doing well; he was a natural and gifted teacher. He and Mara had their little son to occupy their hours and soften their grief. I alone seemed to have no work and no purpose to my days. In my bitter hours I wondered if God would ever have need of me and my poor services again.

I missed Bentresh—not with the fierceness of grief, but with this same dull hopelessness which engulfed all parts of my life. I could not write of my sister; the grief was too close, too inward a thing to allow any stepping back, any appraisal. I fear that in my pettiness I felt sorry for myself because she had been taken and had left me to keep stumbling on, trying to sort out the muddle of my own life and all of the others in which I was involved.

Only in my garden did I find succor, the gentle intimations of peace. Even in my sorry state I was not immune to the beauty that hovered there and reached out to my soul. So perhaps it was fitting that Shemnon, coming out of the mists of the lost past, should find me there.

I should have sensed his presence, but I did not. When he spoke my name a terrible thrill shuddered through me and I turned, thinking to find nothing but a cruel ghost which my own mind had conjured. Yet, there he stood, looking fierce and beautiful, his burnished locks shaven, warrior fashion, his body slim and hardened with the discipline of the years. I drank the sight of him in through my very pores, and when he gathered me into his arms the years fell away, and his touch seemed to open the constricted passages of my heart.

There was no awkwardness between us though, in truth, we were strangers, at least in all practical ways. The reality of his presence revealed the great gulf that existed between his life and mine—and yet this sense of harmony, of unspoken understanding.

When I heard Himni approach, I hoped against hope that he would see the good that existed here and do nothing to spoil. Shemnon sensed what I would not have him realize, and I felt ashamed when my husband, driven by his own insecurities, denied Shemnon welcome and behaved like a boor. Gathering my dignity about me I ignored him, and myself led our old friend through the house—room after room lavish with earthly treasures to dazzle his eyes. Dazzle they did, yet there was a sadness upon him as he gazed upon things which had no meaning to him and would serve no function in the life that he lived. I felt ashamed, suddenly, of all I "needed" to consider myself happy. And yet how soothing to my spirit the things of beauty around me could be. Only when we entered my workroom did he relax, for here the splendor and opulence gave way to function and the beauty of that which is natural and close to the earth. He was not dismayed, nor was he distant and judgmental. When he turned his sea gaze on me and said, "I remember your need for beauty," I knew that he was saying he understood. And yet he was concerned for me, angry at anything which had hurt or disappointed me. And I understood the feelings of helplessness that tortured his soul.

Himni followed us. It saddened my heart that he could not trust me, could not graciously allow me to bestow a few moments of my life upon Shemnon, when the abundance of my years were all his. I knew my old friend, and I was watching his eyes. He would not have acquiesced to Himni's demand that he leave us, and I tremble to think of what might have happened if Rensi had not appeared, coming up through the dusk of the garden walk to surprise us and take the whole thing in hand. How noble he appeared, defending my honor and Shemnon's; he had never seemed more dear to me. I left him to his unpleasant task and slipped into the shadowed garden, where all now seemed hallowed and still.

After my first great shock, I had guessed at Shemnon's purpose in being here, so I asked him to speak of the child, watching the pleasure that traced itself over his features. I would have happily diverted him from conversation centered on me.

"The child is a wonder," he said at last, "and if you did not exist, Nefer, I would have come for the sacred privilege of holding him in my arms and bringing some measure of joy to his mother's heart. But it is you, your spirit, which drew me hither."

Then I tried to explain to Shemnon what life here had been like for me, what joy I had taken in my children and in playing my own small part in building a city, an earthly kingdom where God could visit his temple and bestow his blessings on man. He listened, his blue eyes clear and unclouded, his spirit in tune with mine. Somehow the telling, the very unburdening, loosened the fetters that had closed round my heart and my mind.

"I have loved Himni," I told him, "but I have loved

you also, and I have tried to love God and move in the
direction of the pure and noble where Rensi walks."

He understood. He told me of the things he and
Rensi had spoken of that same day. He revealed but
little of his own struggles, but I knew something of
them through my conversations with Mara. Yet when he
told me of the manner of his son's dying and of Jarom's
grave on the hilltop, I saw him through new eyes. I
knew then that the beauty I had recognized was of a
high, noble nature, refined in the very fires of life. And I
knew we had never truly been without one another, nor
had he been without God. God had whispered to his
spirit and sanctified his sufferings, as he does for all of
his children who choose good over evil and seek for
light amid darkness. And I knew my Heavenly Father
was reminding me of the power of his love, of his presence in our lives, though at times we may know it not.

"O how great the holiness of our God!" How many
times had Nephi's brother Jacob taught us this, praising
our God and the Redeemer he would send? "For he
knoweth all things, and there is not anything save he
knows it. And he cometh into the world that he may
save all men if they will hearken unto his voice. And
whoso knocketh, to him will he open."

I did not quote Jacob to Shemnon, but my spirit
spoke to his spirit, as when we were young, and
together we communed with the highest within ourselves. I asked him to kneel with me in prayer, and the
benediction of the God of Israel rested upon our sore
hearts.

"Will I see you again?" I asked, being but human.

"That remains in God's hands," he replied.

Then he left me, but I could endure the parting
because of all I had seen and all I had felt. There was no
darkness left in me, only a tender gratitude and a joy
laced with tears—but then, is not joy but the thrilling of
our souls toward heaven, as they embrace the bitter to

know the sweet, the struggle to know the triumph, the pain to partake of the peace?

I never discussed Shemnon's visit with Himni. As far as he was concerned, it had never happened at all. He carried on with life as usual, and I fell back into my place. The safe, routine order of things seemed to be restored, but not so! For my life shone with a purpose which the common days could not dim. Rensi and I spoke often of Shemnon, recounting with pleasure his visit, recalling the words that had been spoken and thinking of the grave on the hill, nurtured and protected at such great cost.

"I could wish for Bentresh to have been here to know this," I confessed to Rensi, "though I know the foolishness of that, since she is with her son now." And the peace of that knowledge, that acceptance flowed through me even as I spoke.

Mara and I rocked her little son in the cradle his grandfather had left behind and spoke of Shemnon's tenderness, his sacrifice, his vision. I would smooth the wood with my hand, delighting in the cool, silken feel of it, and think of the goodness of life which had brought my blood and Shemnon's together in the love of my son and his daughter, uniting so much promise and possibility. And my spirit yearned toward the future, which I could not see.

I gave in at last to the great, unseen design of things and loosened my insistent grasp, letting His hand guide where I could not see. Time became unimportant; indeed, time slid away from me. More babies came. A daughter, whom Seth and Mara named Rachel in honor of Mara's mother. This disgusted Himni, of course. But he grew more and more prosperous, and his means provided lavish gifts for the children and a fine new house for the struggling young teacher and his growing family; and I knew, in his heart, Himni took pleasure in that.

Five years passed with an ease that alarmed me. A second son was born to Seth and Mara and given the name of Jarom, and this brought joy to us all. And Isabel's faith was rewarded, for Onihah kept to his sober ways. I believe that virtue restored his sight, and he was again able to see the true beauty—both physical and spiritual—of the girl he had wed. He began to cherish her as one can only cherish a thing of great value which once had been lost. A daughter was born to them, and Isabel called her Bentresh. I think that alone proved the true nature of Onihah's repentance, for he embraced the child, bestowing all the tenderness upon her which my Bentresh, in her anguish, had been unable to call forth. Esther and I fussed mercilessly over the child, perhaps in part because our own daughters were nearly grown. Ruth of the large oval eyes, like pools of warm honey, was now fifteen years old. Already many young men had expressed interest in obtaining her gentle, modest beauty, and, indeed, she would make some good man a prized wife.

Then there was Awhere. It was now the year 550 before the coming of Christ, fifty years since Lehi traveled into the wilderness, leaving a doomed and unhappy Jerusalem behind. My daughter was twenty years old and had still shown no interest in marriage, and no man had caught her eye or caused sufficient flurry in her young heart to make an impact.

Another year passed. Then one night of dark storms and noisome winds a stranger appeared at our door, a young man in distress, who had apparently lost his way in the black rain. His frightened horse had missed his footing on the uneven ground and had thrown him. I let him in, wondering how he had managed to make it as far as the house. The lightning cracked in bright threads above the horizon, and the lad winced in pain as I helped him lower his bruised body onto a chair. He could not put his weight on his left leg, and there was a

deep red gash along the length of his arm. I called for
Awhere to run the distance to Rensi's and have one of
his field hands go for a doctor. But it was I who braved
the elements, for she had dropped down on her knee
beside him—she who could not stand the sight of blood
or of suffering. I left her crooning over the flushed, surprised lad, wetting cloths with cool water and cleansing
herbs to tend his injuries. I burst through Rensi's door
with little ceremony, standing wet and shivering, while
puddles formed at my feet. Rensi is a quiet and calm
man, but he can be quick and efficient when need
demands. After he had sent a man on his way, he urged
me to drink the hot tea he had prepared for me. I sat
down with a sigh.

"This is the one," I said. "Something tells me that."

"Do not be silly, my dear." He smiled indulgently,
but I could not share his nonchalance.

"The boy is a native," I said, "perhaps from one of
the local tribes near here."

"His skin is dark-shaded and loathsome?"

"Rensi, please!"

He reached over and covered my cold hand with his
compact, warm one.

"Besides, I know nothing about him. He wanders in
from the night—"

"Yes. Some force brought him to your house. If
Awhere is drawn to him, then might not that impulse be
right?"

I sighed again. "Himni would have none of it, you
know that."

"Are you courting trouble, my dear?"

But I was not, as things turned out. Lamoni was an
engineer, building roads across the high mountains to
where our people would build new settlements, and he
was not so young as he looked.

"Thirty-three," Awhere chirped, "but he looks
younger than I do. Is not Father older than you?"

"Eight years," I responded, "which sometimes seems eight hundred. Not twelve, Awhere."

"Really, Mother. It makes no difference at all."

Of course, she was right. What matters age where affairs of the heart are concerned?

"You will go with him?"

"Yes. We will raise a new city out of the wilderness, as you did here."

The voice of youth. I had forgotten what it was like and, looking into her shining eyes, was given a bitter reminder that I could not now enter the world of the future which she inhabited.

"So, you will break your own path," I conceded, "knowing more than your parents did; that is how it should be. But do not forget to make place for those things which are most important, for they never change."

"Mother, really!" There was an indulgence in her tone which both stung and frightened me, and then I knew.

"Lamoni is not one of us, is he?"

"If you mean a converted Nephite, no."

She sucked in her bottom lip, looking petulant as a child. "And does that not concern you at all?" I pressed.

"Not as it concerns you, Mother. I have faith in Lamoni. He has a good heart. He listens when I speak of the teachings of Nephi." She shrugged her smooth, rounded shoulders. "Some day . . ."

I turned away to hide the misery which was making my mouth tremble.

"Your love means everything, Mother. I could not do this without it."

"It may be all that you have," I murmured.

She knew what I meant and was silent, but she did not know all. Himni would oppose her—that was certain. So she would forfeit his support. But she had already forfeited something much more important: the guiding voice of the Spirit, that real strength which sustained and uplifted. She would stumble on without it, never knowing what she was missing. With a grieving heart I kissed her cheek, knowing I had no power or right to interfere in her life. She had her own choices to make, her own mistakes, her own triumphs, her own way to find.

Himni was so harsh that even I withered before his anger and entreated Rensi to intercede for us, but even his words were to no avail.

"If you marry this man you will cease to be my daughter," he told Awhere. "I will no longer be shamed by my children."

"What of Seth?" she countered, in tears. "He married a Lamanite woman and you have not disowned him."

"I have learned my lesson." Himni's voice was so cold that I shuddered. "I will not make the same mistake twice." Seeing the horror in Awhere's eyes, he added, "Besides, he has redeemed himself somewhat by his sober living and his excellence as a teacher. This man you marry is a common laborer and will bring no honor to you. How do I explain to the other ruling elders the foolishness and weakness of my only daughter?"

It was the same no matter how many times she approached him, except that each time he hardened his heart against her further. So I was not surprised to awaken one morning to find my daughter's room empty, divested of every sign of her, as though she had melted out of existence. I stood a long time staring into the emptiness, feeling the coldness of it seep into my heart.

I spoke no word to Himni, but after three days had passed I went to Rensi in tears.

"He asks nothing, shows no concern, offers no comfort."

"He dare not, for fear of losing this iron control of himself."

"This evil coldness of heart, you mean. I hope it freezes his own blood," I muttered.

"It has, Nefer, it has."

Rensi's quiet words startled me. I began to observe my husband more closely after that day. It was true. His very skin appeared gray and sallow; his eyes were dull, with no lights in them; even his movements exhibited a weariness, a clumsiness he could not disguise.

For a week he was thus, two weeks. Nothing seemed to alter, and we heard no word from Awhere. Mara comforted me, and together we prayed, which was really all we could do.

Then one morning Himni awoke me out of a deep sleep. There was no light in the east yet to herald morning's approach, only a cold inky darkness that pressed like a weight on my eyelids. I struggled to rise.

"You must be quick, Nefer," Himni chided. "For the caravan stands waiting and I leave within the hour."

I sat up, rubbing my eyes. "Whatever do you mean? You are speaking madness, Himni."

He glanced at me, his gaze businesslike, impersonal. "I go to meet a ship and examine a cargo." He rubbed his hands together. "If all goes right, I shall make more money in three months than I have made in the past three years."

"Why did you not tell me before?"

His eyes met mine briefly. There was a glow of excitement in them which was foreign to me. "You are put out with me since Awhere's disappearance. You would have opposed anything I presented—if only to vex me."

"You are unfair!" I cried. "I have been unhappy; I cannot help that."

His eyes had gone cold and clear again. "Come now, Nefer. You despise me and the things I care about, you always have. And yet you are happy enough to spend the riches I bring back to you." He chuckled under his breath, and the sound made me feel ill inside.

"Himni, how long will you be gone on this journey?"

"Six weeks, eight weeks, I am uncertain—it is not easy to tell."

I sank back, speechless, watching him go about his preparations in a sort of blank daze.

"Have you a kiss good-bye for me?" he asked suddenly, turning toward me, and yet making no move to cross the distance and come to stand by the bed.

I rose and went to stand beside him, struggling to control the anger and dismay which I felt. "Take care of yourself, Himni. I will miss you."

"No, you will be lonely," he replied. "And that is not the same thing, Nefer."

He kissed me, but only a light touch against my cold lips.

"My affairs are in order," he said, as he turned away from me. "Just in case."

"Of course," I murmured, as I continued to watch him and then trail him out to the door. He did not kiss me again. He did not express concern for my welfare or how I would fare during his absence. I knew he was punishing me for siding with his daughter, albeit silently, for failing to stand beside him as an obedient wife, no matter what his actions might be. I knew him well; he was looking forward to the freedom of this journey. He would put me out of his mind and enjoy the company of men who thought and acted as he did, who wanted the same things from life. After he returned— well, I would deal with that when it happened. But I had never been so afraid. The estrangement between us was real, and I wondered sadly how such a rent in the delicate fabric of our marriage could be repaired.

c·ɔ

Days passed. I grew accustomed to my aloneness. At first I hoped Awhere might hear of her father's absence and come to me, but such hopes proved to be fruitless. I worked in my house and my garden and spent time with the people I loved. But there were too many hollow places within me which no activity, however meaningful, was able to fill. A month passed, then another with no word of Himni. A sense of unease fell upon me, and I began to be worried for him.

It was Seth who came to me with the news. Himni had suffered a massive heart failure when the caravan passed through the high mountains. His friends had buried him there in the thin, cold silences. He had never seen the ocean, never set eyes on the ship. Yet the wealth he coveted found its way back to me to mock my emptiness and my guilt.

Some things God denies us; or perhaps only life itself does; no matter, the results are the same. We are brought up short to stand before our own weaknesses. Some in bitterness turn away. Others of us fall broken, humbled at the feet of that God whose patience must be even greater than his love. And we tremble there, seeking the strength to right ourselves, pick up the pieces, and go on again.

One prayer was answered. Awhere and her new husband came to the funeral, to pay sad and silent homage to the man who would no more interfere in her life. I could not see what was in her heart; I could only pray that Jehovah would touch it, and that he would forgive my small deception. Before she left to go back to the way of living she had chosen, I called her into my room and drew from out of my carved teakwood box a sum of money and a delicate strand of deep jade stones, costly and well set by Himni's own hand.

"Your father left certain instructions, if anything

should happen to him; you know how thorough he was." I held my hand out, and the gems glowed against my white palm. "He wished for you to have these."

I held my breath as she decided. At last she extended her arm. I do not know if she really believed me, but there were tears in her eyes as she accepted the gift.

"Will you come to visit me, Mother? In my new home?"

I nodded. "I would be delighted," I said.

"So would I. And so would Lamoni. He thinks very highly of you."

I kissed her and watched her walk away, wondering if the letting go, the growing wise, the very growing up inside my own soul would ever end.

Mara glided close beside me and planted a kiss on my hair. "You have made Awhere happy," she whispered, "and I can guess the price that it cost you."

"Not so much, my dear," I replied, smiling. "Not so much as you think. He who will one day give his all for us—I believe he rejoices in our giving and opens his heart to us, and then we are filled and wonder what it was we were afraid of in the first place, when we trembled and hesitated."

The love in Mara's eyes as she smiled back was like a strength flowing into me, and I folded my heart around the precious warmth of it against the dark and difficult moments which were certain to come.

Nefer

CHAPTER TWENTY-FOUR

H e is dead. Even a prophet, dear to his people, must reach the end of his days and pass on to that blessed state which awaits him. But, oh, with Nephi's passing the people mourn and assemble themselves together to weep and fast while his body is shrouded and made ready for burial. We are as children again, remembering the wilderness, the days of fear and confusion when he led us, as it were, by the hand. Nephi was one of the mighty ones of the earth—will any like him come amongst us again?

Rensi fears, as do Nephi's brother Jacob and his brethren, that we even now lay the foundation for our downfall in our weak, wicked ways. How is it that so much evil and cunning and selfishness can survive among those who were pledged to purity and obedience.

"Wealth and the desires of the flesh," Rensi says sadly. "We are, each one of us, human and subject to our own natures. In our poverty and travail we turned to God of necessity. Now we have the means with which to indulge and pleasure ourselves. Where is the need for him now?"

Fifty and five years have passed since Lehi and his followers came out of Jerusalem, a free people brought safely to a land of promise whereon we might dwell and serve the God of the land, to whom we are beholden for our very lives, and for all that we are. Now in shame we bow our heads as Nephi's spirit passes from us and we sense our unworthiness before heaven. And every heart mourns.

Nephi has anointed one to be king and ruler after him, and it is decreed that he be known by the name and title of Nephi, that this hallowed name might be held in remembrance among us from generation to generation: second Nephi, third Nephi, fourth Nephi—and wo to that man who wears unworthily the mantle of this power and priesthood so nobly bestowed.

Thus, life will go on. Nephi has gone to his reward, but those of us left behind yet have much proving to do.

"My father, Zoram, will meet him," I said to Seth and Mara, "and his joy will be great. And those noble spirits who have gone before us will all rejoice."

But to Rensi I confided my unhappiness. "What of Himni?" I said. "How does he fare among that realm of great spirits, among those things which did not speak to his heart in this life?"

"You stretch my powers, dear sister," he replied, smiling. "Such things are not for us to know. It is part of our walking by faith, is it not?" He laid his hand over mine. "But one thing is for certain. That is the mercy and love of Jehovah, who will redeem all who come unto him. You may rest assured, Nefer, that Himni is safe in his hands."

We buried our prophet-leader, warrior, statesman, colonizer, builder of cities and builder of men. But, more than anything else, Nephi was a servant of God, and he knew whom he served. Among his last words to us were these, which I have written, and shall treasure for the rest of my life:

"I pray continually for my people by day, and mine eyes water my pillow by night, because of them; and I cry unto my God in faith, and I know that he will hear my cry. And I know that the Lord God will consecrate my prayers for the gain of my people. And the words which I have written in weakness will be made strong unto them. I glory in plainness; I glory in truth; I glory in my Jesus, for he hath redeemed my soul. And I pray the Father in the name of Christ that many of us, if not all, may be saved in his kingdom at that great and last day. And now, my beloved brethren, all those who are of the house of Israel, and all ye ends of the earth, I speak unto you as the voice of one crying from the dust: Farewell until that great day shall come."

The testament remains, and I wonder at the power of this one man whose words, we are told, shall indeed whisper long after we and our children and our children's children are gone, and the Gentiles who are brought by God to this place shall receive his words and honor his teachings. This is a most marvelous thing; I cannot envision it, but sometimes in my heart I can understand—and feel with my spiritual being, if I am not able to see with my spiritual eyes.

I have viewed life differently since Nephi is no longer among us. I seem to do all things with care. I look at my children, and they seem a wonder unto me. Seth and Mara's children are growing. At one time he had thought to leave this city and establish a school of his own. But now that his father is gone he desires to stay near me, and I am glad. I need his strength and Mara's tenderness, and I want his children to know me, I want to be a part of their lives. And recognition has come to him. He is revered as a teacher of men's hearts as well as their minds. He contributes and grows from the giving, and that is good.

Bentresh, daughter of Isabel, blossoms. She is a light in our lives, a gift sent to sanctify her namesake's sacrifice, I am sure. Amon and Esther's Ruth has chosen a good man to marry and, although Hannah has not returned to them, Miriam, Sariah, Rebekah, and Anna have brought much joy to their hearts. There are grandsons now, a new generation to teach and love. And we who have learned so much from our own mistakes are eager to give and sustain where we are able, with a mingling of patience and faith which we did not possess when we were younger. Ah, but so mortal life goes!

It is five years since Awhere wed Lamoni, and a daughter has blessed their union, a daughter christened Neferure, who possesses both dreamy eyes and a fiery temper and will indeed be a handful to raise. Lamoni is a successful engineer, the new city flourishes, and these two are glad to be part of it. Lamoni has not yet become one of us in purpose and practice, but his heart is still good. He truly loves my daughter and this lovely child born to them, and what could be more blessed than that? Time will yet weave out many bright strands, many patterns—and what, after all, is time in the hands of God?

In my own hands time sometimes sits heavily. I am lonely of late. I spend much of the time I have writing, and I feel a power in the words that flow from my heart to my pen. The children of Zoram—look what has already become of them! One man walked into the wilderness and embraced his own dream—and now dozens bear his name, and hundreds after them, and in their lives he will live on, through countless generations which will honor his name. There is power in this continuation of the seed, power we do not understand. In truth, it is one of those things which Rensi reminds me, with one of his gentle smiles, that we are not yet given to know.

But my restless heart has always yearned to see into the future. I cannot let go and consign it entirely to those whose lives will come after me, who are its right-ful possessors. Perhaps this is wrong; perhaps it is only natural. But through my writing I feel that something of my spirit will yet live on; indeed, all we of the exodus, who came out from among the children of Israel and blazed a new path, all these walk over the pages I write. Their voices speak through mine, and what remains here, though weak and inadequate, yet retains some-thing of the reality of their days. And that too is power. For God himself has called precious the records we keep of our mortal lives. I write in faith, praying that God in his goodness will sanctify what I record here to the blessing and strengthening of those who will come, bearing the bounteous harvest of the future in their hands.

It is nearly eleven years since Shemnon came to my garden. It is the year 544, the year which shall be known hereafter and forever as the year in which Nephi died. Himni was fifty-four years old when his life ended five years ago, and I but forty-six. Now I have reached fifty-one years, as the age of earth life is measured. Yet this seems as nothing to me. Though at times I feel weary, bent to breaking with life's burdens, still there is a song in my heart, as sweet and youthful, as filled with hope and wonder, as when I was young. How this can be so, I do not know; my mind does not understand. But my spirit, renewed, seems more alive, more vital with each passing year.

Yet the loneliness of my solitary life is unavoidable, though at times I experience a vague expectancy, as though some adventure, some purpose is waiting for me.

⌣⊃

During the past week two things happened, singular things but strangely connected, and both have
altered my life.

A stranger appeared at my door three mornings
past, introducing himself as a merchant from the city
who had been instructed to carry a message to me. The
parchment he drew from his leather pouch was worn
and wrinkled, yet I knew before touching it whose
words it bore, whose hand had sealed it and set it upon
this journey to me.

I went into my small workroom which looks out
upon the gardens and is itself scattered with growing
things, warm with the light from many small windows.
Here I could feel the impress of Shemnon's spirit; here
his voice, itself, lingered, and the sea shimmer of his
gaze.

"Nefer dear," it began, "I send by a trusted hand
this missive to you. Time, as we reckon the calendar,
tells me it has been over ten years since I have set eyes
upon you. Yet the memory of your image is fresh in my
mind, and your voice still vibrates in warm waves,
washing my soul clean.

"Through my gracious Mara I know of the death of
Himni and the marriage of your daughter, and of the
children who come to bless Zoram's line."

He would say no more of my husband, not offer
condolences, nor criticize the dead, nor proffer weak
pity; his spirit walked other paths.

"I raise daily prayers to your god," he continued,
"to protect and uphold you all, and sometimes I have
been given to know a happiness, a sense of reassurance.
But sometimes, too, I dream disturbing dreams, and
when that happens I know that they portend something.

"I will not pretend that my longings do not go out to
you . . ."

His words shivered along my skin like a trail of warm sunlight.

"Yet I do not belong in your world; it is too late, I have too much to do in my own life; I have commitments and vows which are not mine to break."

I knew it was so; I had not been entertaining elaborate daydreams of a life beside Shemnon. He was right. I could not see him here: he would be unhappy, his inner self would be stifled. All the pure and good which flowed between his spirit and mine would be in danger of extinction, or at least of the dull, unhappy muddling which a lack of wholeness in one's life tends to give. And, there was the woman who was wife to him, Mara's mother. There were his Lamanite warrior-sons. I sighed as I read the last remaining words.

"Know, dear one, that my love goes out to you each day, with the prayers which I utter, in the new pale mornings when the earth is silent and expectant and closer to heaven than we imagine. In that far ago day when you and I walked by the sea and spoke of our lives, you said to me that if we desire righteousness, God will show us the way. Surely he has, many times over, and blessed us beyond what we could see. Your wisdom even then was like a shining in your young eyes. Now it rests like the gentle hand of peace on my heart.

"It distresses me, Nefer, to think of you living alone. You are too young, there is too much within you, and I know of one who would welcome your companionship and be worthy of your love and your trust. Think on it, Nefer, and let your heart again flower, as God intends it to do.

"We may meet again in this life, or we may not, as God ordains. But nothing can ever separate me from you. Go in joy, my Nefer, for so I shall picture you as I kneel on my gentle green mountain with the mists of morning swirling up from the sea, and the beauty around me no more lovely than you."

I clutched the precious pages to my breast and sat long in the undisturbed peace of my room, as I attempted to sift through his words and sort out the feelings of my heart. The task was not an easy one, but Shemnon's words held me in their warm weaving, and I felt surrounded, upheld by that peace which he spoke of, which I knew he could understand.

Rensi has been chosen and consecrated at the hands of the high priests as a priest and teacher among the people of Nephi. Surely he is worthy the honor; his whole life has led him steadily toward such a role, such a noble and weighty calling.

This is the second event of a singular nature I refer to. The night after the unexpected arrival of Shemnon's precious message, Rensi came to my door, his face grave but his gentle eyes glowing. He told me what had transpired, I spoke words of encouragement to him, and together we rejoiced.

"I have need of you, Neferure," he said, "in ways more solemn, more demanding than ever before."

I blinked at his words, spoken so calmly, so unexpectedly. Yet I did not understand them.

"I need you beside me," he tried again. "Surely, Nefer," he reached out and captured my hand between his two small, capable ones, "surely both you and I have been lonely these past years, and sore of heart."

I nodded assent. The warmth of his spirit seeped into me through the touch of his hands. "Surely between us there exists a mutual respect, a unity which I believe, my dear, to be precious and rare."

I looked into his eyes; his gentle soul gazed back from the hazel depths of them, and the words Shemnon had written came into my mind: *"I know of one who would welcome your companionship and be worthy of your love and your trust."*

Understanding flooded over me—and with understanding, awareness. I saw what I had not seen before—love, and even desire in Rensi's still gaze. I dropped my eyes and felt a blush of heat along my cheeks and forehead.

"I have loved you for as long as I have been alive, Neferure, loved you in many ways. Why not this one?"

"No!" I answered, wresting my fingers from his and putting my hands to my cheeks.

"And why not?"

"It would not be—seemly. What would people say of us?"

He laughed, and the sound was low and pleasant. "What indeed, Neferure, but that we had come to our senses at last?"

"Bentresh," I said bluntly, perhaps unkindly. "She would stand between us."

"She would stand beside us," he said. "Along with Himni, despite his faults and weaknesses. Along with your parents and mine. The love of all who are dear to us would be woven into our union, dear sister, even that of Shemnon, who sees with eyes more spiritual than you may know."

I met his gaze, and this time did not shrink before the outpouring of love which washed over me like a warm light, which awakened my heart and stirred the deepest feelings within me.

He reached again for my hand, pulled me close to him, pressed his lips gently to mine. There was no sense of shame or embarrassment, only a tingling pleasure that traveled the lines of my body and seemed in harmony with the warmth that I felt in my heart.

⌒

I have agreed to marry Rensi, to live as his wife, his helpmeet, his soulmate, and I know nothing but joy at the prospect—and a deep confirmation of peace.

He spoke truly. People see a rightness in it, and their hearts reach out to support us. I feel no censure, no misunderstanding, only an outpouring of love.

I am happy as I have never before been happy. It seems I sing through my days; anticipation like a sauce to my hours. To live as one with a man, to serve that God whom I seek to know, through Rensi to learn more of Him, to learn more of serving others. Such a life appears sweet to me.

It is fifty-six years since Lehi and his children came out of Jerusalem and, by the hand of Jehovah, were led safely here. Now their seed graces the land of promise, and in their eyes shines the light of a new tomorrow. And that is how it should be. The God of Israel delights to bless his children. In this fair place we raise our voices in praise of his love and his blessings. We, the people of Nephi, rejoice and lift our eyes, in faith, to the future which God has prepared for this land.

Savior of mankind,
— My Savior! —
I take thy hand
And walk at last
By the greater light
Of faith.
I am content
To trust Thy wisdom,
To receive all things
Which come from Thee
To grace my mortal days,
Or to build strength
Through trial:

In thy love
All things are possible.
My Savior, now
I see the deeper wisdom
Of Thy ways
And am content
To wait upon Thy will
And look toward the future
With delight,
Knowing Thy feet
Shall walk upon this land,
Thy eyes smile
On my sons and daughters.
Thus in joy
I lift my heart in reverence
And in praise
To Thee:
My Guide,
My Savior,
And my Friend.

About the Author

Susan Evans McCloud's previously published writings include poems, a children's book, local newspaper feature articles, narratives for tapes and filmstrips, screenplays, and lyrics—including two hymns found in the 1985 Church hymnbook. The author of many novels, she is listed in several international biographies of writers of distinction.

The author and her husband, James, are the parents of six children, and the family resides in Provo, Utah.

Other publications by Susan Evans McCloud:

For Love of Ivy
By All We Hold Dear
Anna
Jennie
Ravenwood
A Face in the Shadows
The Heart That Truly Loves
Who Goes There?
Mormon Girls series
Sunset Across India